EXPOSED
EVIDENCE

EXPOSED EVIDENCE

A
JESSICA FROST
LEGAL THRILLER

R. BARRI FLOWERS

First published by Level Best Books/New Arc Books 2021

Copyright © 2021 by R. Barri Flowers

Author Photo Credit: R. Barri Flowers

First edition

ISBN: 978-1-68512-060-3

Cover art by Level Best Designs

This book was professionally typeset on Reedsy.
Find out more at reedsy.com

To my beloved Mother and Father, Marjah A. and Johnnie H., who gave me the tools needed to succeed at my craft.

And to the love of my life, Loraine, to whom I am forever indebted for her support and tireless commitment to helping me to complete one book after another for many years of concerted efforts.

Praise for R. BARRI FLOWERS

"Flowers may be a new voice in modern mystery writing, but he is already one of its best voices."—*Statesman Journal*

"R. Barri Flowers is among the best of them."—John Lutz, Edgar-winning, bestselling mystery author

"R. Barri Flowers writes with the passion and knowledge of someone who truly knows his craft."—Allison Leotta, former federal prosecutor and crime novelist

"Flowers once again has written a page-turner legal thriller that begins with a bang and rapidly moves along to its final page."—*Midwest Book Review*

"With his amazing background and varied stories, Flowers's tales of crime in paradise will pull the reader right in."—Karen Harper, *New York Times* bestselling author

"Vivid details of police procedure one would expect from an author who is also a top criminologist."—Douglas Preston, bestselling mystery writer

"Gripping writing, wonderfully rounded characters you really care about, and vivid locations."—Peter James, bestselling mystery author

"Flowers always relates an engrossing story in a hard-hitting and fast-paced manner."—Robert Scott, true crime author

I

The Crime

Prologue

T he members of the club sat around the marble table, talking, laughing, and drinking spiritedly, as they embraced their good fortunes and dismissed the bad ones, like they did not matter in the scheme of things. In adopting the motto of "all for one and one for all," they had made a pact that ensured no one would stray from the group without just cause. As luck would have it, they were all on the same page in that what they were doing made perfect sense in taking advantage of the opportunities afforded them in an environment that was tailor-made for their individual and collective skills, imagination, and ingenuity. After plotting their strategy in moving ahead full steam like a locomotive, and seeing no obstacles they couldn't overcome, the club members joined hands in reiterating their support for one another in a bond that had proven all but unbreakable, save for one misfortune that was totally out of their control, insofar as being able to control the unpredictable. And, therefore, didn't count in their stated objectives and generous prospects that lay ahead. In the end, they raised their glasses and toasted one another, before turning the page and forging full speed ahead, without looking back.

* * *

After making her way through rows of black alder trees, she stepped into the clearing. The sun had begun to set, making it just dark enough for her purposes. Her eyes adjusted before zeroing in on a lonely owl who, staring back at her, seemed mildly curious before flying off into the reddish sky.

She sucked in a deep breath and walked toward the apartment building not far from campus till reaching her destination. She went to the ground floor corner unit and turned the doorknob until the door opened. Stepping inside, she was immediately hit by the skunky and familiar odor of marijuana, offset somewhat by the mid-October breeze entering through a crack in the living room window.

She walked quietly across the cork flooring in loafers, sidestepping contemporary furnishings, and into the one-wall kitchen, where dirty dishes and empty glasses were piled up in the apron sink, as someone apparently couldn't be bothered to put them in the dishwasher. On the laminate countertop sat a nearly empty bottle of red wine. Nearby was a bamboo knife block full of knives. She grabbed a serrated knife, admiring for a moment its ten-inch blade as if a work of expensive art, before moving toward the bathroom. The light was on, as if someone intended to return but got sidetracked. She did the honors, shutting off the light, and headed down a short hallway toward the bedrooms.

Peeking in one fully furnished room with jewel-toned walls and potted plants, she saw that the panel bed was made and room was otherwise tidy. She moved to the other bedroom. The door was open. Gazing inside, exterior lighting filtered through the open faux wood blinds and fell onto the platform bed. It was occupied by a female who lay asleep haphazardly atop the duvet cover, as if passed out. She was wearing a short wine-colored nightgown with long, lean legs separated ever so slightly. A halo of thick blonde hair surrounded her pretty young face like an angel.

Entering the partially furnished room, she moved quickly up to the bed. Hesitation stilled her for a moment, maybe two, like a concrete barrier, as she weighed the consequences of her actions. She knew enough to understand that if she went through with it, there was no turning back. But why should there be? Her blood boiled with renewed fury. When you played with fire, you deserved to get burned. The bitch had to pay dearly for what she had done—with her very life. So there, the decision to move ahead had been made, as if ever truly in doubt.

"May you rot in hell!" she spat venomously, like a woman possessed by

4

the Devil himself. Or simply psycho. At this point, she didn't care.

The female on the bed opened her bold blue eyes at the last moment, horror crossing her face as though seeing her worst nightmare come to life. But it was too late to prevent her fate.

She brought the knife down hard into the young woman's chest, unleashing a blood-curdling scream that practically shook the foundation of the entire apartment. Unmoved, she yanked the sharp blade out and brought it down again and again, and again and again, ignoring the bitch's feeble and futile attempts to ward off the blows; wanting her to feel the pain and know she was about to die.

Finally, there was a deathly silence, aside from her own heavy breathing, and a motionless bloody body below, the lifeless eyes staring back at her as a final act of resignation.

Chapter One

Jessica Frost sat on pins and needles in the courtroom as she always did whenever a verdict was about to be rendered. One she firmly thought would work in her favor. Yet, as a criminal defense attorney at her own firm, she never took anything for granted. Even when it seemed as though she had poked enough holes in the prosecution's case to sink like a ship that had been struck smackdab by a torpedo. It was all but impossible to believe that serious reasonable doubt hadn't been established in this trial.

Her client, thirty-nine-year-old teacher Roslyn Whitman, had been accused of molesting one of her female teenage students at Hubbard High School in northwest Creighton Hills, a bustling city in Southern Oregon. Problem was, the accused not only had a history of making such accusations against other students who got on her bad side, but the case was built almost entirely on circumstantial evidence against a woman who had not only passed two lie detector tests, but had a solid alibi that contradicted the timeline established by the accuser.

As far as Jessica was concerned, this should never have been brought to court. *But what do I know?* she thought facetiously, brushing away from her forehead a jet-black tendril from piecey bangs that went with a short pixie haircut. Or, more to the point, what didn't she know? She never underestimated her opponent, Thorne County prosecutor Madeleine Griffin. African American and well put together, she was slightly intimidating to Jessica on the professional stage. Madeleine seemed to take every case almost more personally than she did. If anyone could convince the jury that Roslyn was guilty as sin, it was surely Madeleine.

Jessica shifted almond-shaped blue eyes toward her as though sensing Madeleine was already looking in her direction like a tiger in search of prey. She was right on the money. Tall and attractive, the forty-two-year-old prosecutor had long and layered brown wavy hair worn in a ponytail updo and enviable hazel eyes. Dressed in a sharp designer mauve pantsuit and black ankle boots; she offered Jessica a competitive, confident, and, perhaps misleading, friendly smile; as if to say, *Better luck next time.* Not one to back away from a challenge, Jessica gave her a thin-lipped grin in return, while thinking audaciously, *I'm ready whenever you are.* She doubted they would ever be friends. At least not so long as they represented opposite sides of the legal spectrum. But she believed there was a healthy respect both ways and could live with that.

Jessica recalled that her father used to say when he practiced law for more than thirty years, before proudly passing the torch onto her, that she could do every bit as good in defending the innocent and preventing them from being unjustly convicted as prosecutors could in putting away the guilty. She took the job very seriously and wanted to do right by not only the one person who believed in her the most, but every client she took on. That notwithstanding, Jessica felt the prosecution had every right to work just as hard on the other side in trying their case while leaving it up to the system of justice to decide who would prevail. She gazed at the uneasy brown eyes of her client, a slender woman with brunette hair in a chin-length bob, and squeezed her hand in a show of support.

Judge Ralph McVeigh, a stout man in his mid-fifties with silver hair in an Ivy League haircut, was handed the verdict by the bailiff. He looked at it impassively, giving Jessica no hint of which way the pendulum had swung. She held her breath anxiously. After the verdict was returned to the jury foreman, the judge asked the defendant to rise.

Jessica rose with her client who was shaking like a leaf as her very freedom and good name dangled in the air like a tree branch. *Without hope, what do we have left?* Jessica thought, heart racing as always at this moment where the tide could just as easily flow one way as the other.

"We, the jury, find the defendant...not guilty..."

This was repeated three times and, finally, Jessica could exhale. She gave Roslyn a hug and received a bigger one in return.

"Thank you so much for believing in me," she whispered tearfully.

"Someone had to," Jessica responded equably, feeling a sense of satisfaction with the outcome, along with adding another victory to her admittedly impressive resume. In five years of practicing law, she had come out on the short end of the stick only twice and those had come from plea bargains in which her clients hadn't a prayer of getting off scot-free.

"Congratulations, Counselor," she heard Madeleine Griffin say in a less than euphoric tone.

Jessica turned to face the prosecutor, who was a couple of inches taller than her own five feet, eight inches, and every bit as slender. Offering a gracious smile, while tugging at the gray houndstooth jacket of her skirt suit, worn with gray leather mules, Jessica responded sincerely, "Thank you, Madeleine. Better luck next time." *So long as I'm not your opponent in court,* she thought, half-jokingly.

"Count on that!" Madeleine wrinkled her nose. "I hate losing!" She sneered at Roslyn and walked away stiffly with her brown attaché case.

"Well, you're free to get on with your life now," Jessica told her client, hoping she hadn't allowed Madeleine to get to her as the losing side.

"I'll certainly try, but I'm afraid the damage has already been done," Roslyn said glumly.

Jessica took her words to heart, realizing that even when a client was victorious, the residual effects from being wrongfully accused and charged might never truly go away. This was a sad reality she had come to know all too well in her years of practicing law. But she had also learned to take each victory for what it was worth and not dwell too much on the negative. This strategy had seemed to work both in her professional and personal life.

* * *

The notion of lasting effects was still on her mind as Jessica left the Thorne County Courthouse in downtown Creighton Hills and crossed the parking lot, before getting into her red Subaru Impreza sedan. It had been three weeks to the day that she broke up with her married boyfriend, Hugh Holliman. She had clung to Hugh's sweet talk and false promises that he would leave what he had described as an overbearing and manipulative wife whom he had never really loved. But that was all shot to hell when the wife and the mother of his children actually confronted Jessica and declared in no uncertain terms that she wasn't going anywhere and neither was Hugh, no matter his indication to the contrary. She demanded that Jessica find some other man to sleep with and leave hers alone.

That was when Jessica knew, as the blunt words sank in, hitting her with the force of dynamite exploding, it was time to cut her losses and move on. No matter the pain in letting the man go. She felt she was better than being someone's part-time lover, even if she had allowed herself to get emotionally and physically attached to him. When Jessica laid this on Hugh, expecting him to pour on the charm in keeping a good thing going, for him at least, instead he seemed more relieved than upset, making no effort to try and talk her into continuing their affair.

And so, just like that, it was over, as though the relationship had never existed in the first place. She hadn't seen or spoken to the successful financial advisor since. *Even if I miss the gentleness of his touch and warmth of his breath on my cheeks and so much more, I won't ever seek him out again,* she promised resolutely. *He made his choice and it certainly wasn't me. I have to live with that and am better for it.*

Jessica bit back the thoughts and drove away from the building. She really had no reason to feel sorry for herself. After all, she was by most accounts a raven-haired, blue-eyed, modern-day Scarlett O'Hara in *Gone With the Wind* type beauty without the Southern drawl, who had put herself through law school, had a successful practice, and her own spacious home in a nice part of town. All at the relatively young age of thirty-four. She didn't need a man in her life. Certainly not one who would cheat on his wife and make Jessica believe he was worth doing to another woman what she would never want done to herself.

But I am a woman with needs like anyone else, the kind that only a man can provide, she thought. *I just need to stay away from those who aren't in trouble, intimidated by an attractive, successful, confident lady. Or are otherwise bad news.*

At a stoplight, Jessica checked her cell phone for messages. Nothing grabbed her attention. She considered touching base with a client or two, but figured that could wait. When the light turned green, she drove a different route than usual, without giving it much thought, and spotted a bar called Dusty's at the corner of Wellington and Twenty-Sixth Street. Hadn't been there before. Not that she had gone to every bar in town. In this case, she was out of her normal path from the courthouse. On the spur, she decided why not live dangerously, just this once, and pulled into the small parking lot, and into the first spot she saw. Afterwards, Jessica checked her appearance in a compact mirror, then dabbed a little *eau de parfum* spray on the base of her neck, and headed inside, for better or worse.

Chapter Two

At six-nineteen p.m., Officer Guy Bean responded to the 911 call at the Cherryton Apartments on Oswego Drive, near Wryer College, a private liberal arts institution on the southside of Creighton Hills. A neighbor had complained about a woman screaming her head off, as the caller put it, in Apartment 140. *So what else is new?* Bean thought, not taking it too seriously. She was probably getting her jollies with some guy she picked up on or off campus that evening. Or maybe it was the other way around. Bean figured the so-called screamer was caught up in the throes of hot sex and probably high as a kite. He used to be pretty bad himself at raising some hell back in the good old days of his youth. But this was now. Over forty and still holding onto his dark hair, married, and with three kids to support, it was his job to investigate every call that came his way, including those that proved to be false alarms.

After pulling his vehicle up to the three-story building at six-twenty-nine, Bean exited and headed to the first-floor unit in question. Right off the bat, he saw no sign of forced entry. A good step in the right direction. Indeed, the door was partially ajar, as if to invite him in. He knocked anyhow. There was no response. Pushing the door open further, he could see nothing out of the ordinary in the lowly lit unit. And no one within his view.

"This is the police," he said. "We received a call about noise coming from this apartment. Is anyone home…?" Maybe the occupant had stepped out and visited a neighbor, the officer considered, leaving the door open for a quick return. Or was asleep. Bean called out again. No response. Warning bells went off in his head that a woman could well be in distress and unable to call out. Erring on the side of caution, he removed his Glock 19 service pistol and stepped inside, identifying himself again while flipping on a light and surveying the scene.

Apart from noticing the dirty dishes in the kitchen, Bean couldn't help but notice the knife missing from the knife block on the counter, as it stood out like a sore thumb. Still, that meant little in and of itself to cause alarm as he moved further into the apartment. Then he heard a noise coming from a bedroom and approached with caution. The door was open. He homed in on a tall and attractive, dark-haired white female in her early twenties. She was standing over the bed, holding a bloody knife in her right hand, as if there was nothing better to do.

Bean immediately shifted his gaze to the young, blonde-haired white female lying on the bed in a nightgown. She was covered in blood from what appeared to be numerous stab wounds. The tormented look in her ashen face told him all he needed to know. She had been the victim of a horrific attack and may or may not live to talk about it.

"Drop the knife!" he ordered, entering the room and pointing his gun at the suspect. She stared at him blankly, as though in a state of shock. Or perhaps resignation that she had been caught, quite literally, red-handed with the murder weapon. Bean wasn't sure if she heard or understood him, but he sure as hell was not going to take any chances with her. He repeated the order vociferously, "Drop the knife," adding brusquely, "Now!" The last thing he wanted to do was shoot her before she could be arrested for what appeared to be coldblooded murder. But he would if he had to.

She apparently got the message and dropped the knife to the floor, blood splattering from it in the process. Bean quickly moved to handcuff her while reading the suspect her rights.

Words slithered from her mouth that were barely discernible to him. It sounded like she said, "I didn't kill her—"

* * *

"Buy you a drink?" Jessica heard the man ask in an ultra-smooth baritone voice, practically before she had even taken a seat at the bar.

That was quick. *Maybe a little too quick*, she thought. Or not. Fortunately, she was in the mood to be pursued by a very good-looking man in his mid-thirties. He was tall, Jessica imagined, at least six-three, even in his leather chukka boots; wore his medium-length dark hair in a messy tapered style, surrounding a square-jawed, clean-shaven face; and was sexy as hell in bootcut jeans and a checkered sport shirt that fit snugly on a muscular frame. She considered it a welcome departure from the expensive, crisp suits her former lover always wore, as if being without was not an option.

"Sure, why not," Jessica told the man with a smile as she gazed into his mesmerizing deep gold-flecked gray eyes.

He grinned back tantalizingly. "What are you having?"

Jessica thought she picked up on a Midwestern accent. Or was that by design as a way to charm the ladies? It was working. Normally, she ordered a cosmo, daiquiri, or an aviation cocktail, depending on the mood. But, this time, she decided to be adventurous. "Whatever you are, as long as it's not beer." She hated beer. Reminded her too much of the rowdies she used to hang out with in college and her early work career. Thanks, but no thanks.

He gave her an accepting the challenge type of pleased look. "In that case, two scotch on the rocks."

She watched as he sat next to her and wondered if he was married, single, or married but still looking for action. Hugh quickly came to mind. Just as quickly, she removed him from it. "Scotch on the rocks it is," she agreed.

The man ordered the drinks and said, "By the way, my name's Liam."

"Jessica." The lawyer in her was happy to limit the intros to a first-name basis with no reason to pry further. She assumed he was comfortable keeping it that way too.

"I'm guessing you don't come in here often?" He chuckled tersely, as if regretting the question. "I know that sounds like a cliché. Or pickup line. In this case, I come here often and, at the risk of digging a deeper hole for myself, seriously doubt if I'd ever forget your gorgeous face."

Jessica couldn't help but laugh. Even if his easy use of clichés was anything but original, she was flattered nonetheless. "You guessed right," she let him off the hook. "I happened to notice the place when I was about to pass by and decided to check it out."

"Good for you." He grinned again. "Me too. I can always use the right company."

"Oh, really?" Jessica lifted a thin brow. "How do you know I'm the right company?"

He laughed. "I have good instincts."

She laughed back. "Nice answer." Jessica got a warm feeling at the way he was staring at her. Clearly, he was hoping to get lucky. And, given the fact that she was trying hard to get her ex jerk out of her system, the man before her just might get his wish.

The drinks came and he asked, holding up his glass, "Are we drinking to anything in particular?"

She smiled, thinking devious thoughts shamelessly. "How about us?"

"Yeah, I like that." He flashed straight white teeth in a sensual way. "Us, it is."

They clinked glasses and Jessica downed the scotch. It burned as it went down her throat, but she wasn't complaining. She wondered what her drinking mate did for a living. Or maybe it was better if she didn't know anything about him. That way they could just keep it light and fun. No regrets.

"How about a second round?" he asked, as if reading her thoughts and seemingly in complete agreement.

"I'm game," she said, in the mood for a little celebrating and alcohol.

He ordered the drinks and they came. Beneath the rim of his glass, his eyes fell on her with more than a little curiosity. "What am I missing here—a beautiful woman all alone in a bar, slightly off the beaten path?"

She flashed her teeth self-consciously. "But I'm not alone, am I? I'm sitting here with a handsome man, who was just as alone in this place off the beaten path."

He laughed. "Yeah, that's true. Guess we're pretty much in the same boat." He tasted his drink. "Sorry about the questions. Force of habit."

Jessica couldn't argue that point. Seemed like they had that much in common when it came to the force of habit part. For her, it came with the territory of an attorney's life and times. What was his excuse? She didn't figure him to be a lawyer. So, what then? "Let's just say I'm not quite ready to share the story of my life to a perfect stranger," she told him and sipped her scotch.

His hands went up as though under arrest. "Hey, no problem. I'm enjoying the company all the same."

So am I, she had to admit, maybe more than was advisable. "Just one question for you," Jessica said, believing all was fair in piquing one's curiosity.

He folded his hands composedly. "Shoot."

Could he be a cop? she wondered. Or maybe a robber? "You married?" Seemed a reasonable question, considering they were hanging out at a bar together.

"I was once," he answered succinctly, "but right now I'm free as a bird."

Jessica smiled, happy to hear that he was single, as was she. She wasn't quite ready to jump into bed with another married man. But unmarried and free as a bird might be a different thing altogether. Now was the time to get brazen. "Do you want to go to your place?" She assumed he had a place he called home.

"Thought you'd never ask." He grinned jokingly. "Yeah, I would be happy to."

Jessica finished off the liquid courage, hoping she didn't hate herself in the morning. But this evening, it seemed like the right thing with the right person. "I'll follow you."

Chapter Three

The Crime Scene Investigations Unit arrived on the scene shortly after the call came in that a young woman had been murdered. The blood-splattered body was splayed cruelly on the bed as forensic investigator Blair Rodriguez observed what clearly was overkill. It didn't take a person in her position to see that someone definitely had it in for the victim. And they had obviously caught the victim totally off guard in the ultimate act of cowardice, attacking someone while defenseless in bed.

Nevertheless, Blair could see that the victim didn't go down without a fight of sorts. The numerous defensive wounds on her thin arms were evidence that the victim tried to ward off the blows from a razor-sharp knife, to no avail. Blair cringed at the thought of being on the receiving end of such a vicious attack. At twenty-five, she wasn't much older than the victim, who looked to be in her early twenties, or even younger than that. Her own life could have been snuffed out just as easily, had Blair been in the wrong place at the wrong time. Instead, in the present, it was her job to collect evidence that could be used to help put the perpetrator away.

She gazed down at the alleged murder weapon. Flipping her shoulder-length layered and wavy raven hair to one side, Blair crouched her slender frame to lift the knife carefully with her nitrile gloved hand. Studying the bloodstained blade that she estimated to be at least nine to ten inches, she felt it was much more suitable for carving a turkey or slicing through a loaf of bread than into a human being. She gulped while bagging it as evidence.

A brief scan of the bedroom, which was neat and nondescript beyond the bed and its immediate surroundings, gave Blair the chills as she realized that not much earlier, the victim was a living, breathing, college-aged female, with her whole life ahead of her. Now she was a forever sullied corpse who would have to be cut up even more by the medical examiner to determine the exact cause of death.

As far as Blair was concerned, the answer was in the plastic evidence bag she was holding. And the killer was apparently the victim's own roommate; her motivation, whatever it was, likely to be established in a court of law.

* * *

Deputy District Attorney Madeleine Griffin was still licking her wounds after losing what seemed like an open and shut case, while paying a visit to the Creighton Hills Police Department. She hated not being able to add another W to her column, especially when she was considering running against her boss in the next election for the top spot in Thorne County. But Jessica Frost had come out on top this round, whether justified or not, and there was nothing Madeleine could do about it, except look toward the next case and hope for a different result.

Madeleine noted a detective bringing in someone who reminded her of the bitch who slept with her ex-partner three years ago. She had come home unexpectedly and caught them going at it hot and heavy in her own bed. It totally disgusted her. Instead of listening to her ex, Karen, try and rationalize the cheating, all but blaming Madeleine for being too consumed by her job, she kicked her ass out of the house, along with her floozy. While part of Madeleine wished she had never walked in on them, the better part of her was glad to rid herself of a woman who had been playing her for a fool. She'd moved on with someone who made her happy and practically worshipped the ground she walked on.

She looked again at the handcuffed white female, on the slender side and wearing an ivory cashmere crew, stained with blood, brown skinny jeans, and flats. Her short, dark brown hair was in a flipped style with a part on the side and blue eyes latched onto her own, as if a plea for help. Madeleine couldn't tell if she was inebriated or not. Or simply overwhelmed by her current predicament, but decided the twentysomething woman really didn't look as much like her ex's whore as at first glance. *Too skinny and taller,* Madeleine mused.

Approaching the arrestee and Detective Jackson Payne—an African American in his late thirties, tall and muscular in a cheap blue suit, with a dark line up short haircut and deep brown eyes—she met his gaze and asked curiously, "What's her story?"

Payne, who held the woman by her elbow, furrowed his brow and shook his head. "Not good. She's been arrested for killing her roommate."

"How?" Madeleine was piqued even more while wondering if the roomie was a standard, platonic roommate. Or one with benefits? Did they have an argument that got out of control? Domestic violence related? What?

"Stabbed to death," Payne said tonelessly.

She winced and eyed the suspect, who now seemed to Madeleine to be glaring at her. Or was it the other way around? "Female roommate?" Or had her venom been directed at a cheating or abusive boyfriend?

"Yeah, and you're not going believe who the victim's father is…"

Madeleine caught the gleam of anticipation in his eye, suggesting there was something worthwhile behind it. But she wasn't in the mood for guessing games. "Just tell me."

"She's Judge Ralph McVeigh's kid," Payne responded animatedly.

That threw Madeleine for a loop. She was aware that McVeigh, a hardnosed Superior Court judge, had at least one daughter, having seen him doting over her at the courthouse like she was Queen of the Nile.

"Are you sure about that?" She gave the detective a sharp look before redirecting her attention to the murder suspect.

"Oh yeah," he responded positively. "Saw a picture of her with the judge at the apartment where the crime occurred. ID'd the victim by her driver's license, Kristine McVeigh, age twenty-two." He looked at the suspect. "She confirmed it as well that the person killed was Judge McVeigh's daughter."

That was proof enough for Madeleine, unless the judge himself refuted this. She was shocked at this interesting twist, while aware that as a result it would be a juicy case that was bound to get its fair share of media attention.

She wanted to be the prosecutor in what could be the trial of her career, thus far, were the facts to warrant such. "And the suspect's name is…?" Madeleine disregarded her for the moment, wanting to hear it from the detective.

"Stephanie Dozier."

"I didn't kill Kristine," the young woman blurted out, as if snapped from a trance. "This is all a big mistake…"

Madeleine flipped her lids in a gesture of denunciation. If she had a dollar for every suspect who feigned innocence, only to be proven to the contrary, she would be a very rich woman and living the good life in the Bahamas. As a result, she didn't take such protestations seriously. Instead, she eyed Payne for his position.

"We're on our way to the interrogation room to get to the bottom of this," he said. "But based on the arresting officer's report and evidence collected at the scene, it's not looking good for Ms. Dozier—"

"Just be sure it's all strictly by the book," Madeleine warned, realizing how even little mistakes these days could affect the outcome of this case. "We don't want the suspect crying later about her rights being violated and such." *Especially when the victim was a prominent judge's daughter*, she thought.

"Not on my watch," Payne insisted, an edge to his voice.

"Well, don't let me stop you." Madeleine tried to restrain her eagerness to learn everything she could about the case against Stephanie Dozier. She would watch the interrogation through a one-way window, before proceeding.

* * *

Jessica followed the hot guy named Liam in his brown Chevrolet Trailblazer to a two-story floating house on the Creighton River. Though she was intrigued with the water setting and might have welcomed the grand tour under other circumstances, that wasn't exactly on her mind at the moment. Or his, for that matter, if she read him correctly. Leading her to a spacious first-floor master suite with rustic furnishings, they wasted little time stripping naked. Jessica set aside the self-consciousness she typically experienced the first time someone saw her without any clothes on—even though she was in great shape from jogging and a healthy diet—by focusing more on his six-pack and otherwise firm body. As if she needed to be turned on any more after a couple of drinks and a need to unwind from her workday. Before they could leap into action beyond kisses and caresses, she handed him a condom, having kept protection in her handbag from when she was still with Hugh. Her soon-to-be one-night stand put it on skillfully and without comment and they fell on the king-sized bed and got busy, getting to know each other much more intimately.

Jessica gave in to the sensations that swept through her body with lightning speed as they made love like there was no more tomorrow. She tasted the scotch left marinating inside his mouth from the bar with deep kisses while they traded positions a few times, before she settled in on the bottom and waited for the climax to come. It did not disappoint as both came at the same time, literally rocking the bed and increasing their heart rates till the moment passed and they could come back down to Earth.

Only then, as she lay cuddled in his firm arms like it was the most natural thing, did Jessica snap out of the lustful trap and realize she had just had sex with a complete stranger, albeit a quite handsome and very sexy one, who seemed to have enjoyed what just happened every bit as much as she did. All Jessica could think of was getting out of there as fast as she could. Sexually gratifying as it was being in his bed on his floating palace, she wasn't looking for a repeat performance; much less, getting back into a relationship with anyone. Something told her he felt the same way.

The familiar chime of a text message on her cell phone gave Jessica the perfect excuse to get out of bed. She ignored her nakedness and found her phone. Someone was seeking her representation ASAP.

She turned to her one-night stand, who was clearly enjoying the tight backside view. "I have to go."

"Too bad," he said, showing real disappointment. "I was hoping you'd hang around a little longer. Maybe have an early breakfast and maybe a bit more dessert beforehand."

Jessica nearly laughed out loud at his poetic way of saying he wanted to have more sex with her. Even if part of her was intrigued by the notion, the better part knew when it was time to call it a day and quit while she was ahead. Or at least even. "Afraid not," she told him. "Something's come up that I need to attend to." She gathered up her clothes that were spread across the laminate floor and got dressed quickly.

"I see." He sat up, displaying his broad chest. "So, do you want to get together again sometime?"

Jessica thought about it. But not too hard. What would be the point, since she never expected to see him again? Not unless she happened upon that bar another time, which she doubted. "Why don't we just leave it at two strangers who had some fun, but whose time has come and gone?" On that note, she grabbed her handbag and was soon out the door, without looking back.

Chapter Four

Jessica's services had been retained by a Mr. and Mrs. Bernard Dozier on behalf of their twenty-one-year-old daughter, Stephanie Dozier, who had been arrested on suspicion of stabbing to death her roommate. Both attended Wryer College, a coed liberal arts university in Creighton Hills that was considered one of the best private colleges in the Pacific Northwest, with a high graduation rate and reputation for leading to high-paying jobs. The seriousness of the accusation notwithstanding, it was the victim's name that stood out in Jessica's mind.

Kristine McVeigh.

As in Judge Ralph McVeigh's daughter. The same judge that Jessica had stood before less than twenty-four hours ago and would likely be in his court again, sooner rather than later. News of his daughter's death had spread like wildfire in the legal community throughout the morning. And, along with it, McVeigh wisely taking the high judicial road in public—in spite of grieving the loss of his only child—by insisting that the alleged killer must be allowed to have her day in court, as was her right, with the underlying theme that justice would surely be served to the full extent of the law at the end of the day.

It was within this context that Jessica was seeing her client for the first time as she was led by an armed male guard into the conference room. Handcuffed and wearing a standard jail-issued orange jumpsuit, she looked frazzled and scared, not too surprisingly. Who wouldn't be, given the circumstances of facing a murder rap and all that went with it? Beyond that initial assessment, Jessica saw a tall and slim attractive young woman with short brown hair and blue eyes that were bloodshot, as if little sleep had come her way since she was arrested. Jessica wondered if she had been drinking alcohol or using drugs at the time of the alleged crime. If so, this would likely be a factor that the prosecution would seek to exploit in bolstering the State's case. At the moment, the person before her could easily have been the proverbial girl next door instead of a murder suspect. But, then again, there was no clear portrait of who was capable of committing cold-blooded murder. Or who was merely in the wrong place at the wrong time.

Which category did she fall into?

Jessica stood from the metal table and eyed the burly guard. "Please remove the cuffs." He frowned, and did so begrudgingly. "Thank you," she told him stiffly.

"I'll be right outside the door if you need me," he muttered.

Jessica appreciated that but did not feel the need for his protection in this instance, able to defend herself if need be. "We'll be fine." She waited till he'd left and then greeted the client as if an old friend. "I'm Jessica Frost," she told her evenly. "Your parents hired me to represent you."

Stephanie gave her an impassive look, as if she expected no less of them. "Are you going to get me out of here?"

It was what every client wanted to know without preamble. No hello. No thanks for coming, or any other pleasantries. Jessica got that, knowing how traumatic it was to be in a jail setting if one had never experienced it before. She wished she could simply wave a magic wand in response to the question posed. Alas, no two cases were alike. "I'm going to try," she promised while adding candidly, "but it can't happen until tomorrow at the earliest at your arraignment when we can request bail." Even in so saying, Jessica knew it would be an uphill battle, given the nature of the charge and the fact that the victim was the daughter of a prominent judge.

"I don't want to stay in this creepy place all night," Stephanie whined, wrinkling her dainty nose. "Especially for something I didn't do."

That was going to be my first question, Jessica thought, *are you guilty?* She liked her answer, before being asked. Not that it was unexpected. Few clients ever admitted to being guilty as charged, as if there was a natural resistance to owning up to his or her actions. Still, it was a starting point.

"I understand how scary it must be being put in jail, but that's the way the system works if you're accused of a serious offense, guilty or innocent," she told her candidly. "I'm afraid there's no way you'll be able to get out tonight. You'll just have to be a little patient and we'll see what happens tomorrow. Right now, I need to get some information from you. Have a seat."

When she hesitated, as if wary of sitting on a pin, Jessica sat first in a wooden chair and waited till Stephanie Dozier followed suit.

Jessica went over the facts in her head as she had been told by the girl's parents, in contrast to the police report. Stephanie had supposedly come home to find her roommate, Kristine McVeigh, barely alive, the victim of a stabbing attack. She panicked and tried to help Kristine, only to wind up being arrested for the crime. Jessica studied Stephanie, trying to picture her as a murderess. She couldn't get a read on her at this point, other than the presumption of innocence or maybe not so innocent, but as her attorney, Jessica was prepared to do what she could to work in the girl's best interests. That included having any damaging statements she may have given to detectives without representation thrown out as inadmissible, should this go to trial.

"I'm told you're an honor student at Wryer College?" Jessica usually liked to ease a client into the harder stuff.

"Yeah." Stephanie shrugged modestly.

"What's your major?"

"Environmental Science."

Jessica viewed this favorably. "Sounds good. Gives you a lot of choices in pursuing a career."

"Hope so." Stephanie lowered her chin, as if to wonder if that career would ever take shape.

Jessica pondered too how one wrong move could have life-altering implications for the living and dead. "Why don't you tell me exactly what happened tonight," she said levelly, sitting back as if preparing to watch a movie on television at her house, without the popcorn.

"Okay." Stephanie licked full lips nervously. "When I came home from

24

visiting my boyfriend, I heard a strange noise coming from Kristine's room. I looked in and saw her on the bed…" She sucked in a deep breath. "There was blood everywhere. I saw the knife stuck in her chest. She was writhing in pain and asked me to help her. I panicked. I didn't know what to do… " Her voice broke. "So, I pulled the knife out. I just didn't want to see her suffering like that, you know?"

Jessica could feel the horror she described as if in the middle of the movie, imagining anyone in such a situation might be tempted to do the same, given such dire circumstances. Of course, it was also the worst possible thing an innocent person could have done, if true. "What happened then?" she asked anxiously, wanting to get as much as possible out of her.

Stephanie's eyes watered. "I froze. Everything just seemed to go blank for a moment there. It was so surreal. I just couldn't believe anyone would do that to Kristine. Next thing I knew, the policeman was pointing a gun at me and ordering me to drop the knife." She sighed. "The weird thing is I didn't even know I still had the knife in my hand."

Jessica jotted down notes. "Did you tell the officer that when you were arrested?"

"Yeah, but he just gave me a weird look and said I did it."

"Did you at any time confess to the crime?" Jessica asked straightforwardly, aware that some suspects fell right into a trap like a cornered mouse when wilting under a harsh police interrogation.

"No, definitely not!" Stephanie spat. "I wouldn't have done that. I'm totally innocent."

Jessica was inclined to believe her, having no reason not to at this point, in spite of the authorities' belief to the contrary. But if she were truly innocent, it meant someone else was guilty of murder. And currently free, while Stephanie was on the hot seat as the culprit. Jessica needed to extract a few more critical details from her client to get the ball rolling in the right direction. "What time was it when you arrived at the apartment?"

Stephanie thought about it. "It was around six-thirty or so, I guess, based on the time I believe I left my boyfriend's apartment and how long it took to walk home, which is four blocks away."

Jessica looked at her. "And your boyfriend's name?"

"Brody Krane."

She jotted this down. "Did you see anyone lurking outside the apartment or running from it when you got there?"

"No," Stephanie answered apologetically. "I had things on my mind and wasn't really focused on anyone else."

Jessica would ask later what exactly was on her mind to not be observant of her surroundings and someone whom she may have inadvertently let off the hook for a deadly assault. "Was there any indication of a forced entry when you entered the apartment?"

"The door was unlocked," she responded matter-of-factly. "We never locked the door, except maybe when we were both there late at night."

That's sure convenient for someone wanting to kill Kristine, Jessica mused. Someone who would have known the door was unlocked, playing right into the killer's hands. She favored Stephanie with a direct look. "Were you drinking or using any drugs this evening?"

Stephanie dithered. "I smoked a joint with Brody," she admitted. "But I didn't get high, not really."

Jessica took that with a grain of salt. Even if she had smoked marijuana prior to the murder of her roommate, it didn't necessarily equate to committing murder. Or contributing to that mindset. Especially since Stephanie seemed cogent enough in her thoughts and actions before and since her arrest. "Did you and Kristine get along?" Jessica asked, imagining this was one of the first things a detective would have asked her, in trying to establish motive.

Stephanie hesitated. "Yeah, for the most part. I mean we fought sometimes like any roommates. But I certainly wouldn't have killed her because of it."

Jessica gazed at the young woman sharply. "Do you know of anyone who would want to kill Kristine?" she asked point blank.

"I've asked myself the same question," she claimed. "No one comes to mind. Kristine had lots of friends and no enemies that I knew of."

"Someone obviously had it in for her," Jessica stressed, given the apparent viciousness of the deadly assault.

"I guess so." Stephanie grew teary-eyed. "No matter what it was, she didn't deserve to die—not like that."

"You're right, she didn't." Jessica agreed that no one should be stabbed to death for any reason. Yet it happened to Kristine McVeigh. So, who killed her and why? Using her own intuition and the pure facts of the case as she knew them, thus far, Jessica decided that Stephanie wasn't the killer. Nevertheless, something told her that she was holding back for some reason. "If there's anything you know at all that can help me to help you get out of the predicament you're in, now is the time to say it," Jessica pressed her.

"I don't know why this happened to Kristine," Stephanie maintained. "I wish I could tell you more. I just know it wasn't me who killed her..."

"All right." Jessica felt she had been through enough for now, though aware it would likely get worse before it got better. Wasn't that often the case when one was being charged with murder? "I will do everything in my power to get you off the hook on this, as long as you're totally honest with me at all times."

Stephanie squared her shoulders. "I understand."

Jessica gave her a comforting smile and stuffed her notes in her briefcase. She stood and waited for her client to do the same. She put out her hand as Stephanie's official lawyer and they shook on it.

"Stay strong," Jessica told her, knowing how difficult that could be, all things considered.

The guard came in and escorted the arrestee out. Jessica followed suit, fully aware that she had her work cut out for her. She was up to the challenge, as this was her life. Even if it lacked in some areas, such as being in a committed relationship with the right man. Hugh certainly fell far short. Liam, her one-night stand, might have had potential had they gotten to know one another outside of bed. Some things were best left to the imagination. Right now, her focus had to be on one thing. Or should she say one person behind bars for something the accused most likely didn't do.

Chapter Five

By the time Jessica got to her residence on Elkwood Circle, she was exhausted after a long day that began victoriously, morphed into a sex romp with a hot stranger, and ended with a new case that figured to be anything but easy breezy. From what she understood, Stephanie Dozier would be formally charged with the murder of Kristine McVeigh tomorrow and there was no getting around it. But between that and a full-blown trial, if it ever got that far, Jessica hoped to prove that they were barking up the wrong tree with her client, while a real killer was out there waiting to be unmasked and apprehended.

She kicked off her mules, allowing her bare feet to feel the coolness of the eucalyptus hardwood flooring throughout the two-level prairie-style home, overlooking a golf course. Jessica had purchased it a year ago in the upscale Bremley Heights section of the city. She loved everything about it, including the open floor plan, high ceilings, great room, large casement windows, and brick fireplace. Outfitting the place with a blend of shabby chic and modern furnishings, the house truly felt like home. Though she hadn't taken up golfing yet, she did enjoy making use of the running and hiking trails on the grounds, which had a creek and an abundance of Oregon maple and Pacific dogwood trees.

Jessica stepped into the gourmet kitchen, cut on the light, got a half-filled bottle of Chardonnay out of the stainless-steel refrigerator, and poured herself a glass. Taking a sip, she thought about the man she'd made love to a few hours ago. She could still smell his masculine woodsy scent on her. Maybe she should have given herself a chance to get to know him better. They could have even talked about seeing each other again. Or would that have only caused her more pain down the line by falling for another handsome, sexy man, only to be let down and frustrated? Maybe there didn't need to be a future, only the present, which was now the past, with no complicated strings attached.

The chimes of her doorbell startled Jessica. It was nearly eleven p.m. Who was visiting her at that hour? Liam crossed her mind. Nope. He had no idea where she lived and she'd made sure no one had followed her when leaving his place, just in case he turned out to be some psycho stalker disguised as a good-looking and desirable hunk. Jessica took a breath, realizing she was letting her thoughts wander too far and wide.

When the bell rang again, she padded across the floor to the door and put her eye up to the peephole. She did a double-take when she saw that it was her former lover, Hugh Holliman, on the other side of the door. *He's got some nerve*, she thought, miffed. After debating for several seconds that seemed like hours as to whether or not to open the door, Jessica unlocked it and twisted the knob.

"What are you doing here?" she asked, unsmilingly, while glaring at him through the doorway.

Hugh was nearly forty with coarse salt and pepper hair in a Quiff style and a neatly trimmed balbo beard. He had on one of his typical tailored dark suits on a tall frame, along with lace-up derby shoes. His blue eyes crinkled. "I missed you," he said simply.

While part of her missed him too, Jessica was not about to admit it. Or let him back into her life. Thanks, but no thanks. "Does your wife know you're still pining for your ex-mistress?"

His face sagged. "She knows."

"And she's okay with it?" Jessica was curious as to his response, if for no other reason.

Hugh averted her gaze. "Claire doesn't know I'm here," he admitted shamelessly.

"Figured as much." Jessica pursed her lips. "You need to go."

"I want us to try to find a way to at least still be friends," he said in a tone of voice that sounded like he was grasping at straws. "I need you in my life, Jess."

"No, you don't," she countered, not about to fall for his charms again. "And I sure as hell don't need *you* in my life. You have a wife who loves you and clearly you love her, even if you won't admit it. I won't be a side dish for you anymore. It's over for us, Hugh. Now do us both a favor and never show up at my door again. Give me at least that much respect—and your wife, too."

He sighed, running a hand raggedly over his mouth. "If that's what you really want—"

"It is," Jessica insisted, standing her ground and proud of it. She wondered how she could have ever decided it was acceptable to be with a man who was married to another woman. Maybe it was a commitment phobia. More likely, she allowed herself too easily to fall for the wrong men. But not anymore. At least where it concerned the one groveling before her. "Goodbye, Hugh," she told him tersely, closing the door.

Jessica heard nothing for a moment or two, as though he was contemplating his next move, and then she heard him walking away, apparently reconciling himself to the fact that it truly was over between them. She felt a sense of triumph, happy to have some closure on that abbreviated part of her life.

She went back into the kitchen and finished the wine while thinking that seeing Liam again suddenly didn't seem like such a bad idea anymore.

* * *

Hugh Holliman felt as though he was caught between a rock and a hard place. He sat in his green Lexus ES Hybrid for a moment in front of Jessica's house, hating like hell that he hadn't done more to keep her as his lover. She got him, unlike his wife and other lovers he'd had over the years. But being with Jessica had put him in a nearly impossible situation. As a married man, happily or not, with two kids, he had family obligations that he couldn't simply walk away from and still call himself a man. He didn't love his wife and hadn't for a long time. Hell, he wasn't sure she still loved him as much as she just wanted to make his life miserable, while threatening to take him to the cleaners should he ever leave her.

The fact that Claire had found out about Jessica and actually confronted her shook him to the core. The last thing Hugh ever wanted was for his now ex-lover and wife to ever meet face to face. Or maybe that was the best thing to happen for all parties concerned, as it had forced Jessica to walk away from their relationship, doubting he could have ever gotten the guts to do the same. He'd made a half-hearted attempt to get back on Jessica's good side and into her bed tonight, telling his wife that he needed to go to the office for some papers. But Jessica wouldn't bend, seemingly determined to put him out of her life for good. Hugh wasn't sure he could merely leave it at that, knowing how good they were together. But Claire had him on a short leash and wouldn't stand for any more of his stepping outside the line.

At least not with Jessica. As it was, he had other options if he so desired. There were almost too many damned hot women looking for love in all the wrong places. Admittedly, he was guilty of the same affliction, against his better judgment. Hugh couldn't help but wonder if it was possible that he could somehow find his way back into Jessica's life once the dust settled in or over his marriage.

He started the car and drove off thoughtfully.

Chapter Six

Madeleine went into the Thorne County District Attorney's office at nine a.m. sharp, prepared to make her pitch for trying Stephanie Dozier for the murder of Kristine McVeigh. Given the heinous nature of the crime and the perpetrator being caught in the act with the murder weapon in hand and the victim's DNA likely all over her to strengthen the case, it was pretty much a no-brainer that they would not go lightly on the suspect. Especially considering that the victim was none other than Judge Ralph McVeigh's daughter. Madeleine wanted the accused to be held accountable, not only for a vicious criminal act, but also to send a very clear message that such crimes in this county would be dealt with to the fullest extent of the law. The public demanded no less. And for her part, she didn't want to disappoint.

"I want you to take on the Stephanie Dozier case," District Attorney Evan Pembroke uttered before Madeleine could even sit down in front of his large double pedestal desk and use her often reliable powers of persuasion. She gazed at the seated D.A., who was in his early fifties, but looked older in spite of his brownish, side-parted, preppy haircut. He looked up at her with baggy blue-gray eyes and seemed to take it in stride. "Think you can handle it?"

Madeleine assumed the question wasn't a literal one. Hadn't she proven time and again that she was more than up to the challenges her job required? She gave him a heartening smile. "Yes, I can definitely handle this. I'll be happy to prosecute the case," she said even-voiced as she sat down before him. She realized there were a few other talented prosecutors he could easily have handed this plum assignment to. Thankfully, she didn't have to remind him of her nearly flawless career record as a trial lawyer to win him over.

"Your last one didn't go so well," Pembroke mentioned, as if having second thoughts, in threatening to burst her bubble.

Madeleine narrowed her eyes, surprised that he should bring that up and offer her the case in practically the same breath. "The jury failed to grasp just how serious child molestation can be when an innocent-looking woman is the accused," she explained, realizing how hollow that sounded, even if there was more than a grain of truth in it. Especially when coupled with a competent attorney having her back, such as Jessica Frost.

"I understand that Stephanie Dozier is an attractive coed, gets good grades, with no criminal record and, as yet, no clear-cut motive," the D.A. said. "A jury may also find it hard to believe that she would just up and stab to death her roommate, as if it came out of nowhere."

He was testing her resolve and confidence. *I can ace this*, Madeleine thought with self-assurance. "Stranger things have happened," she said wryly. "We both know that people fly off the handle all the time and it doesn't always end well."

"That's true." Pembroke paused. "But this seems like overkill."

She couldn't argue with that, knowing that the victim was stabbed at least twelve times, according to a preliminary report by the medical examiner. "It was definitely overkill," Madeleine stated. "In my experience, when someone is killed in such a way, it often involves a classic love triangle," she theorized. "Though we're still looking into this, it has all the earmarks of jealous rage. Throughout history, young women have been known to do vicious things in the name of jealousy, anger, and revenge, as it related to the all-consuming power of love—and that includes committing murder as the ultimate payback."

Pembroke's brow furrowed. "If true, what a terrible price to pay, especially for the victim." He leaned forward. "There should be no bail for the accused. Judge McVeigh is a personal friend of mine. This is tearing him up, understandably so. He wants to see justice done and his daughter's killer locked up until such time that she is found guilty—if, in fact, the jury agrees."

That was a given as far as Madeleine was concerned. Of course, Dozier's defense attorney, whoever that might be, would see things differently and try for bail, even if unlikely due to the cruelty of the crime. "We're all certainly on the same page here," she told her boss, certain that the judge at the arraignment would also see it their way.

"Good." Pembroke sat back. "By the way, I understand that Stephanie Dozier is being represented by Jessica Frost."

Madeleine barely blinked at the news, though it did give her a start. "Why am I not surprised?" she said nonetheless, when thinking about it. "Jessica seems willing to take on anyone if it suits her fancy or the price is right." *Maybe I should have gone into private practice and sold myself to the highest bidder*, Madeleine thought. As if. She would much rather be on the right side of the law than not. This case was no different.

"Let's just make sure the outcome is in our favor this time around," Pembroke warned in no uncertain terms. "Neither of us can afford a slip up on this one."

"Understood." Loud and clear. Anything less than a conviction and she could kiss her chances at moving up the ladder in the District Attorney's office goodbye.

* * *

Jessica arrived at the courthouse at five to one. She'd had a restless sleep last night, tossing and turning between dreams of being stabbed to death herself and making love to a man she hardly knew. *That's an understatement*, she thought, considering neither took the time to get to know one another, other than in bed. That last bit caused Jessica to blush.

She expected the arraignment to be pretty routine. Whether that meant she could get her client bail, even a high one, remained to be seen. She would certainly get no help from her opponent.

Jessica didn't have to guess who that might be. Before she could reach her client, she was cut off by none other than Madeleine Griffin.

"Didn't expect to see you back in the ring so soon, Jessica," she quipped humorlessly.

Jessica turned this around aptly. "I could say the same for you, Counselor."

Madeleine grinned. "When duty calls, I jump on it."

"Guess we're not so different after all," Jessica said in a sincere tone.

"I wouldn't go that far. My job is to keep dangerous people off the streets. Yours is to find a way to circumvent justice by any means necessary."

Jessica frowned. "That's over the top, even for you, Madeleine. You know as well as I do that every defendant is entitled to counsel. My job is to stop you from railroading innocent people, so I guess we'll just have to keep bumping heads."

Madeleine fluttered her lashes. "I doubt very much that your latest client is innocent of anything," she said rudely. "Quite the contrary, I see her as someone very guilty of brutally murdering her roommate."

Jessica gritted her teeth. *I won't allow her to get under my skin*, she thought, which was obviously her intention. "I suppose innocent until proven guilty has somehow gotten lost in the shuffle with you, Counselor?" She allowed that to sink in for an instant of soul searching. "Now if you'll excuse me..."

Jessica skirted past the prosecutor and made her way to where Stephanie Dozier was already waiting, still dressed in jail garb and otherwise looking worn down. Forcing a smile, Jessica wanted to try and keep her client thinking positively. "How are you holding up?"

"I just want to go home," she said emotionally.

Jessica wondered if she meant back to the apartment scene of the crime. Or to Boise, Idaho, where she was from. "I know this is difficult," Jessica conceded, "but let's try to get through it and face whatever happens head-on." She realized that was easier said than done when facing a murder charge. Jessica had prepped her client in advance on what to do and say before the judge, wanting to minimize the damage as much as possible for a felony arraignment.

Thorne County Circuit Court Judge Loretta Watkins entered the courtroom. She was a slender woman in her forties with chestnut hair in a lob cut. She looked out over the courtroom before sitting on her throne. Jessica had seen her a time or two, chatting amicably in the hall with Judge McVeigh. Nothing unusual there from one judge to the next. This would likely not fare well, though, in terms of getting Jessica's client released on bail, but she would try her best.

After a few routine opening remarks, the judge read the single current charge of murder in the first degree. She eyed the defendant. "Do you understand the charge, Ms. Dozier?"

Stephanie lowered her eyes. "I do, Your Honor."

"And how do you plead?" she asked.

Stephanie looked at Jessica and back at the judge. "Not guilty, Your Honor."

Judge Watkins noted this for the record and then turned to the subject of bail, deferring to the prosecutor to present the State's best argument in this regard.

Madeleine glared at Jessica and her client, before facing the judge. "Your Honor, a young woman—Kristine McVeigh—was viciously stabbed to death in her own bed. We believe the person responsible is her roommate, the defendant, Stephanie Dozier, who was quite literally caught standing over the victim while holding the murder weapon. Given the horrendous nature of the offense, in which Ms. McVeigh was stabbed repeatedly, and the threat posed to the public by releasing the suspect, the State asks that there be no bail."

"I expected as much, Counselor," the judge said equably. She turned to Jessica. "And what's your view, Ms. Frost? I think I can hazard a guess that you're not on the same boat as Ms. Griffin, but let's hear it…"

Jessica took a step forward, as if to somehow separate herself from her opponent in appealing to the judge's sense of fairness. "Your Honor, my client is a twenty-one-year-old honor student at Wryer College. She has never been accused of a crime, much less arrested for one. Ms. Dozier walked in on a dangerous situation, in which her roommate had been seriously injured and had a knife still left in her by the killer. Trying to honor Ms. McVeigh's request that the knife be removed, in too weakened a state to do so herself, my client thought she was doing the right thing in showing mercy and hoping, at the same time, that she might actually save her friend's life by taking the knife out of her chest. It was my client's misfortune that she happened to still be holding it when the police officer arrived and drew the wrong conclusions. Given those circumstances, while recognizing the seriousness of the charge, I ask that Ms. Dozier be released at a reasonable bail till such time that her innocence will be proven beyond a shadow of a doubt." Given that her parents were well-to-do and indicated that they were willing to put up the money for any bail, Jessica hoped her pitch was good enough to give them that opportunity.

Judge Watkins wasted little time with her answer. Facing the accused, she uttered stoically and without preface, "Bail is denied."

Jessica watched as her client broke into sobs. She placed a comforting arm around her shoulder. "This isn't over," she promised, hoping to bring up the issue of bail again.

Jessica felt helpless as Stephanie Dozier was taken back to jail.

Chapter Seven

L iam Reed sat in his not so roomy downtown office on Westmore Drive, putting away in a virtual file cabinet on his laptop some final notes from the last case he'd worked on as a private investigator. Seemed like a missing wife, presumed dead, had not really been missing after all. Nor was she a victim of foul play. Rather, she had run off to Buenos Aires, Argentina, to be with a man she'd met online and had no plans to return.

Liam leaned back in his camel-colored leather chair, thoughts turning to the raven-haired beauty he'd met at Dusty's last night. Putting aside the fact that they were total strangers—at least in the beginning—there was an air of familiarity about her, though he couldn't quite put a finger on where he might have seen her. Since they never exchanged any vital information, apart from his being divorced, he hadn't a clue to work with. Perhaps she was a celebrity, of sorts, that needed to step away from the limelight. Or maybe had some other claim to fame or even infamy. Maybe it was all in his head. Whatever the case, the last thing he ever expected was to take her home to bed. Good thing he'd changed the sheets that very morning. Must have been a sixth sense, had he believed in that kind of thing.

Then she received a text message and, just like that, she'd left like a thief in the night. While making it clear that she had no plans for a repeat performance. No matter that the sex was incredible for both of them, given the way they reacted to one another during the process. Liam could still smell her, intoxicating and arousing at the same time, and feel her ultra-soft skin against his hard body. He bit back these sensations while continuing to speculate about the mysterious lady. He suspected that she'd been running from something—or someone—on an emotional level. And he happened to be at the right place at the right time.

Not that he could blame her much for wanting a no-strings-attached quickie. He too had been in his fair share of disappointing relationships and felt on the whole that they were more trouble than they were worth. That was certainly true where his ex-wife was concerned. He had met Kelly when they both worked for Homeland Security. He was a criminal investigator and she was a forestry technician. They got along great professionally and thought that could somehow translate well into matters of the heart. It started out that way, but quickly fizzled and they both agreed that they weren't a good match and went their separate ways.

Liam took it even further, deciding at the age of thirty-one that he needed a clean break from his former life in Indianapolis, Indiana; relocating to the Pacific Northwest five years ago. He settled in on Creighton Hills, where he bought a floating house to be near the water sports he enjoyed, and opened his detective agency, tapping on his skills as a federal investigator to earn a decent living. Again, his mind wandered back to the woman he knew only as Jessica. For his part, he wasn't averse to giving it another go with her in the sack, if the opportunity were to present itself again. Better yet, he envisioned getting to know her on a deeper level. Apart from being drop-dead gorgeous and super sexy, in and out of her fashionable clothing, the lady had an air of sophistication about her and clearly had more going for her than great sex and bar company.

Dream on, Liam told himself, getting real. *That ship has sailed.* His reverie was broken as a thin woman came into the office. She was maybe forty, or a little younger, with blonde hair in a layered bob, and wearing a brown dress suit with espadrille wedge sandals.

"How can I help you?" he asked politely.

"I'd like to hire you," she responded firmly.

Liam never saw a paying customer he didn't like. But, in spite of being between cases, he still needed to know what he was getting himself into beforehand. "And your name is...?"

"Jackie Quail."

He stood up, towering over the woman, and shook her hand. "Liam Reed," he introduced himself formally. "Won't you have a seat, Ms. Quail?"

She sat in one of the two rose-colored task chairs across from his reversible U-desk. He sat back down and met her blue eyes. "What is it you want to hire me to do?"

"I need to find out why my brother's dead," she said with a hard edge to her voice.

Sounds simple enough for a start, Liam thought. "When did he die?"

"Last month."

"Name?"

"Sean Quail."

"Hmm." Liam's mind raced. "Why does that name sound familiar?"

"Sean was a professor at Wryer College," Jackie explained. "Until recently, I thought he was pretty happy with his life. Then, all of a sudden, he kills himself. I want to know why."

Liam recalled hearing about the art history professor, who was found hanging in his office. The police had ruled it a suicide.

"Sometimes these things just happen," Liam suggested, though in no way meant to diminish her pain in losing a family member. "Maybe he was under pressure with bills, tenure, lack thereof, or—"

"Or maybe his wife drove him to it," she blurted out as if Liam had never considered that angle.

"He was married?"

"For ten years."

"What makes you think his wife had anything to do with the suicide?" Liam asked curiously.

"I don't know that she did," Jackie replied flatly. "When I've tried to talk to her, she's blown me off. Not sure why." She sighed. "All I know is that my brother was in good health, had a good job, and people who loved him. If he took his own life, there must have been a reason that hasn't come to light. I want you to find out what that is."

Liam was never one to take someone's money merely to fatten his bank account, which was why he always liked to be upfront about the realistic prospects for an acceptable outcome. "I'll be happy to look into this, as long as you know I may come up with nothing out of the ordinary that may make you feel you got your money's worth."

She nodded. "I just want some peace of mind, no matter what you come up with, even if it's nothing at all."

"Fair enough." He informed her of his fees, which were, more or less, on par with the competition, if not a bit lower. After collecting some basic information on Sean Quail, Liam told his new client, "I'll be in touch," and saw her out.

Back at his desk, Liam considered the fact that with the murder yesterday of a female student at Wryer College, this meant two people associated with the school had died in a short period of time. Coincidence? Perhaps, considering the authorities had already made an arrest in the student's death. Another female student, with whom she shared an apartment, had been charged with the crime. But then again, he was never one to take coincidences at face value.

Liam got on his cell phone and opened a local news station app. He clicked on the headlines video that talked about the murder of Kristine McVeigh, the daughter of a criminal court judge, Ralph McVeigh. After a news brief on the case, the video switched to a news conference held by the defendant's lawyer, Jessica Frost. It was the voice that first caught Liam's attention, ringing a bell in his head. Then he saw her attractive face. He clicked on the full screen.

Well, I'll be damned, he thought with surprise. That explained the familiarity. His mystery lady was a successful criminal defense attorney, who appeared to have her hands full in her latest representation. He wished her luck.

Liam's thoughts switched to being picked up at the bar by the lady last night. He instantly felt his libido rise as he recalled their time in bed. He wondered what the chances were that Jessica Frost might show up again tonight at Dusty's.

✳ ✳ ✳

"Seems like you've got another challenging case on your hands," Connie Martinez told Jessica as they sat in a riverside coffee shop on Fisher Way called Café Laney's that afternoon. The two had met at a trial lawyers conference in Portland three years ago and had been friends ever since. Connie, who was a Mexican-American and a partner in the Creighton Hills law firm, Nelson, Martinez, and Associates, had been trying to entice Jessica into joining the practice; thus far, to no avail. Though tempting, right now, Jessica enjoyed her independence in deciding which cases to take and which to pass on.

"Tell me about it." She held a chai latte while looking at her attractive friend, who was the same age, tall, and model thin in a power cream-colored suit; with long and glossy brunette hair with blonde highlights and brown-green eyes. Jessica was glad to have someone to bounce things off of who could relate to the situation. "The story of my life." At least her professional life. Not to say that her personal life hadn't come with its own challenges, for better or worse.

Connie rolled her eyes. "Judge Watkins may as well have just announced to the whole world that her decision to not even consider bail for your client was a personal favor to her buddy Judge McVeigh."

"I know." Jessica made a face. "You should've seen the look on that poor girl's face. She practically crumbled into my arms with disappointment. But there was nothing I could do."

"Comes with the territory, unfortunately," Connie said, nibbling on a croissant. "We all would love to get our clients out of jail, pending trial, if it were within our power. The important thing is to win your case at the end of the day." She paused. "You do believe your client is innocent of killing the judge's daughter, right?"

Jessica's eyes widened, surprised she would ask. On the other hand, even the guilty deserved representation, if only to try and get the best deal possible. "Of course," she made clear in this instance. "The police rushed to judgment in charging her with murder and the D.A.'s office was only too happy to jump on it, as if there was no one else to go after."

"Just asking, girlfriend," Connie said apologetically and lifted her cup of peppermint mocha. "I hope you can prove it."

"So do I." Jessica wasn't under any illusion that it would be easy. Madeleine would undoubtedly pull out all the stops to get a conviction and juries had heard about enough similar cases to believe it was entirely possible for a stressed-out or vindictive, the prosecution would say, college student, to go ballistic on her roommate, for one reason or another. Trusting her own instincts, Jessica intended to prove otherwise in this case; certain that someone else had it out for Kristine McVeigh.

"You could always come to work for our firm, Jess," Connie threw out once again. "I'm sure we could make you a partner and use our resources to tackle this together. Nothing says you have to stick with being a Lone Ranger."

Jessica smiled, always a little tempted when such an offer came her way. "I like being the Lone Ranger," she told her. "Or more like, the Lone Lawyer. I get to be my own boss, take the bitter with the sweet, and not have to worry about being fired if I step on the wrong toes."

"That wouldn't happen with us," Connie assured her, "but I understand. Still, if you ever change your mind, the offer stands—"

"And I love you for it." Jessica flashed her teeth sincerely. Admittedly, she liked the idea of one day working side by side with her friend. Perhaps at some point, she could lure Connie away from the firm to partner up with her in their own two-person law practice.

Jessica adroitly moved away from the subject of law and lawyers, to an equally tender topic. She told Connie about Hugh showing up at her door last night.

Connie shook her head with disgust. "What a jerk! Hope you told him where to go—as long as it wasn't straight into your bed...?"

Jessica gave her an amused grin. "You bet," she said gratifyingly. "I sent him back to his wife, where presumably he'll stay."

"Either that, or he'll find someone else to cheat on his wife with."

Jessica wouldn't put it past Hugh to find another mistress. *After all, isn't that what most adulterous men do when one became unavailable?* she mused. It certainly appeared that his wife had failed in her attempt to make them one happy couple. What could she do to change that?

"You what?" Connie's lower lip hung down, finding herself eager to hear more.

Jessica had saved the best for last, revealing her one-night stand. "It just seemed right at the time," she said guiltlessly.

Connie chuckled. "He must have been a real hottie, and then some."

Jessica blushed. "Oh yeah, he was pretty hot to trot—especially in bed," she added boldly.

"Maybe I need to try that some time," Connie said, sipping her drink. "My love life could certainly use a boost these days."

That was news to Jessica. "You're not still with that pilot hunk, what's his name?"

"Geoffrey Montgomery." Connie frowned. "We were never exclusive. Besides, with his hectic travel schedule, it would never have worked for the long term."

"Probably not," Jessica agreed, though feeling sorry for her, as if neither of them were capable of standing on their own two feet without romance in their lives.

"So, are you planning to see him again?" Connie asked curiously.

Jessica pondered the question. The answer had once been an unequivocal no. But she had to admit there was definite chemistry between them, even for such a short experience. And little of the drama she had experienced with Hugh. Maybe seeing Liam again might not be such a bad idea after all. "One never knows," she responded ambiguously, while already making plans to go back to that bar tonight, hoping he might be there.

Chapter Eight

Before Jessica could think about reuniting with Liam, duty called. Her first priority had to be her latest client, Stephanie Dozier, in giving her the best representation possible. That started with talking to Stephanie's boyfriend, Brody Krane, who Jessica established was a senior at Wryer College, on the timeline and her client's state of mind prior to the murder. Jessica drove to the apartment complex on Hagaden Road. After parking in the lot, she considered the story Stephanie told about the events of the evening in question. Would Brody back her up?

Upon climbing three flights of stairs, Jessica knocked on the door to Unit 318. It opened and she looked up into the face of a muscular male in his early twenties, with blue eyes and black hair in a high fade with a textured top. He was dressed in jeans and a T-shirt. "Brody Krane?" she asked.

"Yeah, that's me. Who are you?"

"Jessica Frost. I'm representing Stephanie Dozier."

He frowned. "How's she doing?"

"Not too well, as you might expect." Jessica met his eyes. "She named you as her boyfriend."

"Yeah, I am," he acknowledged tensely.

"I need to talk to you about what happened last night. Do you mind if I come in?"

"Of course not." He stepped aside and she walked through and into a cluttered and untidy living room that looked like the typical young guys' pad that she recalled from her college days and first boyfriend, named Pete Kellogg. "Excuse the mess," he apologized. "Blame it on my roommate."

45

"Not a problem," Jessica said, resisting a smile, given the nature of her visit. She watched as he transferred junk from one wide barrel chair to another and invited her to sit, while he remained standing.

"So, are they really charging Steph with murder?" Brody asked, as if in total disbelief.

"I'm afraid they are."

He voiced an expletive. "She wouldn't have killed Kristine," he claimed.

Jessica was glad to hear him say that, as her client would need his support to help her get through this. "According to Stephanie, she visited you yesterday. Is that correct?"

"Yeah." He looked down at his black sneakers.

Jessica did not bother to ask the nature of the visit, which she could figure out. "And what time did she leave?"

Brody shrugged. "I guess around six-ten or so."

"And she walked home?"

"Yeah. I offered to drive her, but she liked the exercise."

Jessica imagined that the prosecution would infer that she'd preferred to go home alone in order to murder her roommate with no witnesses. "What was Stephanie's state of mind when she left here?"

"She was fine," he said tersely and began pacing.

Why am I getting the feeling there's something he isn't saying? Jessica asked herself. "Can you think of any reason at all why Stephanie would want to kill Kristine?" she tossed at him. "Or at least lead the police to believe she had a motive?"

Brody stopped pacing and shifted his weight from one leg to the other. "Yesterday after we had sex, I told Steph that I slept with Kristine."

"Really?" Jessica cocked a brow in surprise as Stephanie hadn't bothered to disclose this to her. "When did this happen...?"

"Last week. It didn't mean anything," he insisted. "Kristine and I both had too much to drink and one thing led to another—"

"How did Stephanie react to the news?" Jessica asked, still wrapping her own mind around this possible motive for murder.

"How do you think?" His chin sagged. "She was pissed. But I still felt I

46

needed to get it off my chest, you know?"

It wasn't Jessica's job to pass judgment on his sexual activities, except where it pertained to her client's guilt or innocence. "So, when Stephanie left here, she was angry at you and Kristine? Maybe angry enough to stab her roommate to death as payback—" Jessica put out there for his reaction.

"Maybe," Brody conceded sourly. "I swore to her it was just a one-time thing and she was the one I wanted to be with. She seemed to accept it...but then I hear that she was arrested for killing Kristine. What am I supposed to think...?"

Jessica asked herself the same question, as she got to her feet. Taking the high road of innocent till proven guilty, she gazed at him and said evenly, "That the person you say is your girlfriend would not have committed such a heinous act out of vengeance, no matter how it looks—"

He looked shamefaced. "Yeah, I guess you're right."

"I suggest you go see her, show your support," Jessica told him. "In the meantime, I intend to do everything in my power to help Stephanie, no matter the outcome..."

Only after she saw herself out, did Jessica wonder just how straight her client had been with her. *Did I actually sign on to represent a cold-blooded killer?* she mused ill at ease.

* * *

Brody Krane watched as Jessica Frost left his apartment. He began pacing while seriously wondering if Stephanie had actually stabbed Kristine to death. In spite of what he told the defense attorney about believing Steph could not have killed Kristine, he wasn't so sure he really felt that way. His girlfriend was beyond furious when he fessed up about having sex with her roommate. No matter that it meant nothing to him, other than getting off while intoxicated and just wanting to put it behind him. Probably the worst thing he could ever have done was admit that he—and Kristine—had betrayed her. At the time, though, it seemed the right move to make, if they were to be totally honest with each other in having a real future together after graduation and beyond.

But Stephanie didn't seem to see it that way. Yeah, she made a halfhearted effort to say she forgave him and didn't want to end their relationship. Yet her body language and smoke practically coming out of her ears told him that it would take much more to get back on her good side. When it came to Kristine, however, Brody had the feeling that forgiving her was not in Stephanie's vocabulary. She intended to have it out with Kristine, one way or the other. While he had expected that it was possible the two might actually come to blows, he sure as hell didn't figure that Kristine would end up stabbed to death. And Steph being charged with the crime. Whether or not her attorney could get her out of this remained to be seen in Brody's mind. If his girlfriend really did take things this far, he couldn't pretend it didn't happen and want to continue to be in a relationship with her. But if she wasn't guilty, he owed it to Stephanie to try and be there for her. Right now, it was anyone's guess as to which direction this was headed.

* * *

Jessica waited for Stephanie to enter the room, anxious to hear what she had to say in light of the new revelations. *Until such time, I will withhold judgment,* Jessica thought, even if she felt dutybound to continue representing the coed and murder suspect.

When Stephanie came in, she looked nervous, as though expecting to be called out on her glaring omission in the case against her. After they were left alone, she asked hopefully, "Do you have any good news for me?"

"I'm afraid not." Jessica sighed before cutting to the chase. "I spoke to Brody Krane—"

Stephanie jutted her chin. "What did he say?"

"He confirmed that you and he were together shortly before the time your roommate was murdered." Stephanie reacted while remaining mute. "Brody also said he confessed to having sex with Kristine and that you were, as he put it, pissed."

Stephanie made no attempt to deny this. "Wouldn't you be if you found out that your boyfriend cheated on you with your roommate?"

"Yes," admitted Jessica, even as she considered her own experience as the other woman in a doomed relationship. The old adage, *hell hath no fury like a woman scorned*, came to mind. Had Stephanie taken things to that level of anger? "That's not the point. You should have told me this yourself when given the chance of putting everything on the table."

"If I had, would you have still wanted to represent me?" Stephanie shot back. "I know how it would have looked had I come clean about being angry that someone I trusted had slept with my boyfriend behind my back."

"Were you angry enough to kill her?" Jessica asked bluntly. Her tone softened when she added, "I will still represent you to the best of my ability, no matter what you say in confidence. I just need you to be straight with me..."

Stephanie's shoulders slumped. "I didn't kill Kristine, I swear to you," she contended. "Yes, I was furious with her and intended to have a good talk about what happened between her and Brody. I never had any thoughts about committing murder and throwing away my future in the process. Especially when Brody still wanted to stay together, choosing me over her." She sucked in a deep breath thoughtfully. "When I got to the apartment, someone else had already been there...and attacked Kristine... But it wasn't me—"

Again, Jessica couldn't help but believe her client's claim of innocence, even with the disturbing new twist in the case that Madeleine would surely use to her advantage, should the prosecutor put Brody on the stand. *I can't exactly prevent this*, thought Jessica realistically, even if he were a hostile witness under oath. It also made it risky to have him as a defense witness subject to cross-examination. She regarded her client, giving her the benefit of the doubt. "All right. If there's anything else you need to tell me, now is the time to do it..."

Stephanie contemplated this for a long moment or two, before saying meekly, "I've told you everything."

Jessica nodded to that effect while wondering if something else might materialize that made her question her client's innocence. Or, if the opposite might occur, information that could work in Stephanie's favor in casting doubt on her guilt in the eyes of the jury, or even the prosecution.

Chapter Nine

At Dusty's, Liam nursed his drink, wondering if lightning might strike twice and Jessica would make her presence known. Though she had suggested it was one and done with them, he held out hope that she might rethink this, wanting a repeat, if not compelled by a desire to get to know him better. Maybe he was getting carried away with his charms and bedroom skills. No harm in fantasizing, admittedly intrigued even more by the lady lawyer. When there was no sign of her after finishing off his first scotch on the rocks, Liam had decided against a second and was about to call it a night, casting aside his wounded ego, when he heard the familiar voice say, "My turn to buy you another drink."

He turned and saw Jessica standing there, looking as gorgeous and inviting as ever. Liam couldn't help but put a broad grin on his face as he replied, "Some offers, you simply can't refuse. Go for it."

She beamed and yelled to the bartender, "Another scotch on the rocks for the gentleman and I'll have the same."

The bartender, a thirtysomething female with crimson hair worn in a loose beehive, replied, "Coming right up!"

Jessica sat beside him. "Surprised to see me again?"

"Yes and no," Liam confessed. "I thought last night might have been the end of the line. But then again…well, I hoped you missed me as much as I did you." He grinned. "Guess I was right…"

"Maybe." She blushed. "Let's just say I was curious as to whether or not you would be here and thought I'd check and see."

"Glad I didn't disappoint," he said, feeling the same about her in reverse.

Moreover, Liam wondered when would be the best time to let the cat out of the bag about his knowledge of who she was. Maybe after a drink. Or two.

After the first round of drinks arrived, Jessica said casually, "So, anything exciting in your life since we last met?"

He chuckled, thinking about his latest client and her dead professor brother. "Not really. My life is truly boring, except when I get to spend time with a very pretty lady."

"Hmm." She tasted her drink. "You have a way with words."

"I'd rather have my way with you," he spoke boldly, sensing they were of the same mind. But just in case they weren't, Liam said sincerely, "But conversation is welcome too."

Jessica smiled. "Who says there can't be both?"

"Not me." He smiled back. "Your place or mine?"

"Yours," she said swiftly.

Though curious about where she lived and the other circumstances of the lawyer's life, Liam certainly wasn't going to argue the point. He finished off his drink. "My place it is."

"Can't wait," Jessica said eagerly, downing her own drink.

Like before, Liam led and she followed him back to the floating house. He had purchased it two years ago, attracted to the price and setting on the river. For much of his life, he had been around water—from fishing with his dad growing up to being on the swim team in high school to once owning his own sailboat. But, for now, he welcomed his current residence as a place where he got to bond sexually with an attractive lady and so much more to her to uncover.

The sex was just as hot and heavy as the first time and Liam did as much or more exploring as he allowed himself to be explored intimately by Jessica. Only when they were both thoroughly exhausted from going a few rounds did they slow down to catch their breaths and regain equilibrium. Whether or not this was something to build on or simply another one-night stand turned into two nights, Liam would go with the flow, feeling it was better not to get his hopes up or down.

He also knew it was time for him to come clean with Jessica as she lay

52

comfortably in his arms. Touching her bare shoulder, he said levelly, "I have a confession to make—"

"Uh oh..." Jessica's voice wavered. "What is it? Or do I want to know...?"

"I happened to catch on my cell phone a local news update that showed you, Jessica Frost, talking about your legal representation of murder suspect, Stephanie Dozier." He paused. "Probably should have mentioned it at the bar, but..."

"But you figured if you had, I might not want to sleep with you?" she asked bluntly, lifting up onto an elbow.

He grinned sheepishly. "Something like that," he admitted. "Didn't want to spoil the first name only basis of our get-togethers."

"It's okay." Jessica touched his chest. "As it's a high-profile case, locally speaking, I couldn't expect that it would escape your notice." She chuckled. "The somewhat anonymity was fun while it lasted."

Liam breathed a sigh of relief. "So, we're good then?"

"Not quite, Mister..." She gazed at him. "As you now have me at a disadvantage, I'd like to know the full name of the man I just made love to—again—and what it is you do for a living. I assume you work?"

"I do, some of the time." He laughed, recognizing that all was fair in love and play, not necessarily in that order. "Liam Reed. I'm a private detective. Used to work for Homeland Security, in case you're wondering. Burned out and moved on."

"I see..." Her eyes wandered up and down him before returning to his face. "Nice to meet you, formally, Liam Reed."

"You too," he said, even if knowing each other informally had worked quite nicely.

She locked eyes with his. "You did say you were divorced, right?"

"Yes, very much so. Eight years now." He could tell that this was important to her. "We gave it a try, but it didn't work out, so we stopped trying and moved on."

"Just checking." Jessica gave a reflective nod. "So, maybe I could tap into your services once and a while...?"

"Anytime." His voice had a mischievous slant to it as Liam took her in lustfully.

"Not those services." Jessica laughed. "Been there, done that."

"Just checking." He wondered if that meant their sleeping together—if being in bed jumping each other's bones qualified as sleeping—had run its course. Hopefully not. "So, do you think your client is innocent of killing her roommate?" Liam asked curiously. He understood that lawyers for hire took on cases even if they believed the client was guilty, as everyone had a right to representation, like it or not.

"I don't usually discuss cases with lovers, but if you must know, I don't believe she is guilty of murder."

Liam went through some of the facts he'd read. The police apparently caught her client holding a knife over the victim, a judge's daughter. What was he missing? "Seems like the prosecutor has a strong case."

"Don't believe everything you see online or television," she warned. "We're only at the beginning stages of the investigation. It's my job to punch holes in the police and prosecution's case, with the goal of clearing my client's name."

"Good luck." He meant that, trusting her intuition and wanting to see justice served and not a miscarriage of it.

"Thanks. It'll take more than luck, but I'm in for the long haul, so we'll see how it goes. Anyway, enough about my work." She raised her chin. "Working on anything you care to share...?"

Though he also usually kept his work confidential, Liam felt comfortable in some quid pro quo here. "As a matter of fact, I was just hired by a woman to look into her brother's suicide last month. His name is Sean Quail."

"Sounds familiar."

"He was an art history professor at Wryer College," Liam pointed out.

"Ahh yes," recalled Jessica. "Didn't he kill himself in his office?"

"Yeah. The sister seems to believe there's something more to it than meets the eye."

"What do you think?" Jessica eyed him curiously.

"I have no opinion yet," he told her honestly. "But I will say that the professor's death occurred just weeks before the death of Wryer student,

Kristine McVeigh. Assuming your client is innocent, do you suppose there could be some connection there?"

"Not sure how there could be," Jessica answered candidly, running her smooth leg across his. "One was a confirmed suicide; the other was a homicide."

"You're probably right," Liam conceded. "Just putting it out there. Call it my suspicious nature."

"I'll try to keep an open mind. If you come up with anything, please let me know."

"I will." He kissed between her small but firm breasts, becoming aroused. "In the meantime, are you up for another go at it...?"

"Hmm..." she murmured. "Maybe."

Liam took that as a yes and went from there.

Chapter Ten

Madeleine watched quietly in the wee hours of the morning as her beautiful wife, Genevieve, slept peacefully in their farmhouse bed. They had purchased the Dutch Colonial home a year ago, one month after tying the knot, after dating for nearly two years. Madeleine had fallen in love with the torch singer the moment she first laid eyes on her at a jazz club called Sweet Times on Eighth Street in downtown Creighton Hills. At thirty-two, Genevieve was ten years her junior and biracial, with long, shiny black hair in box braids. She had performed with some of the best jazz artists coast to coast and Madeleine was happy to spend time with her given Genevieve's busy schedule of playing in clubs, concerts, casinos, cruise ships, and jazz festivals around the world. Moreover, given her own workload as a prosecutor, Madeleine knew they both needed their own space. The fact that neither crowded the other or was territorial was what made them work. She gladly took whatever was afforded them in being together. Such as here and now.

She leaned over and kissed Genevieve softly on the lips, awakening her. "Didn't mean to wake you," Madeleine lied.

Genevieve smiled, turning her big brown eyes on her. "Come here," she demanded, wrapping Madeleine in her arms. "Let's not let this time between gigs go to waste."

Beaming and desirous, Madeleine concurred. "Yes, let's not."

They kissed and made love before falling asleep in each other's arms. With morning sunrise, Madeleine slipped out of bed, allowing Genevieve to continue her beauty rest. After getting dressed, Madeleine grabbed a quick bite to eat in the French country style kitchen and walked across the natural stone tile flooring and through the minimalist living room, with its abstract furniture and picture windows, and was out the door. She planned to meet Genevieve later for lunch. For now, she had to continue to prepare for her case against Stephanie Dozier, while trying to stay at least one step ahead of her lawyer, Jessica Frost. And, at the very least, in line with the determination of Judge Ralph McVeigh that his daughter's death not go unpunished. No pressure, right? In reality, the pressure was always there for Madeleine, ready to boil over at any time like steam in an engine. But she was prepared to do battle with the goal to be victorious in the name of justice.

Madeleine drove her aquamarine BMW 228i xDrive Gran Coupe to work, parking in the lot of the Criminal Courts Building, before heading inside. She had only gotten situated in her office before Detective Jackson Payne arrived on schedule. "Hey," she said to him in a friendly tone.

"Hey." He sat in the side chair to her L-shape wooden desk, stretching long legs.

Madeleine gave him a brief smile, as she and Genevieve had hung out from time to time with Payne and his girlfriend, Sheila, before getting down to business. "What have you got on the Dozier investigation?" she asked anxiously.

"The evidence toward guilt continues to pile up," he responded surely. "According to forensics, Stephanie Dozier's DNA was all over the murder weapon, along with her prints."

Madeleine had expected as much, considering the suspect was apprehended after being caught with the knife in her hand at the crime scene. "Anything else?"

"Yeah." Payne smoothed a thick eyebrow. "Looks like we had a love triangle between Kristine McVeigh, Dozier, and the suspect's boyfriend, Brody Krane."

"Really?" Madeleine's interest perked up. "Do tell?"

"According to Krane, a senior at Wryer College, majoring in agribusiness management, he hooked up with McVeigh and made the mistake of telling

Dozier."

"How did she take it?" Madeleine asked, already sure she knew the answer.

"He says she flew off the handle," the detective answered. "Before he could smooth things over, Krane claims that Dozier left to confront McVeigh. Obviously, that didn't work out so well—at least not for the murder victim."

Madeleine agreed. "Kristine McVeigh definitely took the brunt of Dozier's rage for sleeping with her boyfriend. Sad as that is for something that happens in life, people cheat and are cheated on; it gives us a key angle to use in the pursuit of justice."

"Yeah." Payne nodded thoughtfully. "And there's more...looks like Dozier's penchant for violence extends at least as far back as high school. Dug into her history at Lakota High in Boise. When she was a senior, Dozier got into a fight with another senior over a dude they both liked. Dozier reportedly threatened to kill the other girl if she didn't back away."

"Hmm..." Madeleine's mind churned. "Clearly a pattern of violent behavior. This just keeps getting better and better." *Not so, though, for the victim of Dozier's violent tendencies,* she thought. Kristine McVeigh's life was over for something that, while the ultimate betrayal, shouldn't have risen to the level of murder. "We can certainly use this to lay the groundwork for a person with anger issues and the ability to become unhinged when threatened in some manner regarding matters of the heart...or other parts of the anatomy—"

"I was thinking that too," the detective said, scratching his pate. "Oh, and one other thing... Another witness has come forward who claims she spotted the suspect pacing around outside the apartment near the time the 911 call came in. She'll testify to that."

"Good work." Madeleine nodded, pleased, knowing that any and every piece of the investigation that fit like a jigsaw puzzle could lead to a conviction. She went over a few facts of the case with the detective before a few minutes of small talk, then back to the grind as an admitted strong-minded prosecutor.

Chapter Eleven

J essica couldn't believe she had slept with Liam a second night, after promising herself this would be a one-time thing. But weren't all promises made to be broken? They clicked and she felt compelled to run with it—again—and had no regrets. The sex was just as terrific and the company engaging. The fact that her identity was revealed was no reason to become unglued. It wasn't as if what happened between them was contingent upon being kept in the dark about each other's lives. As it was, discovering that Liam was a private eye with federal investigator credentials, backed up by his website, was a good thing and could prove to be useful in her line of work. He certainly seemed agreeable to the possibilities of them working together outside the bedroom.

Jessica drove to the apartment complex that Stephanie lived in. Or had, till she was placed under arrest. Getting out of her car, wearing a drawstring pullover top, jogger pants, and trail running shoes, she surveyed the property, taking in the parking lot, the apartments and their proximity to one another, and the wooded area that practically led up to the door of her client's apartment. Moving toward it, she saw remnants of crime scene tape left behind by authorities. At the door, Jessica turned around and tried to imagine which way a killer would likely go to escape once the deed was done. The woods were the obvious answer, short of a killer other than Stephanie being a resident of the complex and, thereby, slipping back into her or his apartment unseen. Jessica thought it was more likely the perpetrator didn't live there, but had scoped out the location ahead of the planned attack.

That's certainly what I would do, Jessica told herself. That way, there wouldn't be too many surprises along the way. The fact that Stephanie was the last person to see Kristine McVeigh alive and happened to be holding the knife that killed her, played right into the hands of the real killer. Or had this person somehow timed this scenario in the calculus of committing murder?

After putting on latex gloves, Jessica turned the knob and opened the door. She went inside the apartment and took a look around. The common indicators of completed police work were still there, but otherwise, the place looked pretty much as she imagined it would have when Stephanie and her roommate were still living there. At least till Jessica got to the bedroom where the crime occurred. While the bed coverings had been removed as evidence, the mattress itself was stained with blood and the room was in disarray from forensic investigators probing for whatever damaging information that could derive. Jessica felt a chill as she thought about the vicious attack that left Kristine McVeigh dead and Stephanie in police custody. The brutality of the crime was something that would play on the psyche of the jurors and work against her client, unless Jessica could produce one or more others who might have had a strong motive for wanting Kristine dead. Short of that would be to throw off the timeline that pointed the finger squarely at Stephanie as the killer.

Jessica went back through the apartment, studying angles, nooks, and crannies that might have served as hiding places for a killer lying in wait for Kristine to go to bed. Or had the killer actually been hiding in plain view with Kristine unsuspecting till it was too late?

Outside, Jessica studied the woods as the likely entry and exit of the culprit, before getting in her car and driving the four blocks to the apartment complex where Brody Krane resided. After parking, she glanced at the time on her cell phone and then, assuming Stephanie would have taken a shortcut to get home, began to walk through the wooded area at a fairly brisk pace. Once in the clearing and right up to the door of Stephanie's apartment, Jessica looked at the time on her cell phone. It had taken her twelve minutes to walk the distance. According to the police report, the 911 call came in at six-nineteen p.m. If Stephanie left Brody's place at around six-ten, as he indicated, that would mean she would have had less than ten minutes to return home, stab her roommate to death, and remain standing there holding the murder weapon till the officer arrived.

It doesn't add up, Jessica thought confidently, even if arithmetic was never her strong point. Had the police conveniently overlooked this in building their case? The prosecution? Even if she allowed for the possibility that Stephanie had sprinted through the woods, Jessica doubted she would have shaved off much more than a couple of minutes at best from her own time. Which would have still put the timeline of the authorities very much in question. Moreover, there was nothing in the police report that indicated that Stephanie was short of breath from the four-block trek combined with the effort it would have taken to stab someone multiple times.

Jessica was buoyed by this experiment, renewing her faith that, in spite of the sketchiness or omissions of her client's statements and infidelity by her boyfriend as a motive for murder, Stephanie Dozier was very much an innocent woman in the killing of Kristine McVeigh.

* * *

Brody was sitting on the other side of the glass partition for the telephone visitation of Stephanie at the jailhouse. He watched as she entered the room, dressed in inmate clothing as opposed to the trendy attire he was used to seeing her wear, and then took a seat in front of him. They both picked up the phones.

"Hey," he muttered tonelessly.

"I didn't think you would come," she said coldly.

Brody sighed and admitted to her awkwardly, "I needed some time to process this." He stared at her.

"I know, I look like crap," Stephanie said, twisting her lips self-consciously.

"I didn't say that." He wouldn't, even if he agreed with her.

"You didn't have to," she told him. "Being in here does that to you."

Enough of the small talk, Brody thought, knowing they needed to cut to the chase. "So, what the hell happened when you went back to your place?"

Stephanie smoothed an eyebrow. "Just like I told the police, I found Kristine lying on the bed with a knife sticking out of her chest. I tried to help her by pulling the knife out. Guess I shouldn't have done that."

He peered at her skeptically. "Is that the real story?"

She made a face. "You think I'm lying?"

"I don't know, Steph," he responded tartly, "you tell me."

"It's the truth, Brody," she snapped. "I swear it."

"We both know you have a temper." He pressed the phone closer to his ear. "I didn't tell your lawyer or the police that you slapped me after I fessed up to you about me and Kristine. I figured that would only get you in hotter water with what they're accusing you of—"

Stephanie jutted her chin. "So, I hit you. Not that you didn't have it coming after telling me you slept with my best friend. That doesn't mean I went home and stabbed her to death. Why would I ruin my life by doing something crazy, so the police could come right on time and arrest me?"

"Maybe you acted on impulse and just decided to be a bitch about it, damn the consequences," Brody theorized, even as he pushed back at the thought that his girlfriend was truly capable of such an act of violence.

"I'm innocent, Brody!" Stephanie insisted. "I thought that you, of all people, would believe me. Obviously, I was wrong." She frowned. "If you're not going to be in my corner, I don't see what the point is of this conversation."

He scowled. Was this some sort of reverse psychology? Or was he really being a jerk and should take Steph at her word? Sucking in a deep breath, Brody said acquiescently, "I'm here for you...I just need you to be straight with me and tell me again everything that happened from the time you left my apartment to what went down afterwards."

Brody listened and, though it sounded believable enough, he still felt unsure in light of the fact that there were no other suspects and Kristine was dead. Even if what happened between them was just a hookup, she didn't deserve to die. Question was, did Stephanie plunge the knife into her repeatedly, as the police believed? Or did someone else do it?

Chapter Twelve

Liam entered the yoga and fitness studio on Pearl Street, where he had tracked down the widow of Sean Quail. Whether or not this would turn out to be a nothing burger remained to be seen. Jackie Quail had intimated that her brother may have been driven to taking his life because of actions or inactions by his wife. While this may or may not have been a crime in and of itself, if true, it could give the client peace of mind. Or maybe only add to her misery.

Liam stepped into a room where about fifteen women were doing yoga exercises on mats. He imagined this was something Jessica would be good at and into in her spare time, when she wasn't being a lawyer or seducing someone like himself. The fact that the seduction was mutual wasn't lost on him. Or the enticing prospects for continuing to see each other, now that the big reveal had been made, insofar as who they were as professionals. He noted that the women were following the lead of a slender woman in her mid-thirties, with dark hair in a boho-chic braid. She wore a purple camisole leotard and was in full command as she moved about gracefully in her bare feet. When she noticed him standing in the back of the room, she abruptly stopped her movement and told the group, "Keep it going. I'll be right back with you."

Liam waited for her to come to him, at which time she asked, "Can I help you?"

"Are you Anna Quail?" he asked, for effect, having already determined this from the information, including her picture, he'd found on her website.

"Yes, that's me." She waited to see what came next.

"My name's Liam Reed. I'm a private investigator. Your sister-in-law, Jackie Quail, hired me to look into your husband Sean's death."

Anna rolled her blue eyes. "Why don't we step outside?" Liam opened the door and followed her into the hall. She rounded on him. "Sean committed suicide."

"Yes, she mentioned that," Liam said. "I also followed up on the official cause of his death."

"So, what are we talking about here?" she pressed, arms folded.

"Jackie has a problem with the nature of her brother's death," Liam pointed out equably. "The details of his suicide were pretty sketchy, at best. She can't seem to wrap her mind around why a happy, healthy, and married professor, with seemingly everything to live for, would take his own life." He paused deliberately. "Apparently, her attempts to get you to help her out here have gone nowhere."

Anna sucked in a deep breath. "That's because I've been trying to put everything that went wrong with my marriage to Sean behind me. Jackie just doesn't seem to get that."

Liam thought about his own failed marriage and how he needed his own period of adjustment, without the disappointments following him around like a hungry tiger. He sensed that it went deeper than that with the widow. "If you can give me something, then I can relay that to my client and we'll both be out of your hair."

"All right, you win." She rubbed her nose thoughtfully. "Sean was in good health, physically, but he was neither happy nor necessarily had everything to live for. My husband made some bad investments and left behind debts that I may never be able to repay. I also believe he was having an affair, though he was never straight with me in admitting or denying it. My guess is that he became overwhelmed with the misery of his own making and took the coward's way out. So, there you have it."

Liam could feel the bitterness and sense of betrayal, thick as ice. He hoped he hadn't made things worse in trying to start her life over. But his client needed the closure she had paid him for. "Is there anyone else I can talk to who might shed further light on where his head was when Sean chose the path he took?"

"You might want to talk with his financial advisor," Anna answered succinctly. "In many ways, Sean seemed closer to him than me, in terms of being aware of what a disaster they'd both made of our finances."

"His name?"

"Hugh Holliman. He has a downtown office on Steel Street."

"Thanks for your time." Liam met her eyes. "Sorry for your loss."

"Don't be," she spoke sourly. "My marriage to Sean was in name only for the last six months of his life. Whatever was broken, there was nothing I could do to fix it." Anna sighed. "I'd better get back to my class..."

Liam nodded understandingly and watched her reenter the room, giving him something to chew on as he headed next to see Hugh Holliman, before speaking to Jackie Quail. En route, Liam wondered if Sean *was* having an affair. If so, could this have played a role in his suicide? Or had the pressure he was under financially been the trigger for ending his life? Maybe it was a combination of both.

* * *

Hugh Holliman was not quite as tall as him, but in as good a shape and well-dressed in an expensive suit. Liam was not a big fan of beards, causing ingrown hairs on his chin and neck, but he supposed the balbo beard Holliman wore was a good fit for him. "Thanks for seeing me," he told the investment advisor after stepping into his spacious office with traditional furnishings and a nice view of the city from a curtain wall.

"Not a problem," Hugh said, shaking his hand with a firm grip. "You mentioned on the phone that this was concerning Sean Quail's death?"

"Yeah," Liam said. "I've been hired to look into the root causes of the professor's suicide. Seems there are some unanswered questions as to why he chose to check out."

Hugh scratched his beard. "Not sure I can be of much help to you."

"His widow seems to think otherwise," Liam put out flatly. "According to her, he got over his head with debts. As you were his financial advisor, I'd like to think you were privy to—if not responsible for—his bad financial decisions."

Hugh flinched. "I don't think I like what you're insinuating."

"So, you're denying any knowledge of this?" Liam asked straightforwardly.

"Of course, I have some knowledge of Sean's financial failings," he spat uneasily, "but take no responsibility for it. My job is to advise my clients. They don't always take the advice. Ultimately, it is up to them to make the final decision on how to invest their money."

Liam wasn't sure he believed that the financial advisor's hands were clean in Quail being driven to the edge, but couldn't prove it. He suspected Holliman knew more than he was letting on. "Quail's widow seemed to think that he was having an affair that may have contributed to his state of mind when he committed suicide. Did he happen to mention anything about that to you?"

Hugh looked uncomfortable. "I wouldn't exactly call it *having an affair*," he spoke tentatively. "Sean was a sex addict, for lack of a better way to put it. And he was willing to shell out thousands of dollars to feed his addiction."

"To whom?" Liam stared at the allegation. "Are you saying he was going to prostitutes, or what?"

"More like the what," Hugh said ambiguously, scratching again into his chin hair. "Sean got involved with one of his students. That's bad enough. But it went further than that. Apparently, she was part of a group that called themselves The Sexy Coeds Club. Sean told me they had a video recording of him having sex with her and were threatening to reveal this to the school, his wife, and on social media if he didn't pay up to keep it silent. This could have ruined him professionally and his marriage."

The Sexy Coeds Club? Liam thought. *Sex with college students and blackmail?* He hadn't seen that one coming. Obviously, Quail got much more than he bargained for in going after a student for his sexual urges. "Did you tell this to the police?" Liam asked.

"No. It didn't seem like a good idea." Hugh ran a hand across his mouth. "I had no proof and saw no reason to soil Sean's reputation any more than it had already been dragged through the mud. Besides, the police did their own investigation and concluded that whatever his motivation was, Sean did, in fact, die by his own hand. Best to just let him rest in peace."

Liam wasn't necessarily in disagreement with that. On the other hand, if there was this play-and-pay-up scheme going on with some college coeds, it needed to be exposed, at the very least. Then it would be up to the authorities to take it from there. Peering at the financial advisor, Liam inquired, "Did Quail mention the name of the coed he was sleeping with who had put the squeeze on him?"

Hugh pondered the question for a moment or two. "I think he let it slip once and referred to her as Kris."

"Kris as in short for Kristine?" Liam thought out loud.

"I suppose."

"A coed named Kristine McVeigh was murdered a couple of days ago," Liam said.

"Yeah, I heard about that," Hugh acknowledged. "Daughter of a judge. You're not suggesting—"

"I'm not suggesting anything at the moment." Liam didn't want to get ahead of himself, though he was finding it difficult not to. "But with the professor dead, followed by a student named Kristine, who may well have been the Kris who was cavorting with and blackmailing Quail, nothing's off the table."

Liam left the office with Hugh Holliman somewhat shaken at the implications, but still firm in not wishing to get involved. While respecting that for the moment, Liam sensed this wasn't the last he would see of the financial advisor. But, for now, he feared that his case had intersected with Jessica's, with the very fate of her client potentially at stake.

Chapter Thirteen

J essica forced a smile when Stephanie entered the conference room looking as though her whole world had come to an end. It hadn't. *Not if I can help it,* Jessica thought. "How are you doing?" she asked gingerly, once they were alone.

"Okay, I guess." Stephanie took a seat, wringing her hands that were free of the handcuffs. Then she frowned. "Kind of bummed out," she admitted.

Jessica sensed there was more to this than the incarceration. "What is it…?"

"Brody came to see me." She paused thoughtfully. "Not sure he believed me when I told him I had nothing to do with what happened to Kristine. It sucks."

"Give him some time," offered Jessica, sympathizing with his and her positions, given the revelations about Brody sleeping with Kristine and the difficult position it placed Stephanie in. "He'll come around." At least she hoped so, knowing that her client needed to feel that someone had her back, other than her attorney and parents. Could Brody man up in that respect? Jessica couldn't help but think about Hugh and how he failed miserably in being between two women, one of whom was his wife. This made Jessica feel all the more guilty in her role as a homewrecker, even if Hugh had done a good job of convincing her that the home had been wrecked long before she came into the picture.

Stephanie shrugged pessimistically. "Whatever."

"I need to ask you a few questions," Jessica said, shifting the conversation to fill in some blanks and reaffirm other things.

"Go ahead…"

"When you walked home from Brody's apartment, which route did you take?" She considered that it could have been the long way, which would have strengthened her case that much more, but suspected it was more likely to be the shortest route.

"I went through the woods," Stephanie responded without prelude, confirming Jessica's belief. "I always go that way so I don't have to deal with traffic and people. Why?"

"I'm trying to establish a timeline for the events before and after," she explained. "Did you happen to run home, walk quickly, slowly…what?"

"I just walked the normal way—not fast or slow." Stephanie frowned. "Why? Do the police think I came home some other way? Or got a ride?"

"I'm not sure what they believe," admitted Jessica, sitting back. "Or if they even bothered to double-check their assumptions and generalities. What I do know is that the official timeline established as to the 911 call and the arrival of the police, contradict the time you left Brody's place and the time it would take to walk through the woods, get home, kill your roommate, and be arrested…"

Stephanie cocked a brow. "How do you know that?"

"I walked the route myself, from Brody's apartment through the woods and right to your apartment," Jessica explained. "Based upon doing this with a fast walk, it still made it virtually impossible that there would have been enough time to do what they are charging you with. In other words, they have a very flawed, if any, case here."

Stephanie's eyes lit with joy. "Does that mean I'll be getting out of here…?"

"Not quite." Jessica hated to dampen her spirits, but didn't want to make any false promises. "My guess is that the prosecution will try to adjust the timeline to fit their narrative and hope that a jury buys it. I'll do my best to make them see otherwise." She paused. "With any luck, some other twist to the case will materialize that we can go with."

Stephanie sulked. "Like what?

"Well, did you happen to run into anyone else while you were in the wooded area?" Jessica leaned forward, gazing at her client.

Stephanie contemplated this. "There was someone running off in the distance."

"Male? Female?"

"I couldn't say." She shrugged. "I really didn't pay much attention. Sorry."

"Don't be," Jessica told her. "You wouldn't have had any reason to believe that someone had killed your roommate. Or that this person might have been fleeing the scene, just as you were arriving." She believed it was more than possible that the real killer had fled through the woods. And may have even intended to set up the victim's roommate for murder.

Stephanie sighed. "So, what now?"

"I keep digging and working on getting you off," Jessica promised, "hopefully, sooner than later…" Her cell phone buzzed. "Sorry, but I need to get this," she said and removed it from her pocket. The caller was Liam Reed. Her first thought was that he was calling to see if she was interested in making it a three-peat in the bedroom. While it was intriguing and made her blush, Jessica turned off the sexual thoughts, under the circumstances. She decided to answer anyhow. "Hey."

"I have some information that makes me think our cases may intertwine," Liam said in a serious tone. "Can we meet?"

Jessica glanced at her client. "Yes." She was certainly more than a little intrigued, but didn't want to meet him at his floating house. Or at Dusty's. "I can be at my office in fifteen minutes. It's in the Eklin Tower on Palin Way, third floor."

"See you there," he said simply, and hung up.

She cut her phone off. "Have to run," Jessica told Stephanie, choosing not to elaborate prematurely.

"All right," she muttered, standing, as if getting used to the routine, as uncomfortable as it may have been.

Jessica stood too. She took Stephanie's hand, which felt cold, and uttered reassuringly, "We'll get through this. Stay strong."

Stephanie nodded, but did not meet her eyes. "I'll try."

When she left the building, Jessica found herself eager to find out what Liam had discovered that may pertain to her case and client.

CHAPTER THIRTEEN

* * *

Liam walked into the corner office that rivaled that of Hugh Holliman's in terms of size, a great view of the landscape through floor-to-ceiling windows, and rustic furnishings on rubber flooring. But the best image was of its occupant, Jessica Frost, who stood by her antique-style desk. She was professionally dressed and the same striking sight for his eyes as their previous get-togethers. Casting that aside, he turned his attention to the subject at hand, saying smoothly, "I came up with some interesting things in my investigation of Professor Sean Quail's suicide."

"Such as?" Jessica met him halfway.

"Such as Quail's wife believed he had squandered their savings with some bad investments and was having an affair."

"Sounds fascinating," Jessica quipped. "How does that relate to my case?"

Liam couldn't blame her for the anxiousness to connect the dots, if any. He felt the same way. Especially given the stakes for her client. Maybe his too. "Anna Quail, the wife, suggested I might learn more from her husband's financial advisor. So, I went to see him and, along with confirming that Quail got in over his head with questionable investments, the professor was also described as a sex addict who was having an affair with a college student named Kris, who was part of a group referring to themselves as The Sexy Coeds Club. According to the financial advisor, Quail was being blackmailed by her. She threatened to expose him to his wife, the school, and through social media, if he didn't pay up."

"Hmm..." Jessica intoned musingly. "You think this Kris could have been Kristine McVeigh?"

"The thought certainly crossed my mind," Liam admitted, "when you consider the timing of the two deaths. Could be coincidental. Or maybe this Kris and her friends got way over their heads and someone wanted to put a stop to it. If true, then it means your client, Stephanie Dozier, could have been made the scapegoat. Or," it occurred to him, "she could be a member of the sex group and was either an innocent pawn to what happened to her roommate or directly involved in the murder of McVeigh." Liam tried to

71

read Jessica's thoughts in digesting his theories, especially as it related to her client. Had he overstepped? Maybe not.

"Not sure I buy the Kris and Kristine McVeigh being one and the same," offered Jessica. "Much less, that my client could also be a member of this Sexy Coeds Club, and involved in blackmail and possibly murder..." She sucked in a deep breath. "But it does present a possible new angle that needs to be explored, with my client currently in jail accused of stabbing Kristine to death."

Liam was content that she was at least willing to keep an open mind, as Jessica was clearly looking for a way to put the onus on someone other than her client for the murder. He couldn't blame her, if she truly believed in the young woman's innocence. For his part, he was intrigued enough to want to see just how much of a hole Sean Quail had dug for himself, before taking the easy way out. "I was hoping you'd feel that way," he said, eyeing Jessica.

"Just out of curiosity," she said ponderingly, "what's the name of this financial advisor to Professor Quail?"

"Hugh Holliman," Liam said and got an unexpected reaction from her. "Do you know the man...?"

Jessica's shoulders slumped. "Until recently, he was my lover—"

Chapter Fourteen

"I made the mistake of getting involved with a married man," Jessica explained apologetically. It felt odd admitting this to her current lover. But, as he happened to be the one who brought to light Hugh's association with Sean Quail and a possible connection to her case, she felt she owed Liam at least that much. "It seemed right at the time, or at least I convinced myself of that, before finally being able to see his lies for what they truly were."

"We all make mistakes," Liam offered, sincereness in his voice. "Believe me, I've been there."

Jessica wondered if it meant he had been involved with a married woman. Or had his ex-wife been seeing a married man? Or was Liam merely speaking in general terms that no one was perfect? "I need to see Hugh," she spoke abruptly.

Liam nodded. "I'll go with you."

She appreciated the offer, but said, "I need to do this alone." She hoped he didn't get the wrong idea, which prompted her to add, "Maybe I can gain more insight into what he knows or doesn't that might or might not be beneficial to my client."

"Did you love him?" Liam asked boldly.

Jessica stared at the question, having asked herself the same more than once. "I thought I did," she admitted. "Now I'm wondering if it was ever anything more than a deep affection borne out of loneliness and being made to feel wanted."

"I see." He angled his face thoughtfully. "Well, be careful. Wouldn't want to see you get sucked in again…"

"I won't," she promised, wondering if his concern was more about protecting her from getting hurt. Or did he view Hugh as a threat to their own sexual involvement, which neither of them had defined in its nature or what it meant for their future.

* * *

Liam walked Jessica to her car, before getting in his own vehicle. He hated to admit it, but a spasm of jealousy ripped through him at the thought of her being with Hugh Holliman. Apart from the man being married and an ex-lover that Liam saw as competition in wanting to get her into bed again, there was something about Holliman that rubbed him the wrong way. Perhaps it was the notion that he was covering for Sean Quail and some transgressions by a group of sexy coeds that could lead to murder. *Or maybe I don't want to be in the middle of another love triangle,* Liam told himself, remembering that his ex, Kelly, had already found someone else even while they were still married. He wasn't interested in doing that song and dance again. By the sound of things, Jessica didn't seem as though she wanted to rekindle her relationship with Holliman. Liam could only take that for what it was worth and see how things played out between himself and Jessica. For his part, he liked the lady and hoped they could keep this going, wherever it led them. He felt she was of the same mind, till proven otherwise.

Liam texted Jackie Quail to meet him at his office. She agreed. They arrived at the same time and, after they sat down, he got to the point. "I did some digging and discovered that your brother was up to his ears in debt."

Jackie's eyes popped wide. "Really?"

"Afraid so. Seems like he made some bad investments that caught up to him."

"I didn't realize he'd had money problems," she moaned. "I could've helped him, had he come to me."

"He had some other issues as well," Liam almost hated to say.

"Such as?" she asked, ill at ease.

"Sean was apparently battling sex addiction."

"What...?" Her mouth hung with disbelief.

"He got involved with one or more college coeds in feeding this addiction," Liam reported. "Sean was being blackmailed by the group, who threatened to reveal what was going on to his wife, the school, and the world itself. This may well have driven him over the edge in committing suicide."

Jackie's eyes welled with tears. "I can't believe this," she cried. "Did Anna know about it?"

"She knew about the money troubles," he responded, "but only suspected Sean was having an affair."

"So, are these coeds just going to get away with this?" she asked, a catch to her voice.

"Not if I can help it." Even in saying that, Liam wasn't under any illusion that he could uncover this sex ring and stop another man from taking his life. By its very nature, those involved—including other men—would not come clean, if it meant exposing their extramarital activities and ruining their lives. He couldn't help but wonder if Holliman fit into this category.

* * *

"Thanks for coming," Jessica said tonelessly when Hugh walked up to the table at Café Laney's. She didn't want to go to his office, knowing it was a place that they had gotten sexual, giving him the wrong impression that this was anything but professional.

"I have to admit, I wasn't expecting to hear from you," he said, sitting across from her in the booth. She had taken the liberty of ordering him black coffee. He lifted the mug and grinned lasciviously. "I'll take you any way I can."

"How about as an attorney, looking out for my client?" she said levelly, ignoring her own mug of coffee.

He lifted a brow. "Not sure I follow you..."

She peered at him. "Why don't you tell me about Sean Quail and what he was up to with college girls?"

"I don't know what you mean," he claimed unevenly.

Jessica made a face. "How about The Sexy Coeds Club, inappropriate sexual behavior by a professor, blackmail...do I need to go on?"

"How did you—?" Hugh pursed his lips. "You've been talking to that private investigator Liam Reed?"

Without him needing to know the extent of their involvement, she acknowledged as much. "We're working together on behalf of my client, Stephanie Dozier, who's been accused of murdering her roommate, Kristine McVeigh."

Hugh sat back. "Yeah, I saw it on the news."

"It's possible that Kristine may be the same person named Kris that you told Liam the professor claimed was blackmailing him after making a video of them having sex," Jessica said, a ring to her voice. "If so, Kris may have been extorting money from other men, causing one of them to resort to murdering her to keep quiet."

"As I told the private eye, I'm not interested in getting involved—" Hugh began.

"Excuse me, but you're already involved in it," Jessica cut in, "whether you like it or not. If you'd rather talk to the police, I'm sure that can be arranged." She didn't necessarily wish to threaten him, but if her ex-boyfriend could help free her client, Jessica was not going to give him a free pass to walk away.

"All right." He wrinkled his nose. "I'll tell you everything I told Reed, which isn't much. Sean was into sex with his students. Or at least the one named Kris. He never elaborated on this, other than saying she belonged to this group of girls in a play then pay scheme that he fell for."

"Did he mention the names of any of the other coeds involved?" Jessica asked searchingly. "Or, for that matter, any of the other men they may have targeted?"

"No, and I didn't ask." Hugh jutted his chin. "What Sean did, outside of investing, was his business and not mine. It was better that way."

"Not for his wife—or sister," Jessica pointed out. She glared at Hugh suspiciously. "Were you also sleeping with college students when you were sleeping with me...?"

"No," he uttered swiftly. "I wouldn't have done that to you."

"Or your wife?" she couldn't resist saying, as if he could be more faithful to one over the other.

"Or her." Hugh tasted the coffee. "Look, Sean made his own choices. I was never part of it."

"I hope you're right about that." Jessica was inclined to give him the benefit of the doubt because of their history. But that hardly meant he was off the hook, should evidence come to light to the contrary. She glanced at her coffee, which she hadn't drank any of, and back at him, while wondering how she allowed herself to fall into his trap of infidelity. "I have to go."

"So, are you sleeping with him?" Hugh stared at her.

She fluttered her lashes. "Excuse me?"

"You heard me. Are you banging the private eye?"

"How dare you!" Jessica glared at him, outraged. "It's none of your damn business who I sleep with. Not anymore."

Hugh curled his lip. "I'll take that as a yes."

"Go to hell, Hugh," she struck back, rising to her feet. "What I ever saw in you, I'll never know. Have a good life—with your wife. That is, assuming she doesn't get smart and kick your ass to the curb!"

Jessica left him sitting there, feeling some sense of satisfaction in giving him a piece of her mind, even as she considered the possibilities surrounding Sean Quail, a coed sex ring, and bloody murder.

* * *

Hugh watched as Jessica stormed away like her pants were on fire. He regretted coming at her like that, acting like a jealous schoolboy. Yes, he missed being with her, more than he cared to admit. But deep down, he knew it was best that he stay away from her, if only for the sake of his marriage. He wondered if Claire would ever have the guts to ask him for a divorce. If so, how would his kids deal with the dynamics of a broken home?

Would the blame fall entirely on his lap?

He tasted the now lukewarm coffee and turned his thoughts to Sean Quail. Did his involvement with a coed temptress and blackmailer—assuming Kris and Kristine McVeigh were one and the same—have a rippling effect, with other men desperate to not fall prey to extortion leading to her murder? The prospect sent a chill through Hugh, wondering how far he would be willing to go were his own marriage threatened in such a way. He hoped he never had to find out.

Chapter Fifteen

Madeleine readied herself for the preliminary hearing as Thorne County Circuit Court Judge Octavia Vanderham sat on the bench, waiting for the two sides to present their arguments in the case against the defendant, Stephanie Dozier, proceeding to trial. The judge was a slender woman, forty-five years of age, with short, blonde-gray hair in a pulled back pixie style. She had a reputation for fairness all the way around—no matter that the victim, Kristine McVeigh, was the daughter of a colleague of the judge—but Madeleine was confident that she had more than enough on the table to keep things moving forward toward a murder conviction.

As such, she wasted no time in making her case, glancing only once at Jessica, who looked tense, and the defendant, whose expression was unreadable, before Madeleine proceeded. "Your Honor, the State intends to show that there is probable cause for going to trial. On Friday, October fourteenth, college student Kristine McVeigh was stabbed to death in her own bed." Madeleine glared at the defendant. "The direct and circumstantial evidence all point in one direction—right at the victim's own roommate, Stephanie Dozier, as the person responsible for taking the life of Ms. McVeigh, whom we think was caught up in a love—or should I say, sex—triangle, involving the defendant's boyfriend, Brody Krane, causing her to strike out in a violent act of jealous rage—"

"That whole scenario—compelling as it sounds—remains to be seen, keeping in mind this isn't a trial," Judge Vanderham warned. She faced Jessica. "Let's hear your arguments to the contrary, Counselor—"

Madeleine watched as the defense counselor, who was tough as nails like herself, prepared to do battle. *This time, Jessica, you may have gotten in over your head with this client*, she thought. *Still, go ahead, take your best shot.* They would see who would be left standing, once the dust settled.

"Your Honor," Jessica began, "what happened to Kristine McVeigh was horrible, with losing her life at such a young age. And no one feels more terrible that she is no longer with us than her best friend with whom she shared an apartment, Stephanie Dozier. The fact that Ms. Dozier is the defendant in this case, accused of committing such a heinous act, is in and of itself a grave miscarriage of justice. Irrespective of any possible ill will between the off-campus college roommates involving a guy, my client tried to do right by her friend by removing the knife wedged within Ms. McVeigh's body. Little could she have imagined at the time that this simple act of kindness and mercy should result in her being charged with murder and forced to defend herself through a court of law. As her attorney, Your Honor, it is clear to me that Stephanie Dozier is not only innocent of the crime, but that the real killer is still on the loose and the motivation for the killing yet to be uncovered."

"We'll see about that, Ms. Frost," the judge uttered evenly. She looked toward the prosecutor and asked expectantly, "Do you have any witnesses to call...?"

"I do, Your Honor," Madeleine said eagerly. She eyed Jessica briefly, almost admiring the smooth and nearly convincing delivery by the defense attorney. But the facts were the facts and no smoke and mirrors in trying to deflect from this reality would change that. She called Officer Guy Bean to the witness stand, allowing him a moment to adjust in the seat, before jumping right in. "Officer Bean, can you tell us about the 911 call you responded to on the evening of October fourteenth and what happened thereafter?"

"Sure." Bean gathered himself. "At six-nineteen p.m., it was reported by a neighbor that a woman was screaming like she was in distress. Being in the vicinity, I responded immediately to the 911 call, and headed straight to the scene—which was the Cherryton Apartments on Oswego Drive, Apartment 140. At approximately six-thirty p.m., I entered the residence; the door was partly ajar. After identifying myself and getting no response, I moved through the apartment until I came to a bedroom…"

"And what did you see in there?" she asked knowledgeably.

"I observed a young woman standing over a bed with a bloody knife in her hand," he recounted. "On the bed was another female. It was clear to me, by the blood coming from various parts of her, that she had been stabbed and was seriously injured, if not dead." He paused. "As I already had my firearm drawn, I immediately pointed it at the one holding the knife and asked her to drop it—twice—before she finally obeyed. At that time, I handcuffed her and placed her under arrest."

Madeleine waited a beat. "Can you identify the person you arrested?" she asked coolly.

"Yes," Bean said positively, and angled his eyes, "it was the defendant, Stephanie Dozier…"

Madeleine gave a look of satisfaction before handing the witness to the defense attorney for what she assumed would be cross-examination.

Jessica was poised as she put forth, "Officer Bean, did you witness Ms. Dozier actually assaulting the victim with the knife she was holding?"

Bean blinked. "No, I did not."

"Did she confess to killing Ms. McVeigh?"

"No, she didn't," he admitted.

"On the contrary, Officer," Jessica stated, "according to your own report, the defendant said she did not kill her roommate. Isn't that correct?"

Bean jutted his chin. "It sounded like that, but she wasn't speaking very clearly," he claimed.

Jessica pounced on that inconsistency. "In the time between when the 911 call came in and you arrived at the scene, is it possible that another person could have stabbed the victim and left the scene before you arrived?"

"Uh, yes, it's theoretically possible, but not likely, given the situa—"

Jessica broke in, "Officer, based on your timeline, eleven minutes is a long time to keep stabbing a person, don't you think?" She didn't allow him to respond. "Isn't it more likely that the killer would have completed what he or she intended to accomplish in minutes, or less, and moved on—rather than waiting there over the victim's body for you to arrive, with the murder weapon in hand...?"

Bean squirmed. "Yeah, maybe under normal circumstances. But the perpetrator, defendant, seemed to be in a state of shock, which could account for why she just stood there after the fact, till I arrived."

Jessica peered at him. "Are you a certified psychologist or psychiatrist in your spare time, Officer?"

He frowned. "No, I'm not."

"Didn't think so." She scratched her nose. "More likely, the defendant, as she has stated repeatedly, arrived at the tail end of that timeline between the attack of Ms. McVeigh and just before your arrival, Officer Bean—and tried to assist her injured friend by pulling the knife out, in what would be a traumatic moment for anyone, and held onto the knife a little too long—to her own detriment, but still as an innocent woman." Jessica sighed. "No further questions, Your Honor."

Madeleine bristled as her opponent turned it back over to her, no doubt feeling as if she had made an impact with Judge Vanderham. *Don't get too excited just yet, Jessica,* Madeleine mused confidently. *I'm just getting started.* She called her next witness, Homicide Detective Jackson Payne, to the stand. "I understand, Detective, that you interviewed the defendant following her arrest. Is that correct?"

Payne gave a small smile. "Yes, that's correct."

"And what were your impressions of her?"

"She struck me as someone who knew she had done something really wrong and was trying to come to terms with it."

Madeleine glanced deliberately at Stephanie Dozier and back. "Did the defendant confess to stabbing her roommate to death?"

Payne sat back. "Not in so many words. But her body language and inability to string together two sentences coherently told me she was flustered the way a guilty person would be when backed into a corner."

Madeleine knew that would never hold up in a trial. Here, though, they only needed to convince one person that this warranted putting the case before a jury. "You also spoke to the defendant's boyfriend, Brody Krane, correct?"

"Yes, I did."

"What did he have to say that was relevant to this investigation?" she asked, knowing what was to come.

"Krane said that after he and the defendant had gotten high and had sex, he admitted to Dozier that he'd slept with the victim, Kristine McVeigh."

"And how did the defendant react upon hearing this news?" Madeleine eyed her sharply.

"According to Krane, she went berserk," Payne stated. "He tried to calm her down, but Dozier stormed out the door for a confrontation with McVeigh." The detective sighed. "She wound up being stabbed to death with Dozier hovering over her, the murder weapon in hand. That's open and shut type stuff for an investigation."

"No further questions for this witness," Madeleine uttered and gave him a little grin for doing his part effectively in the hearing.

"Would you like to cross-examine?" the judge asked Jessica.

Madeleine watched her respond to the affirmative, expecting as much from the defense attorney.

Chapter Sixteen

J essica had reconciled with the fact that, given the low threshold for probable cause at this stage of the case, getting the judge to be on her side was a long shot at best and all but impossible at worst. Still, she intended to give it her all. Especially as she was starting to believe that this was not a crime of passion, but rather a crime of lust, manipulation, and extortion involving Kristine McVeigh. Though she had yet to see if her client was involved, Jessica planned to pursue this line of inquiry while standing by Stephanie as any reputable lawyer would do.

"Detective Payne," Jessica began levelly, "do you truly believe you are qualified to judge a suspect's guilt on, as you put it, her body language and inability to string together two sentences coherently?"

His brows knitted. "Yeah, I think I have enough experience to make that assessment."

Madeleine must be loving this, she thought cynically, and said to him, "Have you considered that as a college student being interrogated by an experienced detective who already had his conclusions drawn, with no representation, my client just might have been too scared out of her wits to think clearly—much less, defend herself as an innocent young woman?"

"I suppose that's possible," he contended begrudgingly, "but when coupled with the facts of the investigation, I'll stand by my assessment of your client—"

"Let's talk about the timeline..." Jessica cleverly switched subjects. "With regard to assessments, I followed the route that my client took through the woods from her boyfriend Brody Krane's apartment. Based on the time he said she left his place and got back to her own apartment, it's a stretch to believe that she could be, essentially, in two places at once. I think it's more likely that Ms. Dozier wasn't even in her apartment when the 911 call came in—meaning that you're barking up the wrong tree, Detective—"

He snorted uncomfortably. "First, I'm not a dog, Counselor. Second, timelines are always estimates and can sometimes be off when they're lined up with evidence that indicates otherwise. Your client had more than enough time to leave the boyfriend and go home to viciously attack her roommate. Sorry."

Jessica almost believed he meant that, even if it came across as sarcastic. She also knew that he was toeing the line between working on behalf of the prosecution and being a detective that was supposed to keep an open mind, appearances notwithstanding. She regarded him hotly. "Did you even try to investigate to see if there were any other suspects in the murder of Kristine McVeigh? Or had you and the D.A.'s office decided that shaky timelines, estimated or not, were irrelevant when it came to pointing the finger at the easiest suspect in a case where the victim was a judge's daughter?"

"It's not about that," Payne claimed in a snippy tone. "We can walk and chew gum at the same time. Our investigation, which is still ongoing, led us to conclude that we have the right person being charged with killing Ms. McVeigh."

"That's your story and you're sticking to it," Jessica said mockingly. "No further questions." If nothing else, she had at least put some things on the table to lay the groundwork for her approach, should this go to trial.

Madeleine was quick to call Blair Rodriguez, a forensic analyst, to the stand. "As a member of the Creighton Hills Police Department Crime Scene Investigations Unit, what is it that you do?"

"I collect forensic evidence left at crime scenes, be it blood, DNA matching, fingerprint documentation, or hair or fiber evidence," she responded coolly.

Jessica listened as the prosecutor asked her a few more lead in questions, such as her educational background and the reliability of forensics, before Madeleine got to the real point at hand. "Did you conduct DNA tests on the knife we believe was used to kill Kristine McVeigh?"

"Yes, I did," Blair answered routinely.

"And what were the results?"

"The DNA on the knife matched DNA from the victim, Kristine McVeigh, and the defendant, Stephanie Dozier," the forensic investigator said persuasively.

Madeleine allowed that to sink in for a moment and then asked, "Were you able to find DNA on the knife that didn't belong to either the victim or defendant?"

Blair blinked. "No. Theirs was the only detectable DNA found on the weapon."

After Madeleine indicated this completed her questioning, Judge Vanderham regarded Jessica and said, "Counselor—"

In taking her turn with the forensic investigator, Jessica saw her client go from tears to being stoic in the proceedings, with Stephanie having to endure the witnesses' assertions that she was guilty of murdering her roommate. With respect to Blair Rodriguez, Jessica realized that it was pointless to try and undermine her DNA findings, as there was no arguing with the science. But there were still a few things that needed to be pointed out. So, she asked what opened the door to other suspects, "Is it possible that someone else could have used the knife either wearing gloves or cleaning off DNA afterwards?"

"Yes, in both instances," Blair responded. "In the former case, trace evidence has not linked the knife to someone else's DNA. In the latter case, as the defendant was holding the weapon in question at the scene of the crime with her DNA and fingerprints on it, it's dubious at best to think that the knife had been cleaned by another person beforehand."

"Except for the fact that if it was the clear intention of someone else to hide their DNA and fingerprints," Jessica pointed out, "then such a person would benefit from doing so, in order to protect his or her identity. Isn't that correct?"

Blair looked away. "Yes. I suppose it is."

Madeleine called the Thorne County Medical Examiner, Doctor Ginger Nishioka to the stand, wasting little time in getting to the heart of her testimony. "Dr. Nishioka, you performed the autopsy on Kristine McVeigh, correct?"

The medical examiner, who was in her mid-forties with dark hair in a short, windblown pixie, touched her silver-rimmed glasses, and said, "Yes, that's correct."

"And what were your conclusions on the manner of death?" Madeleine asked.

"The victim was stabbed to death," she said without prelude. "She sustained fourteen deep puncture wounds from a serrated knife with a ten-inch blade. There were also a number of defensive wounds where Ms. McVeigh tried to ward off the attack, to no avail."

Madeleine made eye contact with the judge before proceeding. "As you know, Doctor, the defendant was believed to be holding the perceived murder weapon. Were you able to match the knife with the injuries to the victim?"

Dr. Nishioka adjusted her glasses and replied, "Yes, in carrying out wound analysis, we were able to confirm through the depth and pattern of the wounds, in relation to the size of the blade and corresponding DNA evidence from the victim and the knife, that it was the weapon used to kill Kristine McVeigh."

"No further questions, Your Honor," Madeleine uttered, glancing at Jessica smugly.

Her own questioning of the medical examiner was meant mainly to open up the possibility that someone other than Stephanie Dozier could have murdered the victim. As such, Jessica began with, "Dr. Nishioka, wouldn't the nature of Ms. McVeigh's injuries in relation to the murder weapon be the same, even if someone else killed her?"

"Yes, they would be," she conceded.

"Thereby, the results of the autopsy, as difficult as they are to hear, would not be any different no matter the killer?"

"Correct." The medical examiner lifted her chin.

"I guess the point I'm making, Doctor," Jessica said smoothly, "is that my client, even during the preliminary hearing, must be presumed innocent, with the possibility that the real killer is still at large."

Dr. Nishioka's brown eyes widened behind her glasses. "I don't disagree with you, Counselor. Your client may well be innocent, no matter the indicators to the contrary. I only report the findings as they pertain to the autopsy and weapon used against the victim. The rest is up to the investigators and lawyers."

Jessica gave a tiny smile in appreciation for this small acknowledgment. "One last question… In your experience as a medical examiner, have you encountered cases where the evidence that supported one conclusion proved to be misleading, if not downright false, in the final analysis?"

The doctor nodded musingly. "Yes, I have encountered such cases."

"Thought so," Jessica said cleverly and glanced at the prosecutor as food for thought, then back at the judge, to signify the end of the questioning of the witness.

After deliberating on the merits of the case, Judge Vanderham said even-voiced, "Upon listening to both sides and the witnesses, I believe the prosecution has produced enough evidence to support probable cause that the defendant, Stephanie Dozier, did, indeed, commit the act of murder for which she is charged in the death of Kristine McVeigh."

After the judge denied a motion to set bail, the case was bound over for trial and a date set for Jessica to work with in defense of her client to prove her innocence.

Chapter Seventeen

Liam watched as Jessica emerged from the courtroom. She looked a little tired, but otherwise definitely not worse for the wear. He understood that the preliminary hearing had gone against her, with Stephanie Dozier's case moving ahead—unless compelling evidence should emerge to throw everything out of whack. Until such time, he threw his support behind the beautiful woman he had been sleeping with at his floating house. They had yet to define what it was they meant to each other—be it just sex, a relationship, or still to be determined. He was just happy to go along for the ride and hope it wasn't too bumpy for either of them.

"Hey," he said after working his way to her.

"Hi." Jessica gave him a guilty look. "You know, you didn't have to come."

"I wanted to show my support." In spite of having already talked about this and his insistence, Liam thought that sounded a bit clichéd. "I think your client is being railroaded and I'd like to help you win the case."

"Thanks. I could use all the help I can get." A frown dampened her spirits. "The preliminary hearing went pretty much as expected—including the judge shooting down any chance that my client might get out on bail anytime soon." Jessica sighed. "Looks like we're headed to trial."

"Maybe so and maybe no," he hinted, a catch to his tenor.

She raised a brow. "Meaning...?"

"I'll explain later. Why don't we go grab a bite to eat? I'm starving."

"Where?"

"There's a great seafood restaurant not far from here called Mahana's Grill." Liam thought it might give them a chance to get to know one another better, outside the bedroom. Or courthouse. "You may have heard of it?"

"I have and love seafood," Jessica declared, then asked tentatively, "So, are we actually talking about a real date here...?"

He wouldn't have quite couched it that way, but supposed the shoe fit, so to speak. "Yeah, that works for me, if you're game..."

She grinned. "Okay, game on."

Liam liked the metaphor as someone who liked to win and seemed to be winning with her. "Maybe we should head out the back way," he suggested, guiding her past others. "Last I saw, the media was out in force, looking to hound anyone associated with this case."

"Great idea." Jessica put her arm beneath his. "Not sure I'm up for that right now."

* * *

She followed him in her car, figuring that was easier than having to come back to the courthouse parking lot to get it. As it was, Jessica had spent half the night in Liam's bed, before bolting to get in a few hours' sleep in the comfort of her own bed prior to the preliminary hearing. Liam had indicated he would be there for her, but she hadn't known if he was serious or not. After all, it wasn't exactly the criminal trial stage of the process, albeit a prelude. *Looks like Liam's a man of his word*, Jessica thought, pleased. Unlike Hugh, who had proven to be untrustworthy to both her and his wife. But what did that mean in the grand scheme where it concerned Liam? Honestly, Jessica had no idea. It scared her to open up her heart again too soon to someone. But just as scary was the thought of having to go it alone as it related to matters of the heart.

She shelved these musings as they arrived at the restaurant during lunchtime, went inside, and were seated by the window that had a nice view of a garden. A big-screen television was on overhead. After ordering and receiving grilled Chilean sea bass and a garden salad, Jessica asked Liam about the *maybe so and maybe no* remark as it related to her case, curious as to what he was up to.

With his own lunch of teriyaki salmon and a Caesar salad, he gazed at her and said with an unreadable expression, "I asked a buddy of mine at Homeland Security to run a criminal background check on Kristine McVeigh and came up with some interesting results."

"Really?" Jessica met his eyes. He had beaten her to the punch in going in a roundabout way to retrieve the information. "What did you learn?"

After forking a bite of salmon, Liam answered coolly, "Ms. McVeigh was actually arrested twice in the past year. Once, for possession of narcotics and, more recently, on a charge of solicitation of prostitution."

"Wow," was the first thing to come out of Jessica's mouth, taking note in particular of the solicitation charge, in considering Hugh's claims about Sean Quail, a campus sex ring, and a coed involved named Kris.

"But here's the catch..." Liam allowed himself to swallow some salad. "In both instances, the charges were dropped abruptly."

"Hmm..." Jessica held up forked sea bass thoughtfully. "Either she's one lucky girl...or..."

They both turned to the TV screen as Judge Ralph McVeigh began to speak, while apparently standing before his home in a crisp dark suit, minus the robe.

"Today, I am not a judge, but a father of a beautiful young woman named Kristine, whose life was snuffed out like a candle well before her time. As you all know, the case against the one accused of murdering my daughter is now headed to trial. I want to make it clear that I will play no role in deciding the defendant's fate. I am not here to pass judgment on her guilt or innocence. That will be left up to the lawyers and a jury of her peers. All I can say is that Kristine did not deserve to die the way she did—whatever the motivation of her killer. For that reason, I and my entire family simply want justice done and nothing more. I ask that our privacy be respected as we continue to mourn Kristine's death and keep living our own lives as best as possible. Thank you."

Liam got Jessica's attention as he asked pointedly, "Are you thinking what I'm thinking?"

How could she not be? "Yes," she responded, reading his mind. "Judge

McVeigh may have pulled some strings to get the charges dropped against his daughter, as his way of protecting her."

Liam nodded in agreement. "If so, it may have been only a stopgap measure at best, assuming Kristine is the Kris that was blackmailing Sean Quail."

"I agree." Jessica used a paper napkin to dab the corners of her mouth.

"So, what's your next move?" Liam asked fixedly over a glass of water.

"To see what my client has to say about this, if anything," she replied contemplatively and finished her food.

Chapter Eighteen

Madeleine was more than a little content that the preliminary hearing had put them on the fast track to a trial. She wasn't particularly looking forward to going up against Jessica again in court, but liked her chances in getting a conviction of the defense attorney's client, Stephanie Dozier. *I've got the law on my side and the strong evidence to boot*, Madeleine thought confidently, as she walked hand in hand with Genevieve in Creighton Riverfront Park. Having taken the rest of the afternoon and night off, she was happy to spend the time with her beautiful and gifted wife.

Genevieve seemed to read into her thoughts as she invaded them in saying, "So, the case is going to trial?"

"Yep." Madeleine gazed at some mallard ducks swimming in the river while a couple of kids stood at the edge tossing pieces of bread to them.

"Do you think it's a slam dunk—though I hate that metaphor—being able to prove that she stabbed her roomie to death out of spite?"

"I believe the evidence will bear that out." Madeleine glanced out at the river. "We'll see how it goes," she said modestly, not wanting to be too presumptuous.

"I caught the judge's heartfelt statement on TV," remarked Genevieve. "Losing a child has to be hell—especially that way."

"I know," Madeleine agreed. She wondered if this was a backdoor way of telling her that you could only lose a child by having one. They had talked about this possibility. Madeleine knew that, at ten years younger, Genevieve was keen on nearing her biological clock and wanting to have a family to share their love. While not opposed to this, Madeleine worried that the age differential and their busy schedules might get in the way of bringing one or more children into the world. Still, she wanted to make her wife happy, so keeping an open mind was key. "Hopefully, when we're ready, we can provide our own child with a loving atmosphere and good values that can help keep him or her safe."

Genevieve beamed. "I like the way you think."

Madeleine smiled back. "Good minds think alike."

"So, does that mean you have the same taste for some sweet baby back ribs?"

Chuckling, Madeleine answered, "Yeah, I think that's something I could go for."

"In that case, why don't we check out that joint, Velma's BBQ Place, on Riverside Drive?"

"You're on." Madeleine squeezed her hand affectionately, glad to take a breather from the prep work for what promised to be a high-profile trial.

* * *

"I didn't expect to see you again so soon," Stephanie said, positioning herself in the chair in the conference room.

"I needed to talk to you," Jessica told her abstrusely, while wondering if her client had, indeed, been on the level with her.

"Okay. What's up?"

It almost seemed to Jessica that she was becoming too comfortable being jailed. Or did that simply come with the territory when one was faced with the reality of needing to adjust to their situation or go crazy? She gave her client a straight look. "Did you know that Kristine had been arrested in the past twelve months for possession of narcotics and soliciting her services as a prostitute?"

Stephanie reacted. "I knew about the arrest for possessing narcotics—she liked using ecstasy or coke sometimes to get high or deal with depression—but not the solicitation."

94

Jessica accepted that for now. "Did Kristine ever go by the nickname Kris?"

"Yeah, all the time," Stephanie said matter-of-factly. "Why do you ask?"

"I have it on good authority that a college student using the moniker, Kris, was involved in a campus sex ring called The Sexy Coeds Club. Apparently, the girls seduced married men—including an art history professor named Sean Quail, who killed himself last month—videoed them having sex, and then blackmailed them to keep it quiet." Jessica peered at her, trying to gauge her client's possible participation. "Did you know about this?" She was going on the assumption that Kris and Kristine actually were one and the same person.

"No." Stephanie's eyes widened. "I took Professor Quail's class last semester, as did Kristine, and heard about his suicide. I can't believe Kris would have been part of—"

Jessica broke in, eyeing her client with misgivings. "You expect me to believe she never talked to you—her own roommate—about this club and its benefits?"

"No," Stephanie repeated, "I swear."

"And you weren't a part of it?" Jessica persisted. "An active member of the sex ring?"

"No!" She sucked in a deep breath. "This is the first time I'm hearing about any of this. I know we were close friends and all, but Kristine didn't tell me everything she was into. She hung out with other girls at school, just as I did." Stephanie ran a hand through her hair. "If I had known this was going on, I would've tried to stop it. Or at least stop her being involved, knowing it would just get her into trouble."

Maybe much more trouble than Kristine bargained for, Jessica thought, inclined to believe Stephanie that she was not a part of The Sexy Coeds Club. Unless proven otherwise.

"Do you think this could have had something to do with Kris's death?" Stephanie asked, an uneasiness to her voice.

"That's what we need to find out," Jessica told her. "Unfortunately, I think it's highly possible that someone Kristine was associated with in this extortion scheme may have been pushed over the edge and killed her rather than pay up…"

Stephanie cringed. "If true, that person had to have left the apartment just before I arrived…" She put a hand to her mouth. "For all I know, the killer was still in there when I got back… And might have come after me with the knife, but maybe was spooked when the policeman arrived and somehow escaped—"

"That's certainly a possibility," conceded Jessica. "I'll need a list of all Kristine's close friends, other than yourself. And any of the professors you shared that she may have seemed to take a special interest in—"

Stephanie nodded musingly. "I'll do my best."

Jessica chose not to pull any punches. "You need to do much better than that…it's your freedom that's on the line here, Stephanie, with the trial right around the corner. If you didn't kill Kristine, that means someone else did. Someone who may have deliberately set you up to take the fall. Or, at the very least, would be more than happy if you're convicted of the crime, letting the real culprit off the hook." By the look on her client's face, it was clear to Jessica that she got the message. Good. Now the question was could they expose evidence that would exonerate Stephanie from the charge of killing her roommate? Jessica steeled herself for what she feared could be a bumpy ride to true justice.

II

The Club

Chapter Nineteen

Jessica observed a group of young women huddled around one another in a lovely courtyard on the Wryer College campus. There were five of them, she counted. All looked to be in their early twenties, and were tall and slender with trendy hairstyles and clothing; attractive, and, yes, Jessica admitted, sexy. She approached and when they saw her coming, stopped talking on a dime, as though confronting an enemy.

"Hi," they spoke in unison, pasting on perfect smiles in the process as if they came with the territory.

"Hello," Jessica said evenly. "My name is Jessica Frost. I'm representing Stephanie Dozier, Kris's roommate." She watched to see how they reacted and interpreted acknowledgment of the name short for Kristine, as well as some uneasiness in their expressions and posture. "I was told that you were friends of Kristine's."

One stepped forward. She had long black hair in a side plait with fringe bangs and bold, blue eyes. "I'm Brittany Delray," she introduced herself. "Yes, we were friends with Kristine...and Stephanie." Brittany looked at a beautiful, green-eyed blonde, her long hair in wispy waves. "This is Danielle Osmond."

"Hey," Danielle spoke equably.

The others identified themselves, one by one, starting with a leggy Latina with brown locks in an asymmetrical short haircut and brown eyes. "Georgina Perez."

"Aimee Atkinson," uttered a model-thin coed with small blue eyes with gold flecks and long, straight red hair.

Lastly, an African American beauty with big sable eyes and black hair in a voluminous blowout style, said, "I'm Cecelia Temple."

"Nice to meet you all," Jessica said, pasting a smile on her face. *Now comes the interesting part*, she thought.

"We're all saddened about what happened to Kris," Brittany spoke again. "And just as sad to think that Steph may have been the one who would do such a terrible thing to her." She frowned uneasily. "Not sure why you would want to see us. If you're looking for character witnesses or something..."

"I'm not," Jessica told her, pausing. "Actually, I came to talk to you about The Sexy Coeds Club."

"Excuse me?" Brittany cocked a razor-thin brow. "The Sexy what?"

Jessica repeated herself and then said straightforwardly, "I have been told that Kris was part of a group of sexy coeds who sleep with married professors, video the sex acts, and then blackmail the men for money. As her close friends, I figured you may know something about this."

Danielle took the lead. "Well, you figured wrong," she insisted. "I don't know where you heard this from, but we don't know anything about a Sexy Coeds Club, or whatever. We certainly weren't part of it. Neither was Kristine." She narrowed her eyes. "Is that what Stephanie is claiming?"

"Stephanie knows nothing about the club," admitted Jessica, giving her client the benefit of the doubt in her denial. *I'm betting it's just the opposite with Kristine's other friends*, she told herself. "But an art history professor, Sean Quail, did know...right up to the time that he committed suicide recently, after telling a business associate about his involvement and being extorted by the club."

"We're not involved in any extortion plot," Cecelia insisted, batting her eyes. "It's crazy to believe we had anything to do with Professor Quail's suicide."

"Maybe you didn't and maybe you're up to your eyeballs in this," Jessica put out forthrightly. "I'm not here to get you into any trouble."

"Then why are you here?" Georgina demanded, folding her arms like a pretzel.

Jessica did not back down. "My client is being charged with the murder of Kristine McVeigh," she voiced sharply. "I think she's innocent."

Aimee ran a hand through her hair haphazardly. "You think one of us killed Kris?"

"No," Jessica made clear. "But I do think that she may have been murdered by someone who had a beef with The Sexy Coeds Club and the way they conducted their business. I believe that Stephanie caught a very bad break and is giving the real killer a free ride." She paused theatrically. "My guess is that Kristine's death may not be the last. If any of you would like to talk to me about this, I'm happy to listen. And I can help you while helping my client at the same time."

"If we knew anything, we would tell you," Brittany said edgily, on behalf of the group. "But we don't. I really hope that Stephanie didn't kill our friend. If you can prove that and point the finger at someone other than us, it would be great for everyone." She looked at the other girls. "We have to go to class now."

Jessica nodded, hiding her disappointment. *I know you're hiding something,* she thought. *Like denying the existence of and participation in The Sexy Coeds Club.* She took out cards with her contact information, handing one to each of them in the hope someone might be more forthcoming without the group pressure. Jessica wasn't holding her breath. But she wasn't prepared to throw in the towel either. Not with her client's life, as she once knew it, on the line.

* * *

They waited till they were alone again, before Georgina Perez said fretfully, "She knows about the club."

"No, she doesn't," Brittany said forcefully. "Can't you see, the attorney was only fishing—trying to do whatever she can to save her client for going down for Kris's murder."

Georgina sensed there was more to it than that and questioned, "But what if she isn't? Who's to say that some psycho isn't out there gunning for us, simply because he couldn't keep it in his pants and is bitter that we're willing to call him out on it?"

"It is weird that Kristine, who was running the show," Cecelia uttered, "would all of a sudden be stabbed to death by Stephanie...I mean, the timing sucks."

"Really?" Danielle begged to differ. "People are killed all the time and often for no sensible reason. They didn't always get along."

"But would Stephanie really take things that far?" Cecelia gazed at everyone, her lower lip hanging open.

Aimee fluttered her lashes. "We all know Kris crossed the line where it concerned her roomie and maybe ended up paying a terrible price." She sighed. "I mean, the police wouldn't have charged Stephanie with the crime if they didn't believe she was guilty, right?"

"That's how I see it," Brittany said, with a catch to her voice. "Even if Jessica Frost knows about The Sexy Coeds Club, she can't prove anything. Or stop us from carrying on. No one is trying to pick us off, one by one. Trust me."

"I agree," Danielle chirped. "So long as we stick together, everything will be fine." She paused. "Kris would've felt the same way if she were still around."

"She's right." Georgina couldn't argue that last point, knowing how committed Kristine was to making sure they succeeded in their profitable, and even fun, endeavor. "Let's not panic and have the club unravel—along with everything it stands for."

The sexy coeds formed a circle and held hands in solidifying their bond, before heading off to class.

Chapter Twenty

On a lark, Brittany Delray decided to pay Stephanie a visit while in jail awaiting trial. They weren't exactly the best of friends, but were acquainted as Kristine's roommate. As the current leader of The Sexy Coeds Club, who replaced Kris, it made sense to keep tabs on someone Kristine trusted, though only to an extent. Watching Stephanie on the other side of the glass separating them, Brittany wondered if this was such a good idea. Especially after her lawyer confronted them about the club and her theory about a vindictive killer on the loose. *Since I'm here, might as well get it over with*, she thought, picking up the phone and waiting for Stephanie to do the same.

When she did, Brittany said in a friendly tone, "Hey," while thinking that she looked worn down. Jail life obviously had not been too kind to Kristine's former roomie.

"What are you doing here?" Stephanie asked, as if she hadn't a clue.

"Just thought I'd come and see how you're doing." Brittany made herself smile. "I would've come sooner, but between classes, volleyball practice, and work, there never seemed to be enough time." She knew that sounded lame, but it was at least partly true.

"No need to explain. It's fine." Stephanie tilted her head. "Not like I was going anywhere. Or had something better to do."

Brittany agreed. She certainly would never want to take her place in a jail cell. "So, how are you holding up?"

"It's pure hell being in here, if you want to know the truth," Stephanie pulled no punches. "But I'm starting to get used to the routine. I only hope it won't last too much longer."

"Speaking of that…" Brittany flashed her a direct look, deciding she may as well put it out there. "Did you do it?"

Stephanie's mouth hung open. "You mean kill Kris?"

"Uh, yeah." It was too late to withdraw the question. Especially since that was why she was in jail. "Everything that I've read and heard about what happened—"

"No, I didn't kill her!" Stephanie made a face, as though this should go without saying. "No matter what they're saying."

Brittany wasn't sure she believed her. Caught in the act, holding the bloody knife, no forced entry, resentful of Kristine, she believed—all seemed to point toward guilt. "Had to ask," she said tonelessly.

"Someone set me up," Stephanie claimed.

"Who?" She eyed her curiously.

"You tell me." Stephanie glared at her suspiciously.

Brittany met her gaze. "I don't know what you mean."

"The Sexy Coeds Club."

"Excuse me?" Brittany played dumb, though surprised she knew about it.

"According to my attorney, Kris was part of this club that has sex with married professors, then blackmails them to keep quiet." Stephanie leaned her face forward. "Are you a member too?"

"I don't know where your lawyer got her information," Brittany suggested. "I don't know anything about some sex club, or Kris being involved. I'm certainly not part of it. I don't need money that badly." She hoped that sounded convincing enough. As it was, Kristine was adamant about keeping her roommate out of the loop, believing she wouldn't be able to handle their extracurricular and lucrative activities. Brittany could see that Kris was right.

Stephanie sighed. "Well, what about the other girls Kristine hung out with?"

"You'll have to ask them," Brittany cleverly dodged the question. Still, she took the opportunity to see what else she could get out of the jailbird. "Why would you think that someone from this so-called sex club would set you up?"

She shrugged. "I don't know. My lawyer believes that someone who might have been blackmailed by the group went after Kristine and, as her roommate, counted on me touching the murder weapon."

"That sounds a bit farfetched to me," countered Brittany, batting her lashes. Even if it did concern her a bit that one of the men they were extorting money from might stoop to that level, she couldn't let this show. "If not you, maybe it was someone with a personal rather than financial vendetta against Kristine."

"Who could that be?" Stephanie rolled her eyes thoughtfully. "Kris didn't have any enemies that I knew of."

I can think of one, Brittany told herself, *and I'm looking at her*. She peered through the glass. "How much did it bother you when you learned that Kristine slept with Brody?"

Stephanie wrinkled her nose. "You knew about that?"

"Everyone knew," she confessed. "It's hard to keep secrets like that from friends, other than you, for obvious reasons."

Stephanie sucked in a deep breath. "I was really pissed," she admitted, with a hard edge to her voice. Softening abruptly, she insisted, "But not enough to kill Kristine."

Brittany didn't respond to that, but could see the rage festering in her like poison, even though the deed was already done and Kris buried. Maybe she did kill her after all and was trying to point the finger in a different direction to get off the hook. "I have to get to class," Brittany said.

Stephanie nodded. "Thanks for visiting."

"I'll try to come again," she lied, knowing that once was enough. Guilty or not, Stephanie would have to fend for herself, with the help of her lawyer, Jessica Frost.

Outside, Brittany breathed in the fresh air. In erring on the side of caution, she thought it might be best if they laid low on extorting money from married professors for a while. But that didn't mean she couldn't go after a lonely and gullible man elsewhere for some extra cash. It would be her secret and hers only. If it worked out, then she could let the other girls in on it.

* * *

Hugh sat at the bar in the Leopard Lounge on Kenton Street. He was nursing a gin and tonic while admittedly feeling sorry for himself. He still missed Jessica. His wife, Claire, wasn't as much interested in allowing him to take her to bed as she was to keep him away from any other woman's bed. In short, his love life sucked. Fortunately, he was still going strong as a financial advisor, using his knowledge of the market to enrich himself and clients, for the most part. There were exceptions, of course, such as Sean Quail, who mismanaged his funds all on his own while feeding his unhealthy addictions.

Hugh's musings were put on hold as the woman sat beside him. She looked to be in her mid-twenties and was a stunner, tall and slender as he liked, with long, layered, golden-blonde hair parted on the side, and pretty blue eyes. She was wearing a black body-hugging tank dress and black strappy sandals. Looking back at him, she offered a smile.

"Hi," she said in a sexy voice.

"Hi, there." He wanted to pretend he wasn't interested in going after her. But against his better judgment was a burning desire to feel wanted and get some action. "Buy you a drink?"

"I usually prefer to buy my own," she claimed. "Simpler that way. But, you seem like a nice person, so…what the hell… Go for it."

Hugh showed his teeth. "What are you having?"

"I'll have a mezcal margarita," she said smoothly.

"Mezcal margarita, it is." He ordered the drink and a second gin and tonic for himself. Turning to his new friend, he said, "I'm Hugh."

"Brittany."

"Nice to meet you, Brittany." He stuck out his hand.

"You too." She shook it and he almost hated to let go of her soft fingers. She smelled good, too. After the drinks were delivered, Hugh had to ask curiously, "I'm sure this sounds like a cliché, but what's a pretty young woman doing here all by your lonesome?" He wondered if she was a call girl. That definitely wasn't his thing. Maybe, in this case, he would make an exception.

CHAPTER TWENTY

"That's so old school." She frowned. "Can't a pretty young woman go out for a drink the same as a little older, quite handsome man?"

"Absolutely! Didn't mean to offend." Hugh liked that she found him handsome, as did most women.

"Apology accepted." She licked her lips after tasting the cocktail. "I feel like dancing. Will you join me?" There was a dance floor and music playing.

Though he wasn't much of a dancer, Hugh found it hard to back away from a challenge. "Sure, I'd love to."

It was a fast song that slowed down in a hurry. Before he knew it, they were slow dancing and Hugh was feeling as if he was in college all over again. He wondered if she could be a student at Wryer College as Sean Quail crossed his mind. Right now, he could care less. They were both adults and he and the attractive lady were entitled to a little fun.

When Brittany invited him to spend the night with her at a local hotel where she had a room, Hugh didn't ask questions. Feeling as horny as hell, he was eager for the release. Afterwards, they would go their separate ways.

* * *

After they both stripped naked, Brittany waited for Hugh to go into the bathroom before positioning and turning on her hidden camera. She had been able to glean from him that he was an unhappily married man—but married nonetheless, who was not looking for anything serious. Of course, serious was the last thing on Brittany's mind too. In fact, he was not her type as dating material. But par for the course as someone who seemed to have money and would have to part with some of it before long. She checked his wallet and saw on his driver's license that his name was Hugh Holliman. She took a picture of the license with her cell phone camera.

By the time he returned to the room, wearing a condom, Brittany was already in bed under the sheets, wanting to get this over with as soon as possible so that she could spring her real plan into action.

Chapter Twenty-One

Homicide Investigator Jackson Payne was not thrilled to be called to work this morning in what was supposed to be his day off spent chilling with his lady, Sheila, at their new condominium on Nottingham Drive. With a baby on the way, they needed all the time afforded them to enjoy each other's company, before having to share it with a child. But duty called. As a fourteen-year veteran of the Creighton Hills Police Department's Detective Division, he knew the ropes. Had to be ready at a moment's notice to investigate crimes of violence that ended very badly for someone. In this case, he'd been told that a young woman was found shot to death in her car on Fourteenth Street, in an area known for its increased gang activity in recent years.

"Too many damned people dying before their time," Payne muttered to himself, as he drove his department-issued dark sedan to the location. Once there, he parked and made his way past the crime scene tape and flashed his ID to a male uniformed policeman that Payne recognized as Officer Guy Bean.

Bean frowned. "Sorry to have to lay this on you to start off your day."

"Comes with the territory." Payne shrugged and glanced at the vehicle in question—a white Subaru Crosstrek. "What do we have here?" he asked routinely, already beginning to put on a pair of nitrile gloves.

"A woman was found slumped over in the car," Bean said. "Appears to have been shot at least twice at fairly close range."

"Who reported the crime?" Payne doubted it was the killer, though this was sometimes the case.

"A construction crew spotted the car. They thought it was left here unattended... Until they saw the victim inside..."

Payne observed the shattered front driver's side window. Opening the door, he winced as he observed a blonde-haired white female in the front seat. He guessed her to be in her early twenties, wearing a dark-colored tank dress, colored red with her own blood. She wasn't wearing a seatbelt, which suggested that she had either just entered the vehicle or hadn't bothered to put one on, as the law required. Either way, her position indicated she was in the driver's seat, but fell onto the passenger side. Judging by the bullet wounds to her head, Payne believed it was at point-blank range and fired from a small-caliber handgun.

He leaned inside the car and grabbed the victim's handbag. Fishing around inside, he came upon a student photo ID card. She attended Wryer College and was named Brittany Delray. It immediately dawned on Payne that another Wryer student, Kristine McVeigh, had recently been the victim of a homicide. Coincidence? Likely yes, the detective decided, when considering that McVeigh's alleged killer, Stephanie Dozier, was already in jail and about to go to trial.

* * *

Jessica did her morning jog around the property, enjoying the fresh air and pushing herself to the limit without going overboard. Though she had once thought that after the Hugh fiasco, it would be difficult to open herself up to another man anytime soon, it appeared as though she was doing just that with Liam. He was probably about as different from Hugh as night and day on the plus side; while on par with him in terms of handsomeness, charm, and sexual attraction. Jessica believed the sexual chemistry was actually better with Liam, even if she had decided it was best to slow things down a bit in that department, if only to see if there was as much substance to build upon. The fact that he was on board with getting to know one another on an intellectual, and even professional, level told her Liam was someone she might be able to have a future with.

After the run, which included bypassing a flock of pigeons that seemed just as enthralled with her, Jessica took a quick shower and headed out to meet with Stephanie. She made it a point to keep in regular communication with her client, knowing that she had become Stephanie's lifeline to the outside world, along with her parents, who visited or phoned as often as they could in showing their love and support.

In the conference room, Jessica waited for Stephanie to arrive. When she did so and they were left alone, the pretty coed furrowed her brow as she sat and muttered, "I got a visit yesterday from Brittany Delray—one of the students Kristine hung out with."

Jessica lifted a brow. "I spoke with her myself yesterday briefly," she admitted, after securing the names of Kristine's friends from Stephanie. "Unfortunately, she didn't have much to say." Neither did the other girls, much to Jessica's chagrin, which she could only assume was a code of silence regarding what they might have been up to.

"She knew about Brody and Kristine having sex," Stephanie said with asperity.

"Really?" Jessica's eyes widened.

"Yeah, Kristine must have bragged about it." Stephanie's lips pursed. "That bitch!"

"Maybe she simply wanted to express her regret," countered Jessica, wanting to give her the benefit of the doubt in putting this out there.

"Yeah, right." Stephanie rolled her eyes.

"It could've come from Brody as well," Jessica offered. "Boys will be boys, too, when it comes to the art of bragging."

"Whatever." Stephanie shrugged, seemingly not too keen on believing her boyfriend would do such a thing. "I confronted Brittany about The Sexy Coeds Club."

"Let me guess..." Jessica hummed. "She denied any knowledge of it?"

"Right. She claimed there was no such club, claiming that you had been misinformed."

"Maybe she's right," Jessica hated to say. "Could be that the Kris connected to Professor Quail is not your roommate, Kristine McVeigh."

"I think Brittany was lying," Stephanie spoke forthrightly. "She's covering her own ass; I just know it!"

"Hold that thought," Jessica said, as her cell phone rang. She took it out of her pocket and saw that it was Liam, with a video chat request. *Better get it,* she told herself, sensing it was important beyond his personal interest in her. "Hey."

"Got some news..." His brows lowered despairingly. "Brittany Delray's body was found this morning. She was shot to death—"

"What?" Jessica reacted, as did Stephanie, who heard every word. "Where?"

"She was in her car in an area near downtown on Fourteenth Street."

"Do they know who killed her?" Jessica had to ask.

"According to my sources, they believe it could be gang-related."

Jessica frowned. "Sounds a little—make that much too—convenient to me."

"You're preaching to the congregation," Liam quipped humorlessly. "With Quail and McVeigh's deaths, this makes three people who have died one way or another recently who were associated with Wryer College. In my book, there's something off here."

"Way off." Jessica agreed, gazing at her client, who was taking it all in and clearly distressed that she was being accused of taking one of those lives. In Jessica's mind, this seemed to be working its way back to the sex ring apparently orchestrated by the group of coeds, who seemed to be dropping like flies.

"Can you meet me at my office?" Liam got her attention. "A friend of mine in the police department with some knowledge of the case has agreed to talk with us—off the record."

"Yes, of course," Jessica said without prelude. He gave her the location. "I'll see you there," she told him.

When she got off the line, Stephanie said swiftly, "Someone's going after members of the club... The same person who killed Kristine—"

"I'm inclined to believe you," Jessica cautioned. "Proving it may be another matter, so long as none of the girls—or men involved—are willing to come forward and confirm the sex ring's existence."

Stephanie cringed. "Am I doomed to simply rot in here for something I didn't do?"

"You just need to be patient," Jessica insisted, even when it was gnawing at her own nerves.

"How can I?" she spat. "This is freaking me out."

Me too, Jessica mused, realizing that soothing words were not going to cut it. So, she tried a different perspective with her client. "If you look at it another way, right now, being in here may be the safest place for you, Stephanie. As long as you're in jail, anyone who views you as a threat—real or imagined—cannot touch you. In order to prove you're innocent of killing Kristine, we have to go through the legal process...till we can turn the tables on the prosecution and your former roommate's real killer—"

Though tightlipped, Jessica believed she had gotten through to her client. Maybe Liam's friend in the department could shed some light on the investigation into Brittany's death and they could proceed from there.

Chapter Twenty-Two

L iam greeted Detective Juan Guillermo of the PD's Evidence and Property Unit with a hearty handshake as they stood in his office. The two had become friends a couple of years ago when their investigations crisscrossed and they discovered a mutual fondness for water activities, such as boating, fishing, parasailing, and river trekking. Guillermo, who was the same height and similar build, and a year older at thirty-six, had brown hair in a crew cut. "Thanks for coming," Liam told him.

"No problem." Guillermo furrowed his brow and added, "Well, there could be one, if this all goes sour."

"It won't," promised Liam, mindful that the detective was putting his neck on the line by providing confidential information. "Not as it pertains to mentioning where I got the info."

"Okay. So, you really think the murder of this latest coed is somehow tied to the case you're working on connecting the suicide of Sean Quail to the killing of Kristine McVeigh?" Guillermo gave him a skeptical look.

"I think it's a distinct possibility." Liam didn't want to sound too confident, given that the murders occurred differently and in different settings, indicating that it was still possible there were two killers. "In my current line of work, I have to rely on gut instincts as much, if not more, than the facts as they may appear."

"I get that," the detective said. "There is something to be said for gut instincts, even for those of us in the PD. But they can only go so far if they're not backed up by the evidence—"

"Speaking of which..." Liam was just about to dive right into whatever information Guillermo had decided to share when Jessica walked through the door. As usual, she gave him a thrill every time Liam saw her face. He wondered if the same were true in reverse. "Hey," he said, as if they were platonic acquaintances and nothing more.

"Hey." She smiled awkwardly. "Did I miss anything?"

"You're right on time." Liam grinned crookedly and made the introductions.

"Actually, I believe we've met before, Detective Guillermo," Jessica said, after they shook hands. "A few years ago, one of my clients used you as a character witness."

"Yeah, I remember." He smiled uneasily. "Dorothy Breck was a good person. Glad you were able to get the case dismissed."

"Me too."

Liam considered just how small their world truly was as members of the local criminal justice and investigative community. He invited everyone to take a seat, as he himself sat on a corner of his desk to be closer to them. "So, Detective, what do you have for us...?"

Guillermo squirmed. "Well, as I mentioned to you on the phone, Liam, the current thinking is that we're talking about separate crimes with the deaths of Kristine McVeigh and Brittany Delray..." He eyed Jessica. "Not saying your client is guilty or not—"

"I understand," she said respectfully.

"But when Liam mentioned the possibility of a campus sex ring involving McVeigh, I did a little digging, unofficially, regarding the evidence bagged in the Delray murder..." Guillermo paused. "It appears as though she video recorded herself having sexual relations with a man. This got me thinking, could her death have been related to extorting men, or this one in particular...?"

"I don't suppose you were able to get a name for the man in the video?" Jessica asked curiously.

"As a matter of fact, I do have a name," he responded, catching Liam by surprise. "At some point, before or after the sex, Delray took a picture of the man's driver's license. His name is Hugh Holliman—"

"Hugh…" Jessica voiced, her facial expression giving her away as to the shock.

"You know him?" Guillermo cocked a brow.

"I thought I did," she muttered. "But lately, I'm seriously beginning to wonder if that was ever the case. What have you gotten yourself into, Hugh?" Jessica threw out pensively.

"I guess that's what we need to find out," Liam spoke edgily.

"Let me know what you come up with," Guillermo told them. "But, as a heads-up, the lead investigator in Delray's murder, Detective Jackson Payne, will certainly be paying Holliman a visit sooner than later. If you want first crack at him, I suggest you not waste any time having a talk with him and see where it leads."

Liam met Jessica's eyes and knew they didn't need to be told twice. "We're on it," he told his friend.

Guillermo nodded and got to his feet. "I better get back to work." He looked at Liam. "Let me know when you want to go fishing again."

"Will do." *Right now, there's bigger fish to catch*, Liam told himself in earnest. Starting with the man Jessica was once hooked on, Hugh Holliman.

* * *

Jessica was downright angry after learning that Hugh had apparently followed Sean Quail's lead in sleeping with college coeds—at least one—only to be burned in the process. *How could I not have seen what a total jerk Hugh was?* she asked herself, heading to his office for an encore confrontation. Would his wife ever wake up and see him for what he truly was and realize that the only person he ever cared about was himself? That notwithstanding, Jessica could only wonder just how far her ex-lover would go to protect his image and keep up appearances as a business and family man if he was faced with a blackmailer.

Riding alongside her was Liam, who seemed just as vested in getting to the truth as she was in relation to Hugh and the possibility that he may have murdered not only Brittany Delray, but could have been involved in the death of Kristine McVeigh, both of whom may have been part of a college sex ring. Jessica considered, though, in glancing at Liam who was looking a bit uncomfortable in the passenger seat of her car, if resentment that Hugh was once her lover may have motivated her current sex partner to want to paint Hugh as the bad guy in her eyes. As it was, she didn't need any help in that department, as her ex seemed to be digging himself quite a large hole all on his own. Still, Liam had nothing to worry about as far as Jessica was concerned. Hugh was so yesterday and she couldn't imagine ever falling into that trap again. Especially now, with him being caught in an unseemly, and possibly murderous, vice of his own making.

When they arrived at Hugh's office, Jessica faced Liam and said, "Let's just see how far this goes with Hugh before jumping to any conclusions, okay?"

"No problem." He pinched his nose. "I'm just along for the ride and to offer moral support, should you need it."

Why do I have the feeling it goes further than that in your way of thinking? Jessica asked herself, but didn't question this. She welcomed his nearness and involvement, whatever the case. "Let's go have a chat with Hugh."

"Yeah, let's," Liam seconded keenly.

They caught Hugh standing by the window, deep in thought, as though his world was about to come crashing down on him. Or was that only Jessica's imagination about what he deserved if he really had allowed his sexual urges and adultery to escalate into murder?

She got his attention and Hugh faced them. "I was hoping to catch you here..." Jessica stated ambiguously.

He hoisted a brow. "You caught me," he said sarcastically, moving toward them. "What's going on...?" Hugh eyed Liam sharply and then gazed back at Jessica. "Decided to gang up on me with him, or what...?"

"No one's ganging up on you, Hugh," she thought to say, "but I'm pretty sure the police will want to speak to you very soon—"

Hugh colored. "What the hell are you talking about?"

"Let's start with Brittany Delray," Liam said, with a catch to his voice. "Does that name ring a bell?"

Jessica could see that it did and made him uncomfortable, as Hugh

116

responded defiantly, "Why should it?"

"Because she was found shot to death this morning," Liam snapped coldly.

Hugh stiffened. "What does that have to do with me?"

"We know you had sex with her, probably last night," Jessica uttered hotly.

"I don't know where this is coming from—"

"It's coming from you!" Liam raised his voice. "You're on a video having sex with the coed."

"There must be a mistake," Hugh claimed with a straight face.

"No mistake, Hugh." Jessica glared at him, astounded at his weak attempts at denial. "Brittany took a picture of your driver's license while you were otherwise preoccupied. The police have it and the recording."

"My one question, Holliman," Liam tossed out strongly, "is whether you were the instigator of Sean Quail's actions or walked in his footsteps in going after college girls for some fun and frolic?"

Jessica didn't give him a chance to respond before she declared, in keeping up the pressure, "No doubt about it. You're in the hot seat, Hugh. With Brittany murdered and you possibly the last person who saw her alive, I'd say you've got some major explaining to do. So, you might as well start right now with us!"

Hugh sucked in a deep breath and lowered his head pitifully. "I met her last night at the Leopard Lounge." He glared at Liam. "And I didn't lead or follow Sean in pursuing coeds for sex. I didn't know Brittany was a college student—she looked older—and she never revealed this to me." Hugh's shoulders slumped as he turned toward Jessica. "I bought her a drink, she asked me to dance, and then to go back to her hotel room. I was feeling lonely, needy, and just went with it. We had sex, said our goodbyes, and I left. That was it."

"We're not the ones you need to convince," Jessica warned. She wanted to believe the man she'd been involved with wasn't capable of murder. But then, who wasn't, if the circumstances and motivation were powerful enough?

"She was alive and well at that point," he insisted. "I swear it!"

"So, you're telling us that Brittany never tried to blackmail you to keep her from releasing the video to your wife?" asked Liam, sounding unconvinced.

"Or on social media?"

"There was never any blackmail attempt, Jess." Hugh met her eyes and Jessica immediately felt inclined to believe him, though she didn't know why she should. Perhaps it was the sense of dread and desperation in his gaze. "If that had been her intent," he stressed, "she would have failed miserably. I would never have succumbed to extortion."

"Even if it cost you your marriage, business, and everything else you held dear?" Liam asked, pushing him hard.

"Even if..." Hugh jutted his chin. "I'm not a murderer." He looked at Jessica again. "I hope after everything we've had between us you believe that."

She glanced at Liam and back, knowing she had been put on the spot, deliberately or otherwise by Hugh. Without giving it too much thought, Jessica responded snappily, "To be honest, I'm not sure I do. I mean, it's not like you haven't lied to me before. What's to say this isn't the same?"

"It isn't." His brows knitted. "You really think I have it in me to take another life to save my own?"

Jessica was unwilling to give him the benefit of the doubt just now, even for old times' sake. Nor was she prepared to outright convict him before the police weighed in. "Right now," she said, "the only thing I believe is that my client is being falsely accused of murdering her roommate, who seems to have been part of a college sex ring. Now another student and possible member of The Sexy Coeds Club has been found murdered as well. Until this is sorted out one way or the other, you won't be able to simply walk away from this, Hugh."

Without saying another word, Jessica gave him that to ponder, as she and Liam left Hugh's office.

Chapter Twenty-Three

"What do you think?" Liam asked Jessica about Hugh Holliman's shaky story during the drive back to his own office.

"Hugh's a jerk, in more ways than one," she answered frankly. "That includes his infidelity and probably questionable business affiliations, if Sean Quail is any indication. But I have to say, he doesn't strike me as being a coldblooded killer."

"I wish I had your confidence in the man," Liam uttered sarcastically. Right away, he realized how it came off. He wasn't some college kid, prone to having a natural distrust of those competing for the affections of the prettiest girl on campus. But the fact was, as a private investigator with a built-in radar for deceit, he was having trouble believing that Holliman's hands weren't dirtier than he'd let on. "Of course, you know him better than I do," Liam tried to soften his position. "I'm just saying—"

"Whatever confidence I had in Hugh has gone out the window," Jessica made it perfectly clear. "That doesn't mean his account of how things went down with Brittany Delray wasn't the truth."

"Which part," questioned Liam, looking at her in the driver's seat, "that Delray never tried to blackmail him? Or he didn't kill her to keep his secret safe, not knowing what she had on him...?"

"Both, of course," Jessica replied matter-of-factly. "Could be that Brittany never got the chance to try to extort money from Hugh, even if that was her intention, because someone else killed her before she could. If true, then Hugh would never have been put to the test in weighing whether or not to resort to committing murder in order to keep a blackmailer from ruining his life. Assuming he had chosen to go down that dark path."

"So you think that someone else Delray—or The Sexy Coeds Club—had been blackmailing could have gone after her?" Liam asked, leaning his head back. "With Holliman being the scapegoat, intentionally or not?"

"Yes, possibly," she answered. "In the same vein as my client."

"That's a lot of scapegoating of innocent people." He didn't mean to imply that Stephanie Dozier may not have been so innocent after all, as much as wondering what the odds were that both she and Holliman were being railroaded by the same person or persons.

Jessica shrugged. "It happens more than you know," she suggested. "All I'm saying is not to rush to judgment till we get the facts sorted out, one way or the other."

Liam liked how she used *we* in her point of view. It meant she wanted him to continue working with her in not only proving her client's innocence, but also solving some related criminality that seemed to be spreading like a virus in what appeared to be a complex case of sex, videos, lies, and murder. "Fair enough," he agreed.

Jessica turned to him and smiled. "Was that so hard?"

"No, not really." He grinned and added half-jokingly, "Just wait till you get my bill."

She laughed nervously. "I'll try not to pass out when I do."

After they got back to the parking lot by Liam's office, he asked curiously, "So, where are you headed next?"

"To have a little chat with Madeleine Griffin."

He lifted a brow. "You really think that will make any difference in the absence of hard evidence?"

"Probably not," she admitted. "But I won't know unless I try. Madeleine needs to know, if she doesn't already, that there are other real possibilities and motivations regarding the murder of Kristine McVeigh that could exonerate my client—if the other side is willing to play fairly."

"Good luck with that." Liam meant it, even if he was still skeptical that the State was anywhere close to pointing the finger at someone else. Much of what he'd heard about the prosecutor, in particular, trying the case, was that she was not very flexible when her mind was made up, short of overwhelming information that could not be easily dismissed. Could Jessica prove him wrong?

"Thanks," she said evenly, and waited for him to exit.

Liam considered leaning over for a kiss, but decided against it. As much as he enjoyed the intimate part of their involvement, he had to respect the boundaries she'd recently set in taking things more slowly as they progressed possibly into something real. He believed she was more than worth the wait. As was he.

Liam got out of the car and waved as Jessica drove off, before deciding to head back into his office for a bit of work left undone.

* * *

Jessica was a little reluctant to meet with Madeleine, knowing she didn't exactly have solid standing for seeking a motion to delay the trial. Much less, have the charge against her client dropped. But if she and the prosecutor were to present a united front, the judge would have to listen, right? To that end, getting Madeleine outside her comfort zone seemed like a smart move. Would her opponent take the bait?

When she saw Madeleine approaching the Tasty Times food truck on Marbury Lane, Jessica waved her over, as though necessary to become noticeable. "Hi," she said, friendly-like.

Madeleine responded in her typical no-nonsense fashion, "This had better be good."

Jessica smiled. "I hear they have some of the best burgers in town. We can put that to the test and judge just how good they are."

"Very funny." Her opponent cracked a smile. "As long as you're buying, I suppose I could have lunch a little earlier than normal for me."

"Consider it my treat." *So far, so good*, thought Jessica, and they both ordered patty melts.

Once she took a big bite out of hers, Madeleine chewed and said straightforwardly, "Okay, now that you've buttered me up a little, what am I doing here?"

Knowing she couldn't delay the inevitable any further, Jessica got right to the point. "I wanted to talk to you about the case against my client, Stephanie Dozier."

Madeleine put her patty melt down and frowned. "That's not appropriate."

"I think it is, all things considered," Jessica shot back, taking a small bite of her sandwich.

Madeleine played hardball. "Unless you're here to tell me your client is prepared to plead guilty to the murder of Kristine McVeigh, I'm not sure there's anything else to say."

"How about the fact that Kristine has had a couple of brushes with the law?" Jessica pointed out. "One in which she was arrested for solicitation of prostitution, only to have the charge dropped."

Madeleine frowned. "The victim's history is not relevant in this instance, Jessica. Going there is low, even for you."

It was obvious to Jessica by her reaction that the attorney was aware of this information and pushed it aside, conveniently. "I agree with you, Madeleine," she countered, "except for the fact that I have reason to believe Kristine McVeigh was part of a college sex ring called The Sexy Coeds Club, and that they were sleeping with married professors and extorting money from them to keep it their little secret. One of those men was an art history professor named Sean Quail, who committed suicide last month. Another member of the sex ring, Brittany Delray, was found shot to death this morning..." Out of respect for what they once had, Jessica chose not to mention Hugh's involvement with her and his possibly being implicated in Brittany's death and the sex ring. If he was guilty of more than bad judgment, it would catch up to him soon enough without her assistance. "In my book, that's more than enough to call into question whether McVeigh's death and Delray's are connected. Since my client is in jail with no bail, that leaves open the possibility that the real killer of Kristine is someone she tried to blackmail and it cost her life..."

"Enough!" Madeleine snapped. She hesitated in taking another bite of the sandwich, as though it was suddenly toxic. "This convoluted story, while certainly entertaining and salacious, doesn't change the fact that we have the goods on your client, including fingerprints, DNA, and holding the murder weapon in the clear vision of the arresting officer. Do I need to go on? Nice try, Jessica, but I think I'll pass."

"Ignoring what's staring you right in the face won't change the truth," she stated, eyeing her opponent sharply. "I've just given you something to chew on, figuratively and literally. The least you can do, in the name of justice, is look into it deeper before dismissing it out of hand simply because it goes against the grain in the case you're building to convict my client."

"You want to talk about justice?" Madeleine scowled. "Justice is having to bury your twenty-two-year-old daughter after she was viciously attacked by someone she trusted. While I'm not working for Judge McVeigh, I do feel his pain. Unless you come up with some hard evidence and not mere supposition to support your position, this is going nowhere." She tossed the rest of her sandwich into a trash can. "Thanks for the lunch—"

Jessica watched her walk away, feeling a little deflated. *I shouldn't have expected a miracle*, she admitted to herself, knowing that if the shoe were on the other foot, it wouldn't have been enough for her to drop the case either. Instead, it was full steam ahead in trying to prove, in court or out of, that Stephanie was not the one who should be behind bars.

After taking another bite of her patty melt, Jessica tossed the rest in the can and headed off.

Chapter Twenty-Four

Detective Payne sat in the interrogation room across from Hugh Holliman, who came in voluntarily, saving them from having to bring him in as a suspect. After waiting a long moment to see just how uncomfortable the man got, Payne advised him routinely about his right to a lawyer, while intimating slyly if he thought he needed one.

Holliman rejected the need for representation and said smugly, "Let's just get this over with."

"All right." Payne peered at him. "Why don't we talk about Brittany Delray." This was where he expected to see the suspect squirm at the mere mention of the dead woman's name. Instead, Holliman seemed to almost welcome the challenge.

"I heard about what happened to her." He sat back pensively. "Look, whatever you may think, you've got the wrong man."

Payne had heard that before, too many times. Meant nothing to him but covering one's ass, as if this was enough to do so. "That's yet to be established," he said curtly. "The fact of the matter is, you are the right man in terms of being identified as someone Ms. Delray spent time with on the last night of her life." Payne waited to see if he would deny it. Holliman did not, but the detective bolstered his case by producing a copy of his driver's license. "She took this picture, before or after you had sex with her in a hotel room, which she also recorded."

Holliman kept his cool, but Payne sensed he had to be sweating beneath the calm exterior. "If that isn't enough, a hotel surveillance camera clocked you entering the lobby with Ms. Delray." Payne leaned forward intimidatingly.

"I have to say, it doesn't look good for you," he said, more for effect at this point.

Holliman ran a hand across his mouth. "I'm not denying that I had sex with Brittany last night, after we met at a club. It was totally consensual and no payment was involved, other than the cost of a drink. When it was over, I left the room, with her alive and well. I had no idea about the video or why she took a picture of my driver's license. Maybe it was just as a keepsake for the time we spent together, brief as it was."

Payne conceded that the hotel security camera backed up his claim that Delray was still alive when Holliman left the hotel alone about an hour after arriving, and Delray doing the same shortly thereafter. Still, the detective sensed that his story was too polished, almost as if he had been prepped beforehand. *Or is that just my imagination?* the detective asked himself. "Where did you go after you left the hotel?"

"I went to my office," he claimed. "Had some work I needed to get done."

"Can anyone vouch for that?"

Holliman hedged. "I didn't run into anyone. Most people had already left the building for the day."

Payne considered this with suspicion, but figured it was plausible. He tried a different angle with the suspect. "Do you own a gun?"

Holliman responded without prelude, "Yes. I keep a firearm in my house for self-defense and to protect my family."

"What's the make and model of your gun?"

"It's a .38 Smith & Wesson Special revolver," Holliman answered.

Payne peered at him thoughtfully. "That's the only firearm you have?"

"Yes," he responded solidly.

"Do you know any reason someone would have wanted Brittany Delray dead?"

"None whatsoever," Holliman insisted. "She seemed like a nice young lady, with her life ahead of her. Why someone would take that from her?" He sighed. "All I can tell you is I'm not your guy."

Payne was inclined to believe him, considering what was known about the murder. But desperation could have led Holliman to wait for the victim to leave the hotel, follow her to her final destination, and kill her with a small-caliber handgun that couldn't be linked to him. "Is that what you plan to tell your wife?" Payne asked brusquely, having learned that the man was married and had kids.

For the first time, the suspect appeared rattled. "It was a one-night stand, nothing more. My wife doesn't need to know any of this."

"Keep telling yourself that," Payne said sarcastically. "We're talking about infidelity that worked its way into a murder investigation. Whether you're guilty or not, this can't be swept under the rug. Your wife is bound to find out, one way or the other. Probably best it came from you and let the chips fall where they may." He left it at that, giving him some sound advice, but suspecting that Holliman may not choose to use it for his own reasons. Whatever the case, Payne turned his focus to other potential culprits in Delray's murder without taking him off the radar altogether just yet.

* * *

Hugh left the building and the police detective's grilling, feeling as if he had successfully made his case for innocence in Brittany's death and turned Payne's attention elsewhere. Being given a heads-up by Jessica and Liam Reed had helped Hugh prepare himself for questioning about the murder. Nevertheless, the fact that someone he'd slept with less than twenty-four hours ago had been shot to death, unnerved him. Was it a random act? Or could this somehow be tied to Sean Quail's suicide and The Sexy Coeds Club? If that were true, how many other coeds were at risk if they continued to try and extort money from married professors? Was that Brittany's intent when she seduced him into her hotel room and bed? Had she planned to blackmail him with the video if he didn't pay up?

In his car, Hugh grappled with this possibility and the fact that she was murdered before it ever reached that point. It certainly worked out for him fortuitously as a wake-up call to his own weaknesses as a man. Being with Jessica was a good thing, he still believed. Not so much with Brittany, as it turned out. Now he needed to decide if coming clean to his wife, Claire, was the best way to go as a preemptive measure, should this thing blow up in his face. Or should he just sit back and see how things played out while a murderer was still at large and possibly out of control in who to go after next?

Chapter Twenty-Five

Madeleine was not happy to have had Jessica Frost lay out her theories regarding the murder of Kristine McVeigh. *Jessica ambushed me, plain and simple*, Madeleine told herself, as she made her way into Jackson Payne's domain. She heard about the tragic death of Brittany Delray. Who hadn't? Madeleine also knew that Payne was the lead investigator into her death. Could it in any way be related to McVeigh's death? Seemed unlikely, as far as the prosecutor was concerned. Yes, she was aware of McVeigh's criminal record. And, yes, Madeleine imagined that Judge McVeigh had called in some favors to get her off. But did this mean that the solid case they had against Stephanie Dozier was suddenly not so solid after all?

When she reached Detective Payne's desk, Madeleine saw him talking on the phone. From the gist of the conversation—something about checking out a film tonight if he could squeeze in the time—she figured he had to be speaking to his girlfriend. Would he ever get up the courage to put a ring on her finger? Or was that too constricting to his freedom? Madeleine thought about Genevieve. Marrying her was probably the best decision she ever made. Or a close second to her career in law.

She cleared her throat to get his attention. Payne turned her way and looked embarrassed as he quickly ended the conversation and hung up. "Sorry about that," he said. "I didn't see you there. What's up?"

"Where are you on the investigation into Brittany Delray's murder?" Madeleine asked pointblank.

"Still in the early stages, but making progress..."

She took a seat on the side of his desk, which was filled with papers, folders, and a couple of mugs, one with coffee in it. "Tell me more..."

"Well, we learned that the victim met a dude named Hugh Holliman at the Leopard Lounge on Kenton Street last night," Payne informed her, "took him to a hotel room, had sex, made a video recording of it, and photographed his driver's license. Sometime after that, Delray was found shot to death in her car about three miles away on Fourteenth Street.

"Hmm..." Madeleine mumbled, while thinking about her little chat with Jessica. "There's a rumor going around that some coeds at Wryer College are engaged in a sex ring with married professors, making a video of them in bed, and then extorting money from them. Do you think this Hugh Holliman could be caught up in that?"

Payne sat back in his task chair musingly. "I don't think so. Holliman is married and definitely an asshole, cheating on his wife with a college-age girl. Furthermore, he's a financial advisor, not a professor. As for recording the sex acts—which, in and of itself, is a violation of the law when nonconsensual—there's no indication that there was an attempt at blackmail."

Madeleine leaned forward. "Do you see any connection between the murders of Kristine McVeigh and Brittany Delray?"

"Not yet," Payne said. "One was stabbed to death, the other shot to death. Apart from that, McVeigh's killer was caught red-handed. Delray's is still at large."

Madeleine's chin fell. "So, Holliman is off the hook in Delray's murder?"

"For now," the detective said. "Ballistics is seeing what it can get from the bullets taken out of Brittany Delray's body. We've also entered them into the ATF's Integrated Ballistic Identification System to see if we can get a hit with the bullets or cartridge casings recovered at the scene of the crime and if they came from the same firearm used in other crimes of violence."

"If not Holliman as the triggerman, what other leads are you following in going after the killer?" she asked curiously, knowing he had an angle in pursuing the unsub.

Payne scratched his cheek. "My guess is Delray's death is gang-related as a retaliatory strike." He glanced at a paper on his desk. "According to the victim's roommate, Danielle Osmond, Delray had an off and on relationship with Jose Rivera, a known gang member. We're trying to track him down, even as we speak."

Madeleine stood, having gotten what she needed to hear. "Keep me apprised on where this goes."

Payne nodded. "Count on it."

"I always do," she said with a thin smile. As an afterthought, Madeleine said, "By the way, on Saturday, Genevieve will be performing at the Sweet Times on Eighth Street. If you and Sheila want to check it—"

"We'll be there," he said, showing his teeth. "Thanks for the invite."

"No problem. Later." Madeleine walked away, her mind racing. As far as she was concerned, Jessica's pathetic attempt to detract from her client's guilt by trying to pin the murder on some sinister character in a college sex ring and extortion plot simply would not fly; which the detective backed her up on. Even if some coeds were foolishly orchestrating this venture, and Kristine McVeigh and Brittany Delray were caught up in it, that hardly exonerated Stephanie Dozier from the persuasive evidence that supported her being the one to stab McVeigh to death. That was good enough for Madeleine to proceed on schedule.

* * *

Danielle Osmond sat in the third-floor student lounge in Kellen Hall, surrounded by the other surviving members of The Sexy Coeds Club, Aimee Atkinson, Georgina Perez, and Cecelia Temple. In spite of the untimely passing of Kristine and now Brittany, it had been a lucrative business and, as the one who had assumed the leadership role with no objections, Danielle saw no reason to disband the group. Even if some were starting to get cold feet, given the hot atmosphere that was circling them like a pack of wolves. It was up to her to keep them in line and get back on track.

Putting on her nicest smile, which she considered her best feature, Danielle said, "Look, everyone's a little freaked out about two of us dying in a short span of time. But that has absolutely nothing to do with what we're doing."

Georgina flapped her lids over big brown eyes. "How do you know that? Maybe someone decided to come after us for pushing him too far—"

"Seriously?" Danielle made a skeptical face. "Have you been locked away in your dorm room? Last I heard, Kristine's roommate, Stephanie Dozier, was charged with her murder and is all but certain to be found guilty at her trial. And Brittany, whom I shared an apartment with and loved like a sister, made the mistake of hooking up with a gang member, even though I warned her it could be a disaster. The detective assigned to her case told me as much. Our group is not the problem. We just need to stick together, be smart about it, and take advantage of the opportunities that present themselves."

Cecelia wrinkled her nose that had an L-shaped ring in it. "Not so sure about that. Even if Kristine and Brittany's deaths are unconnected, I see it as a sign that we should quit while we're ahead."

"We will," insisted Danielle coolly. "But we're not ahead right now. Not really. There's still money to be made and gullible, needy professors who will gladly pay us off and go away. No one needs to be hurt."

"People are already being hurt," Cecelia said, glaring at her. "I don't know why you can't see that."

"Maybe because I'm not weak and ready to run at every little bump in the road," she shot back.

"Then I guess I'm not as strong as you, Danielle. Sorry, but I'm done." She stood up, waiting to see if anyone else would do the same. When no one did, she walked off and out of the lounge.

"Anyone else?" Danielle asked tentatively, hoping that the club wasn't about to disintegrate before her very eyes.

Aimee, who was two months away from her twentieth birthday, was the youngest of the group, but wise and sexually experienced beyond her years, had remained mostly quiet throughout their impromptu meeting. "I say we stay the course," she put forth keenly. "As Danielle said, what happened to Brittany and Kristine is not our fault. If it had been one of us who died, they'd both still be here and insist that we keep it going. You know that. Why shouldn't we do the same?"

Georgina, who had seemed touch and go, appeared to be regaining a backbone. "Yeah, I see no reason to stop a good thing. Since I can't collect on my trust fund till graduation, I can use the money for expenses. I'm still in."

"Same here," seconded Aimee emphatically.

Danielle flashed her perfectly white and straight teeth. "Then we're all in agreement."

"Do you think Cecelia will rat us out?" Georgina asked, eyeing the other girls.

"No," Danielle answered confidently. "We made a pact and Cecelia knows if we go down, so will she. Cecelia will keep her mouth shut."

The three of them put their hands together in a show of solidarity. Only then did Danielle bring up the subject of finding a replacement for Cecelia, given that their numbers had already dwindled enough with Kristine and Brittany out of the picture.

Chapter Twenty-Six

J essica moved steadily on the treadmill at the Creighton Hills Gym. Moving at an even faster pace on the treadmill beside her was her friend and fellow attorney, Connie Martinez. Their mutual love for staying in shape and working up a sweat was the perfect means to get together for a chat.

"That jerk!" Connie mouthed, curling a corner of her lower lip. She was referring to Hugh, whom Jessica had spilled the beans about his latest sexual conquest; along with its implications on her latest case.

"I know," she muttered, increasing the speed on the treadmill. "Going after someone half his age and not his wife is bad enough. But allowing it to be videoed, possibly meant to blackmail him, was just plain dumb." *There, I said it,* Jessica thought, knowing that his error in judgment went well beyond that and could still give him headaches.

"If you ask me, he'll get what he deserves," Connie offered, "if his wife kicks him to the curb and all his bad karma with him."

"Maybe she'll wise up and do just that!" Jessica wasn't about to cut him any slack. Especially when he may have a direct role in her client being jailed for murder, while a sex ring could well be at the center of the deaths of two coeds who were in over their heads with sex, videos, and extortion. Jessica said as much to her friend.

"Sounds like something out of a sleazy novel," Connie said, grabbing her water bottle, while still in full stride.

"Except I believe it to be very real," Jessica stressed. "Problem is, Madeleine doesn't seem to want to touch it. At least where it concerns Stephanie."

"Then you need to force the issue."

Jessica rolled her eyes. "And just how would you suggest I do that?"

Connie took a deep breath. "By finding out as much as you can about this Sexy Coeds Club and how the dots connect to and away from your client. If there is something there, they won't be able to just wish it away like a damned genie."

This caused Jessica to chuckle. "I'm not a magician, but I see your point." She frowned. "Unfortunately, the coeds and the married men they are involved with aren't talking, for obvious reasons—unless, like Hugh, their hand is forced." She sipped from her water bottle thoughtfully. "Then there's the small fact that Kristine McVeigh and Brittany Delray died in different ways. It makes it that much more difficult to tie them to the same killer."

"Who's to say there isn't more than one killer in this deadly game of sex and blackmail?" Connie threw out. "Could be the club coeds pissed off enough men to cause one or more of them to want to strike back, rather than pay up or risk exposure."

"You could be right." Jessica slowed down slightly while mulling this over. "I still say if the murders involved two killers, they must be coordinating the murders to protect themselves."

"And keep your client on the hook for at least one of the deaths," Connie said.

"I was thinking the same thing," admitted Jessica, wiping perspiration from her face.

"So why not hire your new lover to dig deeper?" Connie looked her way. "I mean, apart from being great in bed, that is his forte and, from what you've told me, seems as if he's all in—to stay on your good side."

Another chuckle tickled Jessica's throat. "Not sure Liam's being motivated by staying on my good side, though he's managed to do just that quite effortlessly," she admitted blushingly. "I think it's more when he starts a case, he wants to see it through—no matter where the skeletons are hidden in or out of the closet..."

"Sounds like someone else I know." Connie's voice had a catch to it.

"Touché," Jessica struck back.

"Guess that's what makes us such great lawyers." Connie laughed. "Getting back to your private investigator and potential boyfriend material, when do I get to meet the man?"

That's a very good question, Jessica told herself. It took her three months of seeing Hugh before she introduced him to Connie. Even then, Jessica found it difficult, considering that he had a wife and another life entirely that didn't include her. But with Liam, they were both single, independent-minded people who were good together, while putting no pressure on the other to move at a faster pace. Perhaps it would be good to have him meet her best friend. And vice versa. What was the worst that could happen? Maybe they would get along great and then Connie could press her about taking things to the next level. Such as living together. Or, at the very least, committing to a real relationship.

She smiled at Connie and said, "Why don't we set a date for next week?"

"You're on. Just name the time and place."

"Will do," Jessica promised, knowing she needed to run it by Liam first. She was sure he would jump at the chance to meet someone she was close to as an opportunity to build bridges into her world. Of course, this meant that she too needed to see more of who he was out of bed or as a private investigator. Jessica embraced the thought as she upped her speed and footwork accordingly.

Chapter Twenty-Seven

When Jessica invited him to her house for dinner, Liam didn't bother to pretend he needed to check his busy schedule. Missing her companionship more than he cared to admit—not to mention the great sex, as things had cooled down a bit of late at her request—he agreed readily. He even volunteered to bring the wine, which she accepted.

He showed up ten minutes early, as eager to see where Jessica lived as he was to touch base on her current case and the still-unfolding dynamics that may have had an innocent young woman about to be put on trial for murder. He noted that Jessica lived on a golf course and Liam naturally wondered if she played golf.

Jessica opened the prairie-style front door before he could ring the bell. "Hey," she said, grinning.

"Hey." He grinned back, sizing her up in an attractive doeskin jumpsuit and flats. He didn't underdress, wearing a beige sport coat, with a casual button-down black shirt and russet chino pants, along with brown boat shoes.

"Right on time."

"Force of habit," he quipped.

"Good habit to have." Jessica chuckled. "Come in."

Liam stepped inside, where he caught a whiff of the dinner. At a glance, he could see that the place was impressive, including its trappings and architecture. "Nice," he marveled.

"Thank you." She smiled softly. "I like it, too."

He handed her the bottle of Pinot Grigio. "Hope this works for you?"

"It does," she assured him. "Why don't I pour us a glass before we eat?"

"Good idea."

"In the meantime, please make yourself at home."

Jessica headed off to the kitchen and Liam took the opportunity to check out the downstairs a bit more. Though he was quite comfortable with his floating house, he imagined himself living there with her. Or at least spending lots of time in and out of the residence, as he stood by the great room window gazing at the golf course.

"In case you're wondering..." Jessica said, reading his mind as she walked up to him and handed him a goblet, "no, I don't play golf. But I do jog and hike, and there are boundless opportunities for that within the complex."

"So that's why you're in such terrific shape," Liam said sincerely, tasting the wine.

"Look who's talking," she tossed back. "So, are you a golfer?"

"I play a few rounds every now and then," he admitted. "But I typically get my exercise from water sports and lifting weights."

"I'm not much of a weight lifter, but I'm certainly open to participating in more water sports when I have the time."

"I'll make a note of that." Liam accepted the challenge, while understanding where her current focus was as a defense lawyer. And sometimes lover.

Within minutes, they were seated at a white oak table in the dining room, eating ribeye steak, baked potato, and sautéed brussels sprouts—all of which Liam found appealing to his tastebuds. They quickly went from small talk to the case against Stephanie Dozier, to the chances that Hugh Holliman could have been a party to any type of murderous conspiratorial plot involving infidelity and extortion. For his part, Liam still wouldn't put anything past Holliman if it meant protecting a client. Or himself.

Jessica clung to the belief that her ex-lover was a charming, cheating spouse, but his self-serving behavior didn't rise to conspiring to commit murder. Or framing her client. She added, while cutting into the steak, "If I'm wrong, the police will surely have something to say about it and Hugh will pay the price. Until then, I think someone else, if not more than one person, is responsible for the death of Kristine McVeigh and, quite possibly, Brittany Delray—no matter the case against my client. Or the convenience of believing that Brittany's murder may be gang-related."

"Then we'll just have to go with your instincts and see who's hiding under what rock in taking away the freedom of your client," Liam promised, knowing he wanted as much of a positive outcome here as Jessica. No matter who was brought down in the process.

She smiled. "Where have you been all my life?"

He laughed, liking the sound of that. "Right around the corner—waiting for you to find me."

She blushed. "Glad I did."

"Me too." He sipped wine, feeling mellow. And desiring her. Were they on the same page? Or did she still want to take things slowly?

Liam had his answer when Jessica rose to her feet and said boldly, "Why don't I show you the master bedroom…and, later, we can check out the rest of the house."

* * *

An hour later, they were atop a wingback bed on a soft bamboo sheet, naked, and trying to catch their breaths after mind-blowing sex that more than made up for lost time. Jessica repositioned herself next to Liam's moist body before saying what was almost embarrassing, but did so anyway. "This may not be the most appropriate time to ask this, but why exactly did your marriage end?" She couldn't help but think of the reasons why some marriages lasted—even when that shouldn't have been the case, considering—and others failed. Did his ex simply not want him anymore? Or was it the other way around? Was this a harbinger of things to come?

Liam adjusted his arm wrapped around her. "Kelly and I never really had a real marriage," he spoke thoughtfully. "She had her ideas of what it should mean and I had mine. We tried to find common ground and make it work somehow, but things only went from bad to worse." He paused. "We realized it was time to end it while we were still on speaking terms."

"Thanks for clearing that up," Jessica said, glad to have some context to his divorce and how it went down. She would hate to be in a marriage that was going nowhere, merely for the sake of keeping up appearances or feigning happiness.

"Have you ever been close to marriage?" Liam cut into her thoughts.

She stared at the question before answering honestly with a comical twist, "Not that I can remember." A beat later, she explained, "I have nothing against marriage, per se. I have everything against marrying for the wrong reasons or the ones that seemed right at the time, but end up just the opposite once the dust settles."

"Sounds pessimistic," he said, "regarding marriage and taking chances at finding true love."

"Actually, it's just the opposite," Jessica argued, as she saw it. "I'm very open to marrying someone who respects me, shares my values, is serious about being in a committed relationship, oh, and did I forget to mention, loves me with all his heart and soul."

Liam chuckled. "That's not asking too much."

She touched his toes with hers. "My sentiments exactly."

"Good minds think alike," he said, "in terms of what makes for a good partner, marriage or otherwise."

"Nice to hear." Jessica could feel her heart beating wildly. Was it just hers?

Liam ran a hand along her inner thigh. "Now that we've cleared that up, I look forward to taking on the next chapter of our lives and seeing how things line up with what we want out of this."

"Hmm... Me too," she murmured with arousal. "Speaking of chapters, my good friend, Connie, thinks I'm hiding you."

"Really?" He kissed her shoulder. "You mean like your own private go-to guy?"

"Not quite." Jessica laughed. "Like someone I've brought into my life that she wants to size up as worthy."

"So, let her size me up," he said playfully. "Happy to meet her anytime you like."

"Okay." She set a date for the get-together and imagined it would be eventful and even fun as they began to take things to the next level and see what it brought them as a couple.

Chapter Twenty-Eight

Jessica met with her client, Stephanie Dozier, wishing she had more positive news as they moved closer to the trial date. As it was, the trail leading to the coed sex club had run cold. Or at least become more difficult to crack, as the participants, including the married professors, had closed ranks as if their lives depended upon remaining silent. This made it less likely to Jessica that they would be able to use this angle to get the charge dropped against her client. She conveyed this to Stephanie. "I'm sorry I don't have something better to report," she spoke truthfully, "but I thought it was important that I level with you every step of the way."

Stephanie, who looked as though she had lost some weight, but was still pretty, slouched when saying, "So, someone's going to get away with killing Kristine, while I'm stuck in here, waiting to be convicted for something I didn't do?"

In that moment, Jessica felt for her, as if she was her own daughter. Or perhaps little sister. "Not if I can help it," she responded in a more upbeat tone. "By no means am I throwing in the towel and neither should you. I have a private investigator helping me to try and track down any leads that might point us in the right direction."

"But what if you're continually misdirected?" questioned Stephanie. "How can you ever prove something did not happen, when no one will speak up on my behalf—even my so-called boyfriend—and that prosecutor is hell-bent on ruining my life by making sure I spend what's left of it behind bars?"

Jessica leaned toward her on the other side of the table, locking eyes with her. "Regardless of the obstacles before us, the truth usually comes out at the end," she promised. "The burden is on the State to prove its case beyond a reasonable doubt. I will do my best to make certain there is plenty of doubt to go around. The jury will not simply rubber-stamp the prosecution's case, no matter how convincing, once we dig deep into its shortcomings and demonstrate alternative possibilities. In the meantime, I won't stop trying to show a pattern between the deaths of Kristine McVeigh, Brittany Delray, and Professor Sean Quail, in relation to a campus sex club and extortion ring—with you being an unwitting victim who had the misfortune of sharing an apartment with Kristine and the bad timing of coming to her aid, only to have it turn into your own personal nightmare."

"Thank you." Stephanie actually smiled. "I'm glad my parents chose you to represent me. Gives me hope that I might somehow get through this and be able to go back to school and have a life again."

Jessica smiled back, resisting the urge to give her a hug. As it was, that would be premature at this point. She kept her own emotions in check and said, "Keep thinking such thoughts," she advised her client. "We'll get through this together, no matter the journey that lies ahead."

When Stephanie was taken back to her cell, Jessica made her exit, determined as ever to connect the dots that her instincts told her would lead to a breakthrough that could change everything in their favor.

* * *

Danielle had lunch with the club's newest recruit, Lacee Sheridan. Lacee, a junior, reminded her of herself, tall, slender, green-eyed, with long blonde hair, only styled differently, with loose curls and parted in the center. Basically, gorgeous. In her mind, Lacee was perfect as someone who would have no trouble seducing oversexed, susceptible married professors into cheating on their wives; then paying to keep it their little secret. Moreover, as Lacee was currently between boyfriends, after losing interest in her last one, the timing was right. Whereas, while Danielle was dating another senior and member of the school's soccer team, Paul Forsythe, she didn't see it going anywhere. Besides that, what he didn't know wouldn't hurt either of them.

"So, how does this work?" Lacee asked curiously, as they sat in the residential dining hall at a corner table away from everyone else.

"It's very simple," Danielle told her confidently, while taking a bite of her grilled chicken sandwich. "We cozy up to a target in his office, or even classroom, after everyone else has left, and basically seduce him into wanting us—not that we have to try very hard—and set up a place to meet of our choosing. There, we have a hidden camera secretly recording the action. Once it's over and done with, we present Mr. Married Professor with the evidence of his infidelity and a quick and easy way to make sure it never goes public—"

Lacee scooped up seafood chowder while batting her lashes. "Do they really go for that?"

"Yes, trust me." Danielle flashed her teeth. "We have what they want and they have what we want. Works out great for everyone." *Except for the wives of those cheating bastards*, she told herself. So not their problem.

"Nothing kinky, right?" Lacee asked ill at ease.

"Only if you agree to it, which is a definite no-no for me," she stressed. "Mostly, they just want the tried and true missionary sex and then they rush back home to their wives, whom they never want to ever know what they've been up to. They pay us to keep their dirty secret."

"Cool." Lacee's features relaxed. She lifted up her iced tea and giggled. "Here's to keeping secrets!"

Danielle grinned, lifting her lemon-infused water, knowing she had won her over. "And here's to the benefits to us in doing so!"

* * *

On Saturday night, Madeleine sat at the front table at Sweet Times, joined by Jackson Payne and his very pregnant, pretty Filipino girlfriend, Sheila Wang. They were all glued to the stage as Genevieve, dressed in an elegant periwinkle chiffon maxi dress, sang a soulful rendition of the classic torch song, "It Had To Be You." As far as Madeleine was concerned, she could definitely give such jazz greats at Ella Fitzgerald, Sarah Vaughan, and June Christy, a run for their money, to name a few. But it was when Genevieve stepped out of her comfort zone that she truly separated herself from the pack. Madeleine felt blessed that she was able to call the beautiful lady her own and gave her back as much in return in what she brought to the table. Becoming the first person in her family to go to college and then graduate from Harvard Law School, was no small feat. Nor was joining the Thorne County District Attorney's office, where she had excelled over the years. A victory in her current case against Stephanie Dozier would only further cement her place as one of Creighton Hills top attorneys and sought-after speakers in matters of law and women's empowerment.

"She's great!" Sheila uttered, running a hand through her short brown pixie.

"Yeah, Genevieve's got it going on," seconded Payne, over his pisco sour cocktail.

Tell me something I don't already know, Madeleine thought gleefully, looking forward to taking her to bed tonight. "That's what Genevieve puts out every time she performs," she bragged, tasting her Negroni. "Just sit back, relax, and enjoy the show." She did the same, trying hard not to let her mind wander to the upcoming trial on the docket.

Chapter Twenty-Nine

J essica sat in her office, pondering the case against her client and ways to counter it, when a young woman whom Jessica recognized as Cecelia Temple, one of the coeds Stephanie had pointed out as close friends of Kristine McVeigh, walked in the door.

"Cecelia, right?" Jessica asked knowingly, as the girl approached the desk.

"Yeah, hi." She flung her head back nervously with a big Afro.

"How can I help you?" Jessica kept her voice level, though most curious about the unexpected visitor.

Cecelia hesitated and then said, "I'm here to talk to you about The Sexy Coeds Club."

Jessica remained reserved. "What about it?"

"It's real," she declared. "I'm scared it could be responsible for what's happened to Brittany and, before her, Kristine."

"I see." Jessica was eager to hear more. "Please, have a seat." She waited for her to plop onto one of the chairs on the other side of the desk, before asking, "Tell me about The Sexy Coeds Club."

Cecelia took a breath. "It started about a year ago," she indicated. "First, there were five of us—me, Kristine, Brittany, Nicole, and Danielle—with Kris the leader…"

"Kristine McVeigh?" Jessica asked, to be sure.

"Yes. Aimee and Georgina joined later." Her voice shook. "Anyway, the idea was as attractive coeds we would use our looks and sexuality to trick married professors into wanting to have sex with us. We chose the marks carefully, based on how flirtatious they were in and out of class, and how susceptible they seemed. The hookups were both one-on-one and two of us with one guy. We video recorded it and used that against them to pay up or else—"

Jessica furrowed her brow. "Extortion is a crime," she needed to point out for the record.

"I know," she conceded. "But we thought we could still get away with it. After all, the men had too much to lose to open their mouths…seemed like we had a good thing going until Kristine was killed…" Cecelia was thoughtful. "When Stephanie was accused of and charged with killing her, everyone in the club kind of breathed a sigh of relief, glad some psycho wasn't coming after us… But after Brittany was murdered, I for one, freaked out, wondering if the murders might have somehow been connected and were retaliation for what we were doing."

"What about the other members of the club?" Jessica looked at her. "Were they just as freaked out?"

"Not really." Cecelia frowned. "Danielle, the new leader after Brittany died, insisted that there was no connection and it would be business as usual. But not for me. I quit. Though the money was nice, to give me something extra to go with my scholarship money, it just wasn't worth the risks of exposure and other things. Especially my health and well-being. Everyone else chose to stay with the club."

"I see…" Jessica jotted down a couple of notes on a pad. "Do you think any of them will talk to me?"

"Not likely." She lowered her eyes ill at ease. "There's a strict code of silence, for obvious reasons. Just talking to you, is violating that. I'm taking a big chance…" Cecelia paused tensely. "With you representing Stephanie, as perhaps an innocent person in Kris's death, I just thought you needed to know what was going on."

"I appreciate you coming forward," Jessica told her musingly, recognizing how difficult it must have been to break ranks. "Are all the members, aside from Kris and Brittany, still with the group?"

"Not Nicole—" Cecelia's voice dropped. "Four months ago, she died of a drug overdose."

"Hmm…" Jessica chewed on her lower lip. "Nicole…"

"Nicole Kingsley."

"Was Nicole known to use drugs?" wondered Jessica.

"Yeah." Cecelia wrinkled her nose. "She OD'd on fentanyl, after being introduced to it recreationally at a party on campus."

"Was anyone ever charged in connection to the overdose?" Jessica asked curiously.

"Not that I know of. Drug use is pretty common at schools these days. Hard to know where any of it came from."

Jessica suspected that the overdose death had been a low priority by authorities, in light of other investigations that commanded greater attention. But was this an oversight? "Was Nicole suicidal?"

"She didn't kill herself intentionally," Cecelia insisted, "if that's what you're asking. She loved her life, got good grades, and was going to graduate next year. Why sabotage that?"

Good question, Jessica thought. But even people who had everything going for them still chose to check out, for one reason or another. Was that the case here? Or was it something more sinister? "Do you think Nicole's death could be related to the deaths of Kristine McVeigh and Brittany Delray?"

Cecelia made a skeptical noise. "I don't see how. Nicole's death was accidental, according to the police. Kris and Brittany were murdered—"

Jessica had no reason to argue with that logic. Still, that made three members of the same sex and extortion ring dead in just a few short months. Along with an art history professor, who was sleeping with Kristine as part of The Sexy Coeds Club. Was Nicole's death truly an isolated occurrence?

"Is Nicole from around here?" Jessica asked.

"Yeah. She lived with her mom, a librarian, on Clarkson Lane. We hung out at their house sometimes…till Nicole died."

Jessica made a note to visit the mother and see if she had any thoughts about Nicole's death being anything but accidental, in relation to a possible serial killer out to get members of The Sexy Coeds Club. "Did any of the married professors refuse to pay to keep their secret safe?" Jessica asked, twirling her pen.

147

Cecelia hedged. "There was one guy...a professor in the English department at Wryer College. We decided to let him off the hook because his wife was dying of cancer."

"What's his name?" Jessica met her eyes.

"I don't want to get anyone into trouble," she said, evading the eye contact.

"Neither do I," Jessica tried to reassure her. "At least not where it concerns their sexual activities and transactions to that effect. But one of them could well have taken things to a dangerous level—murder—to keep his infidelity a secret. If that's the case—and you obviously believe it's possible or you wouldn't be here right now—then we need to identify this person, whether it's the professor or not, and prevent any more of your club members from dying."

Cecelia shifted uncomfortably in the chair. "His name is Professor Conrad Ramsay," she relented.

Jessica considered that a victory of sorts in prying the information from her. But she didn't want to stop there. "I'd like the names of the other men involved in the pay after play sex ring," she pressed. "It's possible that one of them could have had buyer's remorse and decided to take it out on the group."

After Cecelia began naming names, she uttered nervously, "This can't come back to me."

"It won't," Jessica promised, and thought, *Unless it becomes necessary in helping to prove my client's innocence.*

As if reading her mind, Cecelia asked doubtingly, "So you really don't think Stephanie killed Kristine, when the police caught her with the knife, standing over her body?"

It was a sensible question, for which Jessica responded candidly, "Looks can be deceiving, especially when someone else who had a reason may have targeted Kristine." *As well as Brittany and even possibly Nicole,* thought Jessica.

"Had to ask," Cecelia said, as though embarrassed for doing so.

"Speaking of my client," Jessica thought out loud, "why didn't Kristine, as the then-leader of your club, invite Stephanie, as her roommate, in on the action?"

Cecelia sighed. "Kris talked about it, but didn't believe Steph would want to do it. She thought Stephanie would see it as cheating on her boyfriend."

Jessica cocked a brow and thought about Hugh and cheating on his wife with him. "Is that why Kristine slept with Brody—to have sex with her roommate's boyfriend, just to prove she could...?"

Cecelia shrugged. "Probably something like that. Kris loved to live on the edge and play with other people's lives—mostly to get back at her father, Judge McVeigh, whom she saw as overbearing in trying to control her life. If he wanted one thing, she would do another, just to piss him off—"

"Hmm..." Jessica hummed while contemplating the parent-child dynamics at play. Even if Judge McVeigh were nothing more than a grieving father, she believed he went to great lengths to try and cover for his daughter's poor choices and predicaments she put herself in—till the very end of her life. Now he wanted Stephanie to bear the burden for Kristine's death. Did the judge truly believe her client was guilty? Could he be turning a blind eye to the real killer? Or might Judge McVeigh himself, frustrated that he couldn't control his daughter and her misbehavior, have simply snapped and stabbed her to death? Though Jessica considered this a stretch to suggest that the judge would resort to murdering his own child, or committing filicide, she also knew that where it concerned family, emotions could run particularly high. That included homicidal behavior as a planned or impromptu act of violence. Was that the case here?

Chapter Thirty

"Judge McVeigh, killing his own daughter, then setting Stephanie up to take the fall?" Liam questioned, sitting beside Jessica on a faux leather saddle-colored sofa on his floating house. "That would be taking judicial overreach to a whole new level, don't you think?"

"That's so not funny." She pushed his shoulder, frowning. "I haven't outright accused the judge of anything," she pointed out. "Not yet anyway." Jessica sipped black coffee. "Okay, so placing the blame on Judge McVeigh for the murder of his daughter, Kris, is a last resort. But you have to admit that, after hearing what Cecelia had to say about Kristine's strained relationship with her father and apparent determination to test his authority at every turn, it does make one wonder just how far the judge might have been willing to go to try and keep her in line. Or stop her altogether from tarnishing the family name."

"Yeah, good point," Liam allowed, tasting his own coffee. Whether he believed the judge committed coldblooded murder and willingly allowed someone else to pay for his crime was a longshot, it did give one food for thought, if nothing else. Still, the notion boggled his mind. "Would a man who has spent practically his entire life upholding the laws of the land in one capacity or another throw it all away by taking the law into his own hands...and against his own flesh and blood?"

"Probably not," Jessica admitted. "Particularly when you consider that whoever killed Kristine McVeigh might also have gone after Brittany Delray and another member of the club, Nicole Kingsley, who I learned supposedly died of a drug overdose last year."

"Interesting." Liam sat back thoughtfully.

"Doesn't figure that Judge McVeigh would be the killer when you look at it that way."

"I agree." Liam put the mug to his mouth. "Still, with the Nicole Kingsley angle, the plot thickens."

"I'd like to pay her mother a visit," Jessica told him. "Maybe she can give us some added insight into her daughter's death. Then we can have a little talk with a Wryer English professor named Conrad Ramsay. According to Cecelia, a former member of The Sexy Coeds Club who dropped by my office, he balked at paying the extortion money. But the girls chose not to expose him, apparently developing a conscience because his wife had cancer. Who's to say he didn't still want to exact vengeance at the mere threat of having his secret tryst revealed?"

"It's worth looking into," Liam agreed, eager to see where these new leads led, if anywhere. "Let's go."

* * *

They took Liam's Trailblazer to the Wryer College Library, where Jessica had discovered Brenda Kingsley was the library director. She was pointed out to them on the second floor, where she was in the course of her duties when they approached.

"Are you Brenda Kingsley?" Jessica asked as she surveyed the tall, thin woman in her early forties with brunette hair in a short and straight style and blue-gray eyes.

"Yes. Can I help you?" she asked.

"My name is Jessica Frost. I'm a criminal defense attorney and this is Liam Reed, a private detective."

Brenda glanced at Liam, then looked unblinkingly at Jessica. "You're the lawyer for that coed charged with killing her roommate..."

"Stephanie Dozier," Jessica acknowledged.

"I've heard about the case," she pointed out. "What's this all about?"

"We'd like to talk to you about your daughter, Nicole."

Brenda flinched. "Nicole… What about her?"

Liam spoke up. "We understand that she died of an overdose last year."

"Yes, that's true," she uttered sadly. "My daughter had a drug problem and couldn't break away from it in time…" Brenda eyed him. "I don't see what that has to do with—"

"We think it's possible that her death may be connected to the deaths of others who were members of a Wryer College group known as The Sexy Coeds Club. These include murder victims, Kristine McVeigh and Brittany Delray." He paused. "Did Nicole ever mention the club to you?"

"No," she claimed, "not in so many words. I mean, Nicole hung out with other girls who attended Wryer, and I suppose they were pretty and sexy like her. Maybe they had formed a club…" Brenda turned to Jessica curiously. "What does any of this, or the murders of those other two girls, have to do with Nicole's death?"

Jessica almost hated to add to the woes of Nicole Kingsley's mother, but there really was no other way, given the situation and possibilities it presented relevant to her client. She glanced around to make sure they were alone, before gazing at Brenda and saying candidly, "Members of the club were seducing married college professors and extorting money from them for their silence."

Brenda's eyes popped wide with shock. "There must be a mistake."

"One of the coeds involved admitted it to me," Jessica said flatly. "We believe a disgruntled professor, or someone on his behalf, may have targeted members of the group as payback. It's possible that your daughter's drug overdose could have been a front for murder," she indicated.

Brenda pushed back against the notion, responding sharply, "Look, Ms. Frost, I'm sure you're doing everything you can to help your client—even looking to place blame elsewhere for the stabbing death of Kristine McVeigh. But the police and the D.A.'s office seem to think they have the right person in custody. And as far as the murder of that other college student, the authorities have said it was gang-related." She sucked in a deep breath. "I was a single mother and did the best I could to raise Nicole. It obviously wasn't enough, as she fell into drugs. According to the medical examiner, my daughter died from a drug overdose. There was nothing about murder in the report. I have to accept that. Now if you'll excuse me, I have to get back to work."

Jessica didn't press further. "Thanks for your time," she told her. And I'm very sorry for your loss."

Brenda nodded and walked away. Jessica watched her thoughtfully.

As they headed downstairs, Liam said, "Maybe we're way off base in trying to link an OD to confirmed cases of murder."

Inclined to agree, Jessica told him, "You could be right. It was worth a try, though."

"Hopefully, we'll have better luck with Professor Ramsay," Liam said when they got outside.

"Perhaps." Jessica offered him a soft smile, but wasn't getting her hopes up that they could pin the murder of Kristine McVeigh on someone else before Stephanie went on trial.

Chapter Thirty-One

J essica and Liam were invited into the cramped office of English professor Conrad Ramsay, who apparently mistook them for a couple there to inquire about a student, perhaps their own offspring. After appraising the man for a long moment—he was in his late forties, tall with a little weight on him, receding dark hair in a buzz cut, and a stubble beard—Jessica said evenly, "Professor Ramsay, my name is Jessica Frost. I'm a defense attorney and this is my associate, Liam Reed. Actually, we're here to talk about The Sexy Coeds Club that you were involved with—" For all she knew, he was still having sex with his students.

Ramsay drew his thick brows together. "I have no idea what you're talking about," he claimed.

"I think you know exactly what we're talking about," Liam said austerely. "So let's not play games here. We know you slept with one or more of the sexy coeds in your class and then they attempted to blackmail you. Do I need to go on?"

"All right, you got me," he relented. Unnerved, Ramsay bypassed them and closed the door, before facing them again. "I didn't do anything illegal."

"Really?" Jessica rolled her eyes cynically.

"They were consenting adults."

"Who tried to extort money from you," she reminded him, "before deciding to cut you some slack because your wife was dying."

Ramsay's chin dropped. "Yeah, they deserve an award for humiliating me and backing down when I refused to pony up to their demands," he muttered sarcastically and looked at her suspiciously. "Who told you this?"

"Does it matter?" Liam turned the question on him. "The point is, it's all out on the table now. Whether this goes any further is up to you..."

Ramsay ran a hand across his mouth. "My late wife, Marilyn, fought a long battle with cervical cancer. I'd never been unfaithful to her. But the more downhill she went, the harder it was for me to deal with it. When a couple of the good-looking students cozied up to me, as if they somehow got it and wanted to relieve my burden, if only for a while, I took them up on the offer. We only got together once and I thought that was the end of it. Then they told me the sex had been recorded on video and, unless I paid them twenty-five grand, my life was toast. With the bills mounting from my wife's deteriorating health, there was no way I could come up with the money. So, I called their bluff, knowing that things couldn't get much worse than they already were." He sighed. "They left me alone. End of story."

"Not necessarily," Jessica countered, a catch to her voice. "Did the sexy coeds you bedded happen to be named Kristine McVeigh and Brittany Delray?"

"What if they were?" Ramsay hesitated. "What difference does it make?"

"The difference between sending an innocent young woman to prison and letting a killer remain free," she responded snappishly, deciding that he had confirmed her suspicions, more or less. Making him that much more of a suspect in their deaths.

He furrowed his brow. "What are you trying to say?"

"Stephanie Dozier, my client, has been charged with the murder of her roommate, Kristine McVeigh." Jessica glared at him. "Brittany Delray was also murdered, with her killer still at large. We're thinking that the two coeds may have been killed by the same person."

"Someone who had a score to settle," added Liam, "after backing him into a corner that could have cost him everything."

"But it didn't," Ramsay pointed out. "They failed to accomplish what they set out to do and I've never looked back. You're looking at the wrong person. I had nothing to do with those deaths."

Liam got up in his face. "For your sake, I hope you're right about that," he warned him. "If any more coeds from the club are harmed and it's linked to you, your problems will be just beginning."

Ramsay backed away. "As I said, I didn't kill anyone and have no desire to target any of the girls, no matter what they tried to do to me."

"But maybe you know another married professor who is capable of harming the members of The Sexy Coeds Club?" Jessica fixed him with an intimidating look. "Looking the other way makes you just as guilty as whoever it is that might be going after the coeds."

"I have no idea what other professors were compromised by the students," he insisted, "or what any of them might be capable of in striking back at the blackmailers. It wasn't exactly the type of thing I wanted to brag about."

Jessica tried to read him, but couldn't with any degree of confidence while giving him the benefit of the doubt. "If you hear about any professor who was involved with the club and seems vindictive, I suggest you contact my office, if not the police," she warned him in no uncertain terms.

The English professor nodded meekly. "I'm not proud of what I've done, okay? If I could do it over, I would take a different path in dealing with my issues."

"That's what all men say who cheat on their wives," Jessica hissed sardonically, picturing Hugh. "I only hope no more naïve young women have to pay the ultimate price for such selfish choices, Professor."

They left him with that chilling thought.

In the car, Liam asked her, "What's your take on Ramsay?"

"He seems innocent enough," Jessica confessed, having pondered this as they walked to the parking lot, "at least of being a murderer. But then, how many times have killers fooled us by pretending to be innocent lambs—only to find out they were guilty as hell?"

"Good point. The jury's still out on the man, as far as I'm concerned. If the motive is strong enough—and it appears to be in this case of infidelity and extortion—someone wants to silence The Sexy Coeds Club members for good. Whether they are willing to acknowledge it or not."

"I agree," Jessica said, convinced of this, "in spite of the case against my client and the fact that the evidence suggests Kristine McVeigh and Brittany Delray may have been the victims of different killers with different motives."

"If there were two killers," Liam said, "chances are they were of the same mind as to their reasoning. I'm with you in trying to get to the bottom of this, one way or the other, before your client is fed to the wolves."

Jessica clutched his free hand and smiled, as much for his support and equal determination to see this through, as being able to touch him, feeling them growing closer with each passing day.

Chapter Thirty-Two

The next day, Jessica drove up to a spot that overlooked the city. She parked next to Hugh's Lexus ES, while noting that he was standing beside the car, waiting for her arrival. She had requested the meeting on neutral ground. It was his suggestion for that location, where they had spent time at the beginning of their relationship. Back when she saw promise in him and a future together. Well, that day had passed and she had no intention of ever falling into his trap again.

"Hey," Hugh said coolly once she got out of her car as he approached.

"Hey." Jessica looked at him and almost felt as though he was a total stranger. She supposed in many ways, he was. Especially now that she had moved on.

"I missed you."

"Don't," she warned, feeling nothing but regret.

His head snapped back, as though she'd hit him. "Forget I said it."

She made a face. "It's forgotten."

He frowned. "So, why are we here?"

"I wanted to talk to you about the case."

"How's your client holding up?" he asked as if to delay.

"Doing the best she can, under the circumstances," Jessica told him. "She has her good and bad days."

"Yeah, I can imagine." Hugh paused. "What else?"

She raised her eyes to his. "Have you told your wife about Brittany Delray?" Or had he dodged this thorny subject, hoping it would somehow go away?

He averted her stare. "Yeah, she knows."

"And...?" Jessica arched her brows anxiously. Had his wife sent him packing after learning he had gotten involved with someone young enough to be his daughter, who was now a murder victim?

"She wants to go to marriage counseling," he muttered, shaking his head.

"Marriage counseling?" Jessica repeated the words as though in a foreign language.

"Yeah, I had the same reaction. Claire believes it's in the best interest of the family if we can work it out."

Jessica waited for him to look at her, before asking curiously, "I assume she knows what happened to Brittany and that it's still an open homicide investigation?"

"I told her everything," he insisted, "hard as it was...I swore to her that I had nothing to do with the murder and that my only mistake was getting caught up in a moment of weakness, letting my guard down."

Jessica crossed her arms peevishly. "Is that what I was too—a moment of weakness that turned into many moments of letting your guard down?"

"No, it wasn't like that with you," Hugh claimed with a straight face. "What we had was real... At least it was for me."

It was for me too, she thought. Till realizing that they had very different definitions of real and what this meant for the future. "Let's not rehash the past," she told him. "Doesn't do either of us any good at this point."

He regarded her with a hard gaze. "I get it. You've moved on?"

She met his eyes. "Yes, I have," she admitted, seeing no reason to allow him to think otherwise. "I think it's for the best, all the way around."

Hugh seemed to want to pry further, but thought better. "You deserve to be with someone who doesn't have divided loyalties."

"Don't we all?" she voiced sarcastically.

"Yeah." He gazed down at his derby shoes.

Jessica sighed and said, "There's been some new developments regarding The Sexy Coeds Club."

"Oh." Hugh's voice lowered.

"One of the members—or should I say, an ex-member—has come forward," Jessica told him, "acknowledging the club's existence. It pretty much squared up with what Sean Quail passed along to you. This was also verified by another married professor, Conrad Ramsay, who got involved with two of the sexy coeds, but managed to avoid becoming the victim of blackmail because his wife was dying."

"So how does knowing the club and the scheming is real help your case?" he asked.

"It gives us a plausible alternative to my client as someone who had a strong motive for wanting Kristine McVeigh dead—as well as Brittany Delray." Jessica lifted her chin. "I know they were killed differently, but that could be simply to throw off investigators in making the connection."

He cocked a brow. "You really believe that?"

"I believe anything's possible," she contended, "especially with the stakes being as high as they were for the men who found themselves caught in a trap of infidelity and extortion—any of whom might have done anything to extricate himself from the risks of being exposed."

"But how will you be able to prove any of this to get your client off?" Hugh asked. "Doesn't the D.A.'s office have what amounts to an airtight case...?"

"They would like you to think that," Jessica conceded. "Doesn't mean it's true. Especially when I can present an opposing point of view in court..." She gazed at him. "I'll need your help with that, Hugh."

His eyes grew. "If you're suggesting—"

"I want to call you as a witness for the defense," she told him bluntly.

"Whoa.... It's one thing to confess, if you will, to my wife," he stammered, "or, for that matter, to you, on what limited information I know about The Sexy Coeds Club. But to state this in a court of law, jeopardizing my reputation as a financial adviser..."

"You have no choice, Hugh." Jessica wasn't about to let him worm his way out of this. "I have a duty to my client to use everything I have in her defense. That includes exposing the college sex and extortion ring, and the ramifications thereof. Besides, you owe me. Our own ill-fated involvement has led us to this very moment in time."

He growled like an angry dog for a moment and then began to pace, before standing still. "All right," he gave in. "I'll testify. Just promise you'll do what you can to limit questioning about my one-night stand with Brittany. Other than being an error in judgment on my part, it did not involve any blackmail attempt or was otherwise related to what happened to her after the fact."

Jessica was not about to make him any promises, knowing she might not be able to keep them. Especially when his involvement may have been deeper than even he knew, or wanted to know. Brittany likely had every intention of trying to extort money from him, if not for the fact that someone shot her to death before the plan could kick into motion. Then there was still his connection with Sean Quail, whose suicide may well have opened up Pandora's box, when it came to murder. "I'll try my best," was the most Jessica could offer him, which Hugh accepted begrudgingly.

When they went their separate ways, a tiny part of Jessica actually felt sympathetic to Hugh, who had seemed to make a real mess of his life. But these sentiments were overrun by the more practical belief that he had been the master of his own mistakes and associations. Moreover, in her view as an attorney, she had to put Stephanie first and foremost, even at the expense of an ex-boyfriend and all he once stood for in her life.

* * *

Danielle had been sizing up married economics professor, Nathaniel Guzman, ever since he made a halfhearted pass at her a month ago. The Sexy Coeds Club did their research on him and knew that the thirty-eight-year-old professor was on his second marriage, had three kids between two wives, and a reputation on campus for flirting with pretty and sexy coeds. As far as they were concerned, that made him the perfect target for helping to finance their lives while in college.

When Danielle invited Professor Guzman to party with her and Lacee in a hotel suite they had booked for that purpose, he readily accepted. By the time he arrived, the hidden video camera was already in place, along with red wine and marijuana, which he indicated were his pleasures.

"Hey." Danielle put on her best smile as she greeted the professor, who was admittedly hot, tall and fit, with long black-brown hair pulled back into a sexy man bun.

"Hi," Lacee murmured to him, wearing a short, pink party dress and pink vinyl pumps.

"Hey, you two." He grinned coolly.

"Ready for some fun?" Danielle teased him, flaunting her own curves in a sexy black chiffon dress and matching two-piece sandals.

"You bet." Guzman looked from one to the other, as if he couldn't decide who was better. "Let's get this party started!"

Lacee giggled. "My thoughts exactly."

"Mine too," Danielle added, and they immediately set about to make him feel at home, starting with removing his chino sport coat.

In no time flat, they were in bed and gave him what he wanted, and then some, while getting off themselves. It was only after the partying was over and Professor Guzman had left the lair and returned home, that they sent him a copy of the video on his cell phone with instructions on how to make sure it never got released to his wife, or the director of the Department of Economics at Wryer College, or the rest of the world through social media.

Chapter Thirty-Three

Detective Payne neared the scene of a fatality that occurred on Macklin Road, not far from the Wryer campus. If the truth be told, he would much rather be at home right now playing with his kid, Jackson, Jr. But, alas, duty called. Maybe this summer, they and Sheila could take a vacation to Maui. Or the Virgin Islands. Or not. It would all depend on whether things slowed down enough that he could be given some breathing room by the department.

He pulled up behind a patrol car. On the other side of the street, Payne noted a gray Genesis G70 with some damage to the front end. A police officer was speaking with an elderly African American male. Nearby, on the grass, was the outline of what Payne knew was a dead body beneath a blue tarp. After exiting his own vehicle, he crossed the street and was met by the twenty-something female officer named Louise Krause. Flashing his ID at her, Payne asked, "So, what are we looking at here?"

"We have a deceased white female," she reported sadly, running a hand across blonde curtain bangs. "The gentleman over there, Ellis Hemsley, struck her with his car. He says she was forced into the street, right in front of him... He's pretty shaken up about it."

"I'll bet," Payne stated sympathetically, assuming it was true. "Had he been drinking? Or on any medication?"

"He said no to both," Louise stated. "A breathalyzer test was administered that supported no alcohol in his system."

"What about the victim?" Payne asked routinely, while knowing that a life lost was a big thing, no matter who it was.

"According to the student photo ID card she was carrying, her name is Danielle Osmond. She attended Wryer College."

Payne was stuck on the decedent's name, Danielle Osmond, which rang a bell in his head like a musical instrument. As he recalled, she was the dorm roommate of Brittany Delray, who was murdered late last year. The unsub was still at large. Coincidence? "I'll go talk to the man," he told the officer.

When he walked up to him, Payne could see that the driver, in his late sixties and wiry thin, with a mini gray Afro, was still unsettled. "Mr. Hemsley," he spoke politely, "I'm Detective Payne."

"Hey." His voice shook.

"Why don't you tell me what happened?"

Hemsley took a breath. "I was just driving along, minding my own business, when someone on a bicycle seemed to deliberately shove that young woman—who was on foot and minding her own business—at the last moment, into the street...right in front of my car..." His face darkened. "I slammed on the brakes and tried to swerve, but there was nothing I could do to stop from hitting her—"

"Did you say someone riding a bicycle pushed the victim onto the road?" Payne replayed this part thoughtfully.

"Yeah, that's right," he maintained.

"Did you get a look at the person riding the bike?"

"Only that he or she was wearing a black bicycle helmet. It all happened so fast..." He wiped his nose. "Afterwards, I saw the person take off and disappear on a side street."

"What about the bicycle?" Payne pressed. "Can you describe it?"

"It was black with red drop handlebars" Hemsley responded assuredly.

"Hmm..." Payne flashed back to the unsolved murder of Brittany Delray. Surveillance video showed a bicycle matching that description pull up to the vehicle Delray was inside of. The bicyclist, wearing a bike helmet, opened fire—before riding away from the scene. In spite of their best efforts, they had not been able to locate the bike. Or identify the rider. Were the bicycles one and the same?

Payne left the witness and driver of the car, and walked over to the spot where the decedent was awaiting the medical examiner to be taken away. Putting on his nitrile gloves, he lifted the tarp slightly for a peek at the dead coed. He recognized the pale face, surrounded by blonde hair, from interviewing her, following the death of Brittany Delray. Had both students been targeted by the same killer? Were they looking at a serial murderer?

Payne couldn't help but recall the video Delray had taken of her having sex with Hugh Holliman, prior to her killing. There had been talk about a coed sex ring and extortion at the time. No evidence had surfaced to support it. Might there be something to this after all that figured into the two deaths? And what about the murder of Kristine McVeigh, Judge McVeigh's daughter? Stephanie Dozier was charged with the homicide and currently awaiting trial. Her defense attorney, Jessica Frost, had insisted her client was innocent and contended that McVeigh's death was connected to a group calling themselves The Sexy Coeds Club. *Maybe I need to take a second look at this,* Payne told himself, while recognizing that time wasn't on the side of Dozier. And that was even more true for McVeigh, Osmond, and Delray—none of whom were able to come back from the dead, as far as he knew.

* * *

The moment Cecelia Temple got wind of the death of her onetime friend, Danielle Osmond, it immediately brought to mind the short lives of other deceased members of The Sexy Coeds Club. Nicole, Kristine, Brittany, and now Danielle had all succumbed to a tragic ending. The last three were homicides, but Nicole's drug overdose death was no less painful. Cecelia couldn't help but feel that for at least three of the deaths, the specter of their extortion sex club hung over them like a funnel cloud, waiting to gobble up the surviving members. Herself included. It was for that reason that she decided to bring together the other survivors, Aimee Atkinson, Georgina Perez, and the newest member of the group, Lacee Sheridan.

They all huddled in Georgina's small dorm room. It was clear to Cecelia that the others were just as unsettled as she was. "With Danielle now dead too," she told them, "there's got to be more to it than just isolated instances."

Georgina, who looked like she wanted to cry, agreed. "Our activities with married professors and then blackmailing them is haunting us," she declared. "We have to stop it—and pray that whoever is behind this doesn't come after us too."

Lacee folded her arms. "I heard that a driver hit Danielle and was cooperating with authorities. The others died in different ways. Do you really think someone is out to get us and clever enough to fool the police?"

"Wake up, Lacee," Aimee admonished her. "Can't you see that we're being targeted, even if there is more than one person after us? It's been reported that someone forced Danielle in front of that car. If so, that makes it murder. How many more of us have to die before you get it through your head—before we all do—that we've pissed off everyone we've taken money from or threatened to?"

"All right, all right," she relented, fumbling with her blonde hair. "We're being hunted down like lambs to be slaughtered. So, what do we do to stop it?"

"We have to go to the police—tell them everything," Cecelia said, nervous about how this would be received, given that it could very well get them kicked out of school. Or even face criminal charges. But anything was better than not living to see their next birthday. Wasn't it?

As expected, everyone but Georgina pushed back on the idea. "There has to be another way..." Aimee pleaded. "If my dad ever found out about this, he'd probably kill me himself—"

"So not funny!" Georgina stated humorlessly. "At this point, we need to cut our losses and take whatever punishment comes out of it."

Lacee stiffened. "Easy for you to say. You have rich parents—except when it comes to financing your lifestyle—and can probably buy your way out of this. Not all of us are as lucky."

"Seriously?" Georgina scowled. "It's bad luck that four members of The Sexy Coeds Club have kicked the bucket. We're all lucky in that we get a chance to save ourselves."

"Or die trying..." Aimee uttered with a shiver.

"Isn't that better than not trying to do the right thing to our own benefit?" Cecelia questioned, looking from one to the next. While wanting to get them all on the same page, she suggested, "We should go see Jessica Frost, Stephanie's attorney. She can help us."

"Why would she want to help us?" Georgina peered at her.

"Because she believes that Stephanie didn't kill Kris. Maybe she's right and someone made it look that way. Or they got a break when Steph found Kris like that and got blamed for it instead—"

Lacee narrowed her eyes at Cecelia. "You really think that lawyer would help us get out of this mess?"

"I think she would try," she told her, without mentioning that she had already broken their code of silence by already speaking to Jessica about the sexy coeds.

"Let's do it!" Aimee declared. "I don't want to die."

"None of us do," Georgina agreed, and Lacee echoed the sentiments.

Cecelia felt good about reconnecting with the club, even under such dire circumstances. "Then it's settled," she told them, and hoped it wasn't too late to help Stephanie, if she really was innocent, as well as themselves. No matter what it meant for their futures.

Chapter Thirty-Four

Jessica was disheartened when learning of the death of Danielle Osmond, a member of The Sexy Coeds Club. Though the police had released scant information, apparently the victim had been killed by a vehicle, after being forced into the street by a bicyclist. This left three of the coeds as murder victims, along with one dying of a drug overdose. Even if, in her mind, the homicides constituted more proof of an assassin at work in eliminating the girls one by one, Jessica knew that it likely would not be enough to get the murder charge against Stephanie dropped by the D.A.'s office. Not when Madeleine had convinced herself that the two were unrelated. As such, the trial would go on and Jessica would have to do her best to defend her client and prepare for an appeal, should things not go their way and more evidence surfaced to prove a serious miscarriage of justice had occurred.

When she got a call from Cecelia Temple, requesting a meeting with her and the remaining members of The Sexy Coeds Club, Jessica agreed, eager to hear what they had to say. She texted Liam to keep him in the loop—deciding it was best to see the coeds alone—before leaving her office and heading to the Wryer College campus. Jessica parked and headed into the Union Building, where she spotted Cecelia, who gave a tentative wave. Surrounding her like a cheerleading squad were mostly recognizable faces from the last time Jessica met with the group. None looked very happy or as smug as before.

"Hey," she said to them.

"Hi," they spoke in unison, ill at ease.

"Can we find a place to speak in private?" Cecelia asked nervously.

"Of course," Jessica said, and they walked to a lounge that was empty and took chairs near the window. Before she heard what they had to say, Jessica told them, "I'm so sorry to hear about your friend, Danielle."

"We're all pretty freaked about it," Georgina said bluntly.

"It's driving us crazy," spoke a tall and attractive blonde, Jessica didn't recognize.

"And you are...?" she asked.

"Lacee Sheridan." She hesitated. "Danielle, uh, talked me into joining the—"

"It's okay," Cecelia told her. "The Sexy Coeds Club. With three of us murdered and another dead from an OD, I'd say the secrecy pact, as we agreed to, is pretty much null and void."

"Yeah," Aimee moaned. "There's no sense in keeping it to ourselves any longer. Not when it seems like someone's really out to get us—"

Jessica lifted a brow. "I think you may be right about that." She was glad to see they were now in agreement, but wished it had come sooner, before their numbers had dwindled.

"We were hoping that if we come clean...name names, payments, whatever," Cecelia uttered, "you could help us..."

"None of us want to die young," Georgina contended.

Lacee added fearfully, "We don't want to be arrested either for what we did...and put in jail—"

"If Stephanie truly didn't kill Kris—and someone we extorted money from did," Aimee stated, "we'd like to do our part to get her released..."

"So, what do you think?" Cecelia gazed at Jessica tensely. "Can you represent us...or at least guide us as we deal with this?"

"Yes, to both," Jessica answered confidently. She didn't need to think about it. Though she wholly disapproved of their extracurricular activities and breaking the law in the process, they didn't deserve to be murdered for it. If helping them meant helping her client get out of a real jam, Jessica was all for it. But with a condition. "I may need one or all of you to testify in court about The Sexy Coeds Club," she cautioned the girls. When they hedged, as though the request was unattainable, Jessica said flatly, "I'm afraid this is non-negotiable. I'll do my best to minimize the trouble you may be in, but Stephanie is about to go on trial for the murder of Kristine McVeigh. Your testimony could well be the thing that saves her from being unjustly sent to prison—"

After a moment or two, Cecelia asserted, in speaking for the group, "We'll do whatever it takes to make all this go away, for Steph and us..."

"Good." Jessica heard what she needed to put things in motion. She collected their contact information and then told them, "Until the coast is clear, which may not be for a while, I strongly suggest you lay low and, when you're out, travel in pairs or more, as each victim has been targeted when she was alone."

All nodded in agreement.

"Oh, and one other thing..." Jessica eyed them the way a grade school teacher might her misbehaving pupils. "Just to be clear, I expect you to put an end to your offers of sex with married professors in exchange for blackmail money. I think we can all agree that it can come at a very high price for any of you—" No one dared argue the point and Jessica left what she hoped was now formerly The Sexy Coeds Club, feeling a renewed sense of optimism where it concerned the case against her client, Stephanie Dozier.

* * *

In doing his part to help Jessica with her case, Liam invited his friend, Detective Juan Guillermo, for an afternoon drink at the Creighton River Club on London Drive. He hoped to pump him for information on the investigation into the death of Danielle Osmond, the latest member of The Sexy Coeds Club, to become a homicide victim.

"We have to stop meeting like this," quipped Guillermo, sipping on a light beer. "Otherwise, I might end up doing desk duty for the rest of my career."

"I won't tell if you don't." Liam chuckled nervously. He tasted his craft beer. "I just want to know where things stand on the Danielle Osmond case—"

"Looks like she was intentionally pushed out in front of a car, with the plan being to inflict enough bodily harm to cost Osmond her life…" Guillermo frowned. "It worked. The poor sucker who hit her had no chance to avoid it."

"I heard that someone riding a bicycle was the instigator," Liam pointed out.

"You heard right," he confirmed. "But what isn't generally known outside of official circles is that a bicyclist, on a bike matching the description of this one, rode up to the car Brittany Delray sat in, and shot her to death…"

"Really?" Liam's eyes grew wide. "So, you think it's the same unsub?"

"Looks that way." Guillermo drank more beer. "We're trying to track down the bicycle and, in the process, the rider." He looked at Liam. "Given that Osmond's a student at Wryer, just as Delray and Kristine McVeigh were, I'm guessing this is playing right into your belief that their deaths are somehow tied to this coed extortion club…?"

"How can it not be?" Liam questioned. "Three members of the club murdered in short order. The only common denominator is that they all happened to be engaged in sexual activities with ready, willing, and able married professors—who had the tables turned on their trysts when the sexy ladies demanded money…or pay in a less desirable way. How does that not add up to an orchestrated hit job?"

"Point taken," Guillermo granted. "At least where it concerns the last two killings…" His chin lowered. "But the same can't be said for McVeigh's murder… No bicyclist was involved. Instead, she was stabbed to death and all the evidence still points toward the roommate, Stephanie Dozier, as her killer. Also, the viciousness of the attack seemed more personal than the others—"

Liam couldn't push back against that reality. So, instead he argued, "Maybe the killer had a more personal reason for targeting McVeigh first and with such venom. Jessica's client had to apparently be in two places at once to pull it off, if the timeline established for the key events is to be believed. A more likely scenario is that Dozier became a convenient scapegoat. Problem is, the same couldn't be said for the murders of Delray and Osmond, since

Jessica's client was behind bars when they occurred. It smacks to me of a serial killer on the prowl that is taking aim, in one manner or another, at The Sexy Coeds Club members—and may not stop until they're all eliminated."

"You could be right." Guillermo took a breath. "If so, Stephanie Dozier really stepped into it when she tried to do a solid for McVeigh."

"It would seem that way," Liam concurred. He was trusting Jessica's faith in her client, as well as his own instincts that told him the case against Stephanie was a little too smooth for his liking. Especially when considering the other real possibility of a determined and deadly foe at large.

Guillermo finished off his drink. "I'll keep you posted on where things go from here."

"And I'll do the same," Liam promised, "should things break in my direction..."

"You better," the detective said. "At the end of the day, we all want to see the right people behind bars."

Liam couldn't agree more. The same was true for Jessica, as they compared notes that night and kept their wits about them while fighting for both her client and a group of sexy coeds, whose lives might be on the line with a common enemy.

"Seems to me that with the girls coming forward to tell their stories, it'll be hard not to think that there may be something to this notion of someone out to get them, before the young extortionists can get them," Liam reckoned, as he lay beside Jessica in her bed, sharing a goblet of white wine.

"You would think so," she agreed, taking the glass from him and sipping wine. "But I'm afraid it may take more than them, and Hugh for that matter, on the witness stand, to convince a judge, much less a jury, that they have the wrong person in custody and on trial for the murder of Kristine McVeigh." Jessica sighed, sliding her bare foot up and down his leg. "We have to try, of course, and hope we can catch a break along the way, where the true killer can be exposed..."

"The fact that the police believe one person is responsible for the deaths of Brittany Delray and Danielle Osmond is a giant step in the right direction," Liam contended. "Logically speaking, when such a connection is established for two young women who knew each other as members of a group that happened to be in the business of seducing married professors and then blackmailing them for hard cash—it doesn't take a rocket scientist to see the symmetry here and consider the strong likelihood that the death of fellow sexy coed club member, Kristine McVeigh, is just as connected."

"Well, said, Liam. Makes perfect sense to me." Jessica chuckled. "Did anyone ever tell you that you'd make a good lawyer?"

He grinned. "Actually, I'd make a terrible lawyer. You see, I don't always play by the rules."

"That's not always a bad thing," she reminded him. "Especially when you're dealing with a criminal justice system that is too often quick to get over its skis in the name of justice and putting people away."

"Good point." He kissed her soft shoulder. "You know, we make a great team."

"Oh, really?" She played footsies with him.

"Are you doubting it?" Liam ran a hand up her thigh.

"Hmm..." Jessica murmured. "Not one bit."

He smiled desirously. "Didn't think so."

They started to kiss and Liam was more than happy to allow nature to take its course, while putting the ups and downs of their professional business temporarily on hold.

III

The Trial

Chapter Thirty-Five

On the first day of the trial, Jessica met in a room at the courthouse with Stephanie's parents, Bernard and Olivia Dozier. Both in their late forties, they had traveled from Idaho, where they had a working farm, to show support for their daughter. Jessica wanted to do her part to calm their fears about the process and prospects for an acquittal, while at the same time not shying away from the worst-case scenario, a conviction and what it may mean for Stephanie's future.

Sitting across the table from them, Jessica said gingerly, "I'm sure you're having butterflies in the stomach right about now. That's normal at the start of a trial. But you will get through this."

Bernard, who was sturdily built and had short gray hair with a side part and chin strap beard, frowned. "What about our daughter? Will she be able to stomach being put on trial for something she didn't do?"

It was an honest question that Jessica took head-on. "Stephanie's stronger than you may think," she told them frankly. "She understands the gravity of the situation and will hold her head high, no matter which way it goes…"

Olivia, a petite woman with shoulder-length crimson hair in angled layers, adjusted her glasses, before saying bluntly, "What are the realistic chances that you can get her off, given the so-called evidence against Stephanie and the mostly negative attention she's received in the media?"

Jessica responded evenly, without needing to give it much thought, "I won't lie to you—it won't be easy. As you noted, the evidence in the case is compelling, to say the least… But you didn't hire me expecting an easy ride. You hired me to give your daughter the best defense. I intend to do just that."

"It's all we can ask," Bernard said, his head down.

"But that doesn't mean I intend to roll over and let the prosecution run roughshod in the courtroom," she stressed. "I believe Stephanie to be as much a victim in this tragedy as Kristine McVeigh. Neither deserved what they received. The jury will have the opportunity to look at the entire landscape before coming to their conclusion on the question of guilt or innocence—"

When Jessica walked out into the hall, alongside the Doziers, they ran into Judge Ralph McVeigh and, Jessica believed, his wife, Rosamund, a tall, slender woman in her early fifties with blonde hair in a low chignon and side bangs. *Uh oh*, Jessica thought ill at ease, as the judge glared at her and the parents of her client. "Judge McVeigh," Jessica said respectfully, clutching her flapover briefcase.

"Ms. Frost." He gave her a steely-eyed look. "You'll forgive me if I don't wish you well as this goes to trial."

Jessica couldn't help but think about his dead daughter's brushes with the law and how he intervened to protect her. Was he still trying to protect her even in death? "I wouldn't expect you to," she made clear and glanced at his wife, who looked uncomfortable.

Bernard gazed at the judge and said, "Stephanie didn't kill her. She's a good girl."

Olivia directed her comment at Rosamund McVeigh. "We're both grieving mothers. There's got to be some other explanation for what happened to Kristine—"

Rosamund favored her husband and turned back to her and said tersely, "We'll leave that to the jury to decide, won't we?"

The judge grabbed his wife's hand and they walked away. Jessica did her best to console her client's parents in the heat of that exchange as they followed the McVeighs into the courtroom for what figured to be a dramatic and, perhaps, eye-opening trial.

* * *

Jessica, wearing a navy dress suit and matching dress shoes, made her way to the defense table. She spotted her boyfriend Liam and her friend, Connie, sitting in the spectator area. Both offered a smile to show their support, which Jessica acknowledged warmly. The vibes were not as friendly when she eyed the prosecutor, Madeleine Griffin. Her tightlipped countenance made it clear to Jessica that she was ready to go toe-to-toe with her—the goal being to come away victorious. *Bring it on,* Jessica told herself daringly, even while knowing that Madeleine had the upper hand in the case she would present to the jury. But what could prove to be the prosecutor's undoing was being overconfident in a case that was anything but airtight.

Finally, Jessica turned to her client, who stood at the table, as though waiting for her arrival before sitting. Stephanie Dozier was dressed for the courtroom and, more importantly, the jury, in a modest charcoal midi dress and pointed-toe flats. Her brown hair had grown and was now in a wavy bob. Jessica couldn't help but think that—with her good looks and tall, slender frame—she could have easily passed for a model, had Stephanie not been about to go on trial for murder. "Hi," Jessica said with a bolstering smile.

"Hey," Stephanie muttered. "I hate that my parents are here, and love it at the same time. Does that make sense?"

"Of course." Jessica took her hand. "They only want what is best for you. So do I."

"Not sure I know what is best anymore." Stephanie's brow creased. "I just want to get it all over with, one way or the other—"

Jessica gave her the benefit of a direct gaze while releasing her hand. "I understand where you're coming from," she voiced sympathetically. "Right now, our sole focus has to be on the trial going only one way—you being acquitted of murder. Giving in to a false charge would only be good for the prosecution—and the real killer of Kristine McVeigh. I need you to stay strong. Together, we can fight this and, hopefully, justice will prevail at the end of the day."

Stephanie nodded and gave a tiny smile of renewed optimism. "Okay."

Jessica considered that a small victory, in and of itself, but knew they would need a major breakthrough if there was any real hope of coming out of this with her client a free woman.

* * *

Presiding over the trial of Stephanie Dozier for the murder of Kristine McVeigh was Thorne County Circuit Court Judge Helen Kuailani-Sinclair. The fifty-year-old Native Hawaiian wife of a renowned seismologist, Ronald Sinclair, had been on the bench for more than a decade and was seen as a prosecutor's judge more than a defense attorney's. Madeleine hoped to work this to her advantage in playing to her own strengths. She regarded the small-boned judge, whose black hair was cut in a short, cropped style, and sporting ombre eyeglasses.

After addressing the court characteristically, Judge Helen Kuailani-Sinclair looked directly at Madeleine, and said, "Are you ready for your opening statement, Counselor?"

"I am, Your Honor," she responded and glanced over at the defense table, where her opponent looked nervous, which was understandable, given her rather weak defense of the defendant. Madeleine approached the jury of six women and six men, while feeling comfortable in a sable, single-button pantsuit and black leather shooties. She wasted no time in making her case. Or at least building the foundation toward it. "Ladies and gentlemen, I have no doubt that you will keep an open mind as the case against the defendant is laid out for each and every one of you to consider every aspect in detail—before rendering a verdict. I also have no doubt that once the hard evidence is presented to support the charge of murder in the first degree, you will reach the same conclusion that I have... And that is, on Friday evening, October fourteenth of last year, sometime around a quarter past six, the defendant, Stephanie Dozier, entered the apartment she shared with the twenty-two-year-old victim and college student, Kristine McVeigh, grabbed a serrated knife from the kitchen, walked to the bedroom of Ms. McVeigh, where she was asleep; and in callous fashion with deliberate intent, viciously stabbed her to death."

Madeleine paused for effect, then continued, "Now, you may ask yourself, why would the defendant, Stephanie Dozier, go after her roommate like that? What could possibly have triggered such a brutal attack seemingly out of nowhere? Well, folks, the answer is as old as life itself, revenge. You see, that very night, the defendant learned from her boyfriend, Brody Krane, whom she was visiting, that he had cheated on her with the defendant's own roommate, Kristine McVeigh. Furious, the defendant snapped. Feeling the rage of betrayal for someone who was supposed to be her trusted friend, she stormed back to her apartment, where she got payback in the cruelest way imaginable—stabbing Ms. McVeigh repeatedly. If not for the arrival of Officer Guy Bean, the defendant, still armed with the murder weapon, would have undoubtedly continued to attack Ms. McVeigh, over and beyond what was necessary to kill her. Which was precisely what the defendant did, before she was taken into custody." Again, Madeleine allowed this to sink in.

"The defendant's penchant for violence didn't just happen overnight," she explained knowingly. "The State intends to show a pattern of such behavior that set the stage for the violent crime that occurred on the night of October fourteenth. When you put all the pieces together, it will be clear, beyond a reasonable doubt, that the defendant, Stephanie Dozier, did indeed commit the act of murder in taking the life of Kristine McVeigh and should be found guilty of said crime, accordingly."

Chapter Thirty-Six

When her turn came, it was clear to Jessica that she had her work cut out for her if she was to get the jury on her side. Admittedly, Madeleine had been effective in painting a picture of a jealous, vindictive, and unhinged person in Stephanie, who used these characteristics as fuel to commit coldblooded murder. If she were a juror, Jessica imagined she might have had a hard time at this point believing that anyone other than the defendant could have been responsible for her roommate's death. *But I'm a defense attorney who happens to believe that very thing*, she thought. Now it was up to her to give the jury something else to think about. While trying to buy time as she and Liam continued to chase leads, few and far between as they were of late, that could lead them in a different direction. And one or more killers still at large.

"You're up, Counselor," Judge Kuailani-Sinclair said, even as Jessica watched a smug Madeleine cross her path, almost daring her to refute her position in the case.

Sucking in a deep breath, Jessica approached the jury in a deliberate manner and began her pitch. "Good morning, ladies and gentlemen," she said smoothly. "If you took everything the prosecution said verbatim, then you might as well find my client guilty right now and call it a day. But we know that's not how it works. An opening statement is just that, an introduction to the case and one's point of view. It is not a blueprint to finding the defendant innocent or guilty on its own merits. As such, it is your duty as jurors to closely examine all aspects of the case against my client and measure that with the counter-arguments that will point in a different direction, in terms of guilt. Only then can you properly render a verdict that must be beyond a reasonable doubt, should it be one of guilt. Otherwise, you are required to acquit the defendant, Stephanie Dozier, and allow her to rebuild her life after what I believe is a miscarriage of justice in having been subjected to a false accusation and months of confinement."

Jessica gave them time to digest this like one might a ham sandwich. Only she didn't want it to come back up, as though tainted food. "I want to make it perfectly clear that what happened to Kristine McVeigh was beyond horrible. No one should ever have to die that way, much less, a beautiful young college coed with her whole life ahead of her. But falsely pinning the murder on another beautiful young woman and college student as well, Stephanie Dozier, who happened to be the best friend and roommate of Ms. McVeigh, won't bring her back. Nor will it do anything to encourage the authorities to go after the true culprit in her untimely death."

Jessica glanced at her client, who was clearly glued to her words, before proceeding. "Now, the prosecution would have you believe that on the evening of October fourteenth of last year, Stephanie Dozier in some jealous temper tantrum, would leave her boyfriend's apartment, walk briskly four blocks through the woods back to her own apartment—only to grab a cooking knife and storm to Ms. McVeigh's bedroom, where she then went on an unprovoked and delirious stabbing attack, showing no mercy whatsoever for someone whom the defendant had lived with for more than a year. Then we are to believe that Ms. Dozier calmly held onto the bloody knife over the defendant's butchered body as she lay on the bed dying, till Officer Guy Bean arrived... As though waiting for him to catch her in the act and, in effect, an admission of guilt.

"Does this seem plausible to any of you?" She cast a skeptical gaze at the jury box. "I mean, who in their right mind would go about it that way—unless you were truly deranged yet somehow sane enough to want the police to arrest you, the court to find you guilty, send you to prison, and throw away the key." Jessica pursed her lips, peeking in the direction of Liam, wondering if he felt she was being too dramatic. Or needed to up her game of credibility a notch. "Well, if the scenario I just laid out was true and the case against her open and shut, then one would have expected my client to confess to the crime and wait to have her punishment meted out. But the defendant did not confess to brutally killing her roommate, Kristine McVeigh, under police interrogation. Quite the contrary, from the moment she was handcuffed and arrested to this very day, Stephanie Dozier has maintained that she did not stab to death Ms. McVeigh. She wouldn't have taken the life of someone she considered close to a sister and chose to live with off campus." Jessica paused coolly. "What my client was guilty of was doing something any of you might have done under the circumstances. She showed compassion for someone who was suffering and asked for her help. The defendant acted impulsively when removing the knife that was wedged deep inside the victim's chest. My client wasn't thinking about being caught with the knife in hand and how this might look to the police. She only wanted to help her friend in the only way she could, after finding Ms. McVeigh in such a terrible state, after the defendant arrived home from spending time with her boyfriend, Brody Krane."

Jessica shifted weight from one leg to the other, while measuring her thoughts carefully. *This is where it gets tricky*, she thought, knowing that once she went in this direction, there was no turning back. But, all things considered, there was really no other choice if she wanted to give her client the best chance possible to win an acquittal. She eyed the jury. "So, if Stephanie Dozier is innocent of murdering Ms. McVeigh, who might be guilty of this heinous act? Well, the defense intends to present an alternative argument. While having no desire to impugn the character of Kristine McVeigh, there is good reason to believe that she was the leader of a group of attractive female college students who called themselves The Sexy Coeds Club. This select club's mission was to seduce married professors, then blackmail them for money. If the marks did not pay, the secret tryst was threatened to be revealed to their wives, the school, and on social media… This would ruin their lives. In fact, the defense will illustrate this with the suicide last year of art history professor, Sean Quail, who hung himself after being under enormous pressure, due in large part to the extortion scheme."

Jessica watched the shocked look on the jurors' faces. She could see the wheels spinning inside their heads as they contemplated where she was heading with this. "I believe that Kristine McVeigh's death is directly related to her role in The Sexy Coeds Club, of which my client had no involvement. I think that someone chose to kill Ms. McVeigh rather than pay up. The defendant being charged for the crime was a convenient means of diverting attention from the real culprit...or culprits of the murder." Jessica sighed before wrapping up her opening statement in giving them plenty to think about. "The defense will connect the dots between the murder of Ms. McVeigh and the murder of another member of The Sexy Coeds Club, Brittany Delray, who was gunned down late last year... Members of the jury, take care to read between the lines and use common sense, along with the shortcomings of the prosecution's case, before you weigh whether or not to convict my client of a homicide that she did not commit."

On that note, Jessica looked at Judge Kuailani-Sinclair to indicate she had finished her presentation. While giving no indication of her own thoughts, the judge turned to Madeleine and directed her to call her first witness.

Chapter Thirty-Seven

Doctor Ginger Nishioka, the Thorne County Medical Examiner, sat in the witness box as Madeleine grilled her about the knife attack on Kristine McVeigh, the depth and nature of the injuries, and other details derived from the autopsy on the victim. Jessica listened patiently as her opponent tried to score points with the jury by illustrating the graphic nature of the murder, including fourteen stab wounds. When her own turn came to question the witness, Jessica's intent was to mitigate the damage as much as possible, while hoping to give the jury some context to the testimony. "Dr. Nishioka, you have pointed out the means by which Ms. McVeigh was murdered in a way we can all understand. But are you able to conclude in that respect that the killer was actually the defendant?"

The medical examiner touched her glasses. "No, that's not for me to say."

"So, the attack, terrible as it was, could just as easily have been carried out by someone other than the defendant, even if she happened to be conveniently holding the murder weapon when the police arrived?" Jessica pressed.

"Yes, I suppose so," she acknowledged.

Jessica waited a beat, then asked, "Did the victim sustain any injuries other than those associated with the knife attack?"

Dr. Nishioka rubbed her nose. "There was some deep bruising on the right side of her face and a welt beneath her left eye," she admitted.

"Could these have been caused by someone hitting or punching the victim?"

"Yes, quite possibly."

Jessica glanced at the jury and back. "Is it possible that these could have been sustained prior to the knife attack?"

"Objection," argued Madeleine, "calls for speculation."

"Overruled," Judge Kuailani-Sinclair said. "It seems like a reasonable question for the doctor that could be as much a benefit to the prosecution as the defense, if not more."

Dr. Nishioka answered, "Yes, it is possible."

Jessica seized on this. "Then is it also possible that the time frame for when the attack began could have been earlier than the time that the 911 call was made?"

The medical examiner paused, before responding, "Yes."

"I ask this," noted Jessica, turning to the jury, "because if Kristine McVeigh's attacker had been in the apartment prior to the timeline established for killing, then it makes it that much harder to square up with the official time it took for the defendant to have left her boyfriend's apartment and arrived home to kill her roommate—" She didn't give Madeleine a chance to object before Jessica uttered, "No further questions..."

* * *

"He's painting me as a cold-blooded monster," Stephanie moaned in Jessica's ear, as Officer Guy Bean testified. "It's all a lie!"

"I know," Jessica whispered back. "I'll have my chance to cross-examine and we'll see if we can undo some of his testimony."

After Madeleine went through her rehearsed line of questioning, she lifted a plastic bag containing a serrated knife, which she identified as Exhibit A. Holding it before the witness, she asked in dramatic fashion, "Officer Bean, do you recognize this knife?"

"Yes, I do."

"Can you tell the court how you recognize it?"

Bean stared at the bag and replied positively, "It's the knife the defendant was holding when I arrived at the scene of the crime and forced her to drop, before arresting her."

Madeleine let that settle in with the jury for a long moment; then walked away from the witness box and Jessica took over, knowing the damage had been done, like it or not. "Officer Bean," she began deliberately, "when you arrived at the apartment complex, did you see anyone else outside?"

"Can't say I did."

"Did you do a scan of the premises for any possible suspects of a possible crime who might have been running away? Or even trying to hide?"

Bean angled his head. "No, I did not," he admitted.

"And why not?" Jessica pounced. "Wouldn't that have been appropriate to see if the distress call might have resulted in someone fleeing the residence in question?"

"Yes, I suppose. But given the nature of the call and seeing no one in my line of vision as I approached the apartment, my priority was to see if anyone in the unit was hurt...and take it from there—"

"Which could have been just what an intruder needed to buy time and escape," Jessica theorized, before Madeleine objected and the judge sustained. Moving on, Jessica asked, "Officer Bean, as the 911 call was logged at six-nineteen and you arrived at six-thirty, do you think this eleven-minute span could give a person adequate time to commit a fatal stabbing attack and leave the scene before the police arrived?"

Bean squirmed. "Yeah, I suppose, in theory. But since the defendant was—"

Jessica interjected, "When you first observed the defendant at the scene, did she appear to be winded?"

"No, she didn't," he replied candidly.

"If she had raced home from four blocks away to fit the timeline established by the prosecution, doesn't it seem logical to you, Officer Bean, that the defendant would have been out of breath when you arrived at the scene—?"

He sighed ponderingly. "I can't really answer that..."

"I believe you already have, Officer," Jessica stated forthrightly, knowing she had backed him into a corner in highlighting an important discrepancy in the prosecution's case. "Did you actually observe the defendant attacking the victim?" she asked the witness.

CHAPTER THIRTY-SEVEN

Bean hedged. "Not exactly…"

"Either you did or you didn't?"

"Well, she was standing over the victim, holding the bloody knife that killed—"

Again, Jessica broke in, "Isn't it possible, Officer Bean, that what you witnessed was a young woman holding a knife that she had removed from the victim to help her while in terrible distress—as opposed to being the person who had actually stabbed Ms. McVeigh and vacated the premises prior to your arrival?"

Bean scratched his jaw, before responding, "Anything's possible. That doesn't make it so…"

"It also doesn't make it so, Officer Bean," she pointed out cleverly, "that just because you assumed that the defendant holding the weapon used to kill the victim—without actually witnessing the killing—was, in fact, the true killer. When it could just as easily have been someone whom you never laid eyes on, given the timeline between the 911 call and your arrival, which was more than enough time to stab someone to death and be on your merry way—" Jessica never gave him a chance to respond as she looked up to the judge and said satisfyingly, "No further questions, Your Honor."

The judge adjourned the trial for lunch.

Chapter Thirty-Eight

Blair Rodriguez was Madeleine's next witness as she tried to make the case for the guilt of the defendant. As the forensic investigator took the stand, Madeleine admittedly found herself distracted. Meeting with her wife for lunch, Genevieve had surprised her with the news that she had signed on for a two-month gig aboard a cruise ship. Worse, was that it would be setting sail in three days. Apart from just starting to get used to having her around, Madeleine had welcomed the much-needed distraction from her work life. Now, once again, it would take center stage as she pursued a conviction of Stephanie Dozier.

After laying out the witness's qualifications, Madeleine got to the root of her testimony. "I understand that you tested the murder weapon for DNA?"

"That's correct," Blair said.

"Was there DNA detected, other than that belonging to the victim?"

"Yes. The defendant's DNA was found on the knife."

"Was there any other DNA on the knife that didn't belong to either the victim or offender?" Madeleine asked knowingly.

"No, there was no other DNA found on the knife," the witness answered succinctly.

"Was the bedding tested for DNA as well?"

"Yes."

"And what did you find?"

"Only the DNA of the victim," Blair answered.

"Let's talk about the defendant's clothing," the prosecutor said. "Was it tested for DNA belonging to the victim?"

"Yes. The victim's DNA was discovered by way of a blood sample removed from the cashmere crew top worn by the defendant."

"Was the victim's DNA found on either hand of the defendant?" Madeleine asked, knowing that was the case from blood on the handle of the knife after the attack.

Blair verified this finding and Madeleine waited a beat and then asked, for the record, "Were any fingerprints found on the murder weapon besides those of the defendant?"

"No, there were not."

Madeleine closed it out with a few more questions that made it clear in her mind that the scientific evidence pointed toward the defendant as the killer of Kristine McVeigh.

* * *

Jessica waited patiently before having her own crack at the forensic investigator through cross-examination. She jumped right in, recognizing that the DNA findings were damaging to the defendant, but still did not mean that someone else wasn't the real culprit in the crime. Now she needed to try and get the jury to at least consider this possibility more than the prosecution would have them believe.

"Would you agree that DNA evidence, no matter how incriminating, does not alone indicate a person's guilt in the commission of a crime?" she asked the witness.

Blair smoothed an eyebrow nervously. "Yes, I'm sure the police rely on other evidence as well when building a case against an individual."

"By the same token, would you agree that simply because a victim's DNA is found on a weapon that the alleged offender is holding, this doesn't necessarily mean that someone else didn't actually commit the crime—is that correct?"

"Yes, that is correct," Blair conceded. "But, as I stated, it's up to the police to make the final determination on whom to charge with a crime."

"If a killer wore gloves in the commission of a crime," Jessica stated, "would this make it more difficult to collect DNA or fingerprints from such individual?"

"Yes," the analyst acknowledged. "But, even then, it's still possible that the person could leave trace amounts of DNA that could be used against—"

Jessica remained calm as she interjected, "If a killer wanted to deliberately try and avoid detection, isn't it logical that he or she would likely wear gloves or even try to wash away DNA evidence from the murder weapon?" she pressed.

Blair exhaled. "Yes, I suppose."

"You testified that only the victim's DNA was found on the bedding," Jessica pointed out. "Is that correct?"

"Yes," she responded.

"Did you also test the victim's body and night clothing for the defendant's DNA?"

"Yes."

"And what were the results?" asked Jessica.

Blair twisted her lips. "There was no DNA from the defendant found on them."

"So, even though the victim was brutally stabbed fourteen times—according to the medical examiner—you're telling us that the defendant's DNA somehow failed to show up at all on the victim, the clothing she had on in bed, or the bedding itself?" Jessica peered at the witness.

"Yes," she admitted, but tried to explain. "It's entirely possible that—"

Jessica cut her off by asking pointedly, "Isn't it more typical that if a killer was not wearing gloves or other protective clothing, his or her DNA in such a vicious assault would be found on or around the victim?"

Blair hedged before admitting, "Yes, it is more typical…"

Before the forensic analyst went further, Jessica moved on. "Can you tell us what blood spatter analysis consists of?"

"Sure. It is a forensic science that involves studying bloodstain patterns, such as the shape, location, and/or volume of blood in establishing such things as the type of weapon or the degree of force that was used in the crime."

Jessica stepped to the other side of the witness box. "In a case such as this one, given the violent nature of the attack, wouldn't you expect the blood spatter to result in a large amount of the victim's blood to be on the perpetrator's clothing and hands...?"

Blair shifted uncomfortably. "Yes, normally, but in some instanc—"

Jessica interpolated, "Isn't it true that only a relatively small amount of the victim's DNA was found on the defendant's cashmere crew sweater and none on the skinny jeans and flats she wore...?"

"Yes, that is true," the witness admitted ill at ease. "Again, this doesn't mean—"

"In my book," Jessica cut in expertly, "it calls into question whether the defendant could have perpetrated the attack if the blood spatter and DNA evidence is inconsistent with other stabbing attacks of this nature..." She ended her questioning there, knowing it had cast doubt on the prosecution's case against Stephanie and opened the door, at least a crack, for someone else to have come into the apartment and murder Kristine McVeigh.

* * *

Madeleine called Sophia Upton to the stand. The seventy-year-old retired dentist was frail, had an ash blonde, short undercut hairstyle, and wore rimless eyeglasses. After establishing her residence at the Cherryton Apartments on Oswego Drive, Madeleine said kindly, "On the Friday evening of October fourteenth, last year, can you tell us what you saw...?"

Sophia sighed and touched her glasses. "Yes. I was walking my dog, Bessie, when I saw a woman pacing outside the apartment building. I remembered thinking that she seemed nervous, for whatever reason."

"And about what time was this?" Madeleine asked, for effect, knowing what was coming.

"It was around six-twenty or so," the witness claimed.

"Is there any reason, in particular, that you can put that time frame down to memory?"

"Yes. I always take Bessie out to do her business at the same time every day. That day was no different…"

Madeleine waited a beat before asking, "Is the person you saw that day in the courtroom?"

Sophia nodded. "Yes."

"Can you point her out, please?"

The witness turned toward the defendant and said firmly, "That's the lady I saw."

"No further questions," Madeleine said concisely, satisfied with the testimony. Jessica took her place for cross-examination, as she sat down, anticipating what was to come.

* * *

Jessica gave the witness a tiny smile and said, "I just have a few questions for you…had you ever seen the defendant before the day in question?"

Sophia eyed Stephanie. "Yes, I believe I had from time to time—"

"So, you hadn't actually met formally?"

"No. As a retiree, I pretty much keep to myself."

"Where were you when you say you saw the defendant on October fourteenth?"

"As, I said, I was walking my—"

"Yes, but exactly where were you standing or walking specifically at the time?" Jessica asked straightforwardly.

"I was near the woods, where Bessie was…relieving herself—"

"And how far would you say you were from the woman you saw pacing?"

The witness stared at the question thoughtfully. "Maybe twenty feet."

Jessica seized on this. "At a distance of twenty feet, around twilight time, it would be hard, if not impossible, even while wearing glasses, to say with certainty that a person one may have seen only on occasion was the same person you saw on the day in question…" Before she could respond, Jessica added, "And it would have been just as unlikely, under the same conditions, to interpret a person pacing as indicative of nervousness…"

"I'm not sure what to say about that," Sophia's voice shook.

"You testified that it was around six-twenty that you saw this female," Jessica went on. "Is that correct?"

"Yes."

"Another witness will testify that the defendant was four blocks away at approximately six-ten p.m. that day," Jessica pointed out. "Walking home, as she did, through the woods at a brisk pace would have taken the defendant at least twelve minutes to get to the apartment complex—or around six-twenty-two, two minutes past the time you say you saw this woman, and a full three minutes before the 911 call came in reporting the victim in distress—" Jessica took a breath and regarded the witness delicately. "As such, isn't it possible that the woman you saw may have been someone else living at or visiting the complex, who may have only looked like the defendant?"

Touching her glasses as she gazed over at Stephanie, the witness answered hesitantly, "Yes, I suppose it could have been someone else I saw."

Jessica left it at that for the jury to ponder, knowing she had achieved her goal of undermining the retired dentist's testimony in further contradicting the overall timeline as established by the prosecution in relation to her client's whereabouts. Though the notion that the witness had spotted another female hovering around the complex was interesting, Jessica suspected this person was most likely innocent herself of anything other than pacing. As it was, she had set her own sights on one of the men being blackmailed by The Sexy Coeds Club as the person exacting deadly revenge on the members, starting with Kristine McVeigh. That notwithstanding, Jessica was steadfast in keeping all options on the table as to who might have wanted Kristine dead and had the means to make this happen.

Chapter Thirty-Nine

When her time came to cross-examine Homicide Investigator Jackson Payne, Jessica was ready to poke some holes into his depiction of her client as someone mentally unstable and at the same time, crafty enough to have been able to perpetrate a crime of violence that left her no room to spare in going from one place to another in successfully carrying out the attack. Only to be caught with the murder weapon in hand before she could make an escape. Though, if one listened to the arrogant detective's prior testimony, to Jessica, one might be led to believe that it was the intention of the defendant to be apprehended, satisfied that the deed was done and prepared to face the consequences of her actions.

I don't believe that to be the case for one minute, Jessica told herself, as she glared at the witness, preparing herself to do battle. "Detective Payne, how long have you been a member of the Creighton Hills Police Department?"

"Too long," he quipped. "Actually, it's going on sixteen years now, the last fourteen have been in the Detective Division—"

"And is it safe to say that in those years you have investigated your fair share of homicides?"

"Yeah, that's fair to say."

Jessica waited a beat. "In those instances, would you say that, by and large, the suspect acknowledged committing the offense when caught with the murder weapon in hand?"

"Yeah, I suppose so." He gazed up at her warily. "Where are you going with this?"

"During your interrogation of the defendant, when presented with the clear facts that she was holding the knife that was used to kill the victim in this case, did Ms. Dozier confess to the crime?"

Payne fidgeted. "No, she didn't," he admitted.

"Did you find that at all unusual," Jessica asked, "given that you had her dead to rights, so to speak, with the evidence and eyewitness account of the arresting officer?"

"Yeah, I guess so. But not all suspects will come clean," the investigator spoke defiantly, "no matter the guilt that's staring them right in the face."

"Or just maybe," countered Jessica, "the suspect, in this case, did not 'come clean' and confess to something she didn't do, no matter the alleged guilt staring her in the face—because the defendant did not kill her roommate and refused to make a false confession to allow you to neatly wrap up your investigation."

The prosecutor objected and Jessica quickly moved on, asking the detective pointedly, "Isn't it true that you had pretty much made up your mind that the defendant was the guilty party in the death of Kristine McVeigh right from the start?"

"Objection," Madeleine argued. "Questioning the detective's integrity as a professional in this case is a low blow."

"On the contrary," Jessica countered, "given what Detective Payne has already testified to, it seems more than fair to believe that he assumed the defendant was guilty and, therefore, didn't put much focus, if any, on any other possible suspects in the murder..."

"I'll allow the question," Judge Kuailani-Sinclair said simply, directing the witness to answer.

Payne's nostrils flared. "As far as guilt and innocence, I base my view on the facts of any case," he stated. "The defendant was at the scene of the crime, holding the murder weapon over the victim, after learning she had been fooling around with the defendant's boyfriend. With no indication of forced entry into the apartment and no evidence to suggest someone else stabbed to death the victim, of course, I made an assessment of the defendant and went with it..." He paused uncomfortably. "That said, I take every case I work on very seriously. That includes leaving nothing on the table when it comes to doing a complete investigation—no matter where it may lead… and to whom. In this instance, it all comes back to the defendant as the killer of her roommate—"

Jessica glanced at her client and could see the anguish in Stephanie's face in being painted as a coldblooded murderer. Needing to counteract the investigator's statement, Jessica moved on. "I understand, Detective, that you were the lead investigator in the murder of Brittany Delray?"

"Yeah, that's true."

"Were you able to find any connection between Ms. Delray and Kristine McVeigh?"

"They both attended Wryer College and were friends," he responded.

"In fact," Jessica stated, "they were more than just friends. The two were part of a group of coeds that engaged in sexual acts with married professors and extortion to keep their dirty little secrets."

Madeleine objected on the grounds of relevance, and the judge demanded to know where Jessica was going with this, which she told her, and overruled the prosecutor. "Has an arrest been made in the Delray homicide?" Jessica asked the witness.

"The case is still ongoing," he muttered.

"I take it that means no arrest has been made?" When he didn't indicate otherwise, she continued, "Isn't it possible, Detective, that whoever killed Ms. Delray as an extortionist might have also gone after Kristine McVeigh to silence her too, while figuring out a way to pin this on the defendant—who has maintained throughout that she was innocent, in spite of the so-called open and shut case against her—thus allowing the real killer to slip through the cracks?"

When Payne took his sweet time to answer, Jessica decided to leave it up to the jury to read between the proverbial lines, and declared, "No further questions—"

* * *

"You more than held your own in there," Liam told Jessica, as they shared a sausage and pepperoni pizza that night at his place. He was impressed at how commanding she could be in a somewhat hostile environment, which told him a lot about the lady.

"I'll need to do a lot better than hold my own," she said sourly, holding up a slice of pizza. "Madeleine seems bent on winning this case no matter what. She's conveniently ignoring the gray areas that give us good reason to believe Kristine McVeigh made herself a target with her sex and money-making schemes—whether Kristine chose to believe she was putting herself at risk or not. Unfortunately, Stephanie fell right into a trap, not of her own making, and in the course of that, it's giving the killer a free pass."

Liam bit into a slice of pizza and said sympathetically, "I'm not the one you need to try to convince."

"I know." She smiled at him. "Don't mind me. I'm just stressing out over this trial and the fact that I don't want to see a young woman go to prison for something she believed was an innocent gesture of compassion."

"Neither do I," he told her sincerely. "That's why we're going to fight tooth and nail on her behalf and not give in to a false narrative." Showing he cared was the least Liam felt he could do for the woman he had fallen hard for. Win or lose, she needed to know that he wasn't going anywhere. "Your client would expect no less and I'll always stand by you as the layers of this case unfold and give way to a just outcome."

"Well said." She took another bite out of the pizza. "Remind me again why I feel so lucky to have you in my life?"

He colored. "I think it works both ways."

"Yeah, you're right, we are a good fit—the dramas of the legal profession, and even private investigation trials and tribulations, aside."

Jessica dabbed a napkin to the corners of her mouth and Liam had a sudden urge to kiss her. He gave in to that urge, leaning across the table, where she seemed just as eager to embrace the moment.

Chapter Forty

Madeleine called Brody Krane to the stand. Though she wouldn't exactly call him a hostile witness, his heart obviously wasn't entirely in it to testify against the defendant. Not that she could blame him for feeling guilty for sleeping with his girlfriend's best friend, causing a deadly chain reaction. Personally, if it were her, Madeleine would have kicked his ass for cheating on her instead of going after the roommate, an easier target. But she would have drawn the line there. Killing the one who betrayed her might have felt good for a moment, but it sure as hell wouldn't have been worth giving up her entire life in the process. That was the defendant's bad choice in attacking the victim, and she would have to live with the consequences. Including facing the man who got the ball rolling simply because he couldn't keep it in his pants.

Madeleine pasted a friendly smile on her face as she asked the witness coolly, "Do you know the defendant?"

Brody gazed at Stephanie and looked away. "Yeah. She's my girlfriend...I mean, ex-girlfriend."

It didn't surprise Madeleine in the slightest that he'd cut her loose when the going got too tough and he could simply move on with another coed who was ripe for the picking. And maybe another betrayal. "So, how long were you two seeing each other?"

"Probably a year."

"Let's talk about the Friday of October fourteenth, last year..." she began. "According to the statement you gave to the police, the defendant came to visit you. Is that correct?"

Brody fidgeted in the chair. "Yeah."

"Around what time was that?"

"Probably about five-thirty p.m."

"And what happened then...?"

He ran a hand across his mouth. "We had sex."

Madeleine thought about lingering on that subject matter as a prelude to the juicier part of his testimony, but chose instead to get to the heart of the matter. "Okay, and when that was over, what happened...?"

Brody rubbed his nose. "I told Steph that I'd slept with her roommate."

"Steph, as in Stephanie Dozier, the defendant?" she clarified.

"Yeah."

"And when you say roommate, you mean the person the defendant shared an apartment with, Kristine McVeigh?"

"Yeah," he answered, eyes cast downward.

"And how did the defendant react to this shocking, no doubt, news...?"

Brody jutted his chin. "She was really pissed."

Madeleine leaned toward him. "Can you please be more specific?"

He lowered his eyes again. "She slapped me and yelled some expletives at me—"

Madeleine looked over at the defense table. She could see by the expression on Jessica's face that she had been caught off guard in hearing this revelation of more violent behavior by her client. *If she conveniently kept this from you, what else is she hiding?* Madeleine thought gleefully.

"I'm sorry, Steph, I didn't want to be here," Brody uttered regretfully, as Madeleine rounded on him angrily. The last thing she wanted was for her witness to play the sympathy card in being loyal to his murderous ex. Too late for that.

"None of us wants to be here," Madeleine hissed. "But we are, because Kristine McVeigh was stabbed to death and we all have to do our part to get to the bottom of it. And that includes you!" Barely taking a breath, she moved past this. "So, after the display of violence and indignation by the defendant, what happened next?" she asked the witness.

Brody paused thoughtfully. "She left."

"To go where?" Madeleine asked artfully.

Jessica weakly objected as calling for speculation, which the judge overruled. The witness answered, "Back to her apartment."

"Did you feel at that time that the defendant was angry enough to do bodily harm to the victim—?"

Jessica objected again, more forcefully. "Your Honor, she's clearly leading the witness..."

Judge Kuailani-Sinclair agreed and Madeleine cleverly withdrew the question, knowing that she had made her point for the jury to consider, when taking into account the lead up to it.

"No further questions," she said pleasingly.

* * *

"I can't believe he turned on me like that," Stephanie grumbled to Jessica at the defense table. "What a creep!"

"Don't blame him," Jessica whispered in her ear. "I'm pretty sure he didn't have much choice in the matter in being called as a witness for the prosecution." She peered at her client. "Why didn't you tell me you hit Brody that night...?"

Stephanie rolled her eyes and shrugged. "I didn't think it was a big deal," she claimed.

"Everything's a big deal when your very freedom is on the line," Jessica admonished her.

"He deserved to be slapped after what he told me he and Kristine were up to behind my back," Stephanie said, furrowing her brow. "I know now I shouldn't have done it. And I'm sorry for not telling you..."

Jessica empathized with the anger she must have felt in the moment, thinking about how she wanted to slap Hugh more than once for leading her on in Jessica's own sordid love triangle. "What's done is done," she told her client, while hoping to mitigate the damage, as it was now time to cross-examine the witness.

When Jessica walked up to Brody, she could tell that he wanted to be anywhere but on the witness stand, being forced to testify against his onetime girlfriend. *I'll try to keep this brief,* she thought, and then said to him, "Mr. Krane, you testified that the defendant came to your apartment at about five-thirty p.m., is that right?"

"Yeah."

"And what time did she leave the apartment?"

Brody sat up straight. "About six-ten."

"Not much earlier...or later?" Jessica asked.

"It was pretty close to six-ten," he maintained.

"And you know this how?"

He tilted his face musingly. "After we got dressed, I checked my cell phone for messages and saw that it was five after six. That's when I told Steph about me and Kristine... I'm sure we only talked for about five minutes, before she stormed out the door—"

Jessica allowed that to sink in for a moment, before asking, "Do you know if the defendant walked home...?"

"Yeah, she did," he spoke confidently.

"How can you be so sure?" Jessica wanted him to answer for the record.

"Because she walked to my place from the library. She called me from there to tell me she was coming over..."

Jessica faced the jury. "As the witness has testified that the defendant left his apartment at approximately six-ten p.m. on the day in question, and walked the four blocks home to her own apartment—the shortest route, which I tested myself, was through the woods. Walking quickly, it took me twelve minutes to arrive at the apartment." She paused. "We know that the defendant couldn't have run there, because Officer Bean testified that she was not out of breath when he spotted her standing over the victim's bed at approximately six-thirty. Since the 911 call came in at six-nineteen p.m., this meant that the defendant would have had only nine minutes to walk from the witness's apartment back to her own place in order to have murdered Ms. McVeigh... Or, in other words, given this timeline, it would have been technically impossible for the defendant to have achieved this feat."

Jessica could only hope that the jurors were able to do the math for themselves in pushing back from the prosecution's sequence of events and realize that the case against the defendant did not add up to murder.

Chapter Forty-One

Kimberly Chung was called to the stand by Madeleine. The twenty-two-year-old flight attendant had been Stephanie Dozier's high school rival, whom the defendant once came to blows with regarding a male student both had been dating. Madeleine thought it was important to show a pattern of violence the defendant engaged in that the jury could digest like food that went down just right.

She eyed the pretty witness, who had long locks in a caramel balayage hairstyle and a dimpled chin, before asking her politely, "Do you recognize the defendant?"

Kimberly glared at Stephanie. "Yes, I recognize her. We went to Lakota High School together."

"Were you friends?"

"Hardly." The witness tautened her lips. "I never liked her. She never liked me."

Good to point out, Madeleine mused. "Tell me about an incident that occurred between you."

Having already gone through this in advance, Kimberly said evenly, "We got into a fight. She accused me of trying to steal her boyfriend..."

"And were you?"

"He wasn't hers to steal," Kimberly argued. "Johnnie O'Keefe was a senior at the time. He also liked playing the field. That included me, Stephanie, and other girls. But Stephanie didn't see it that way. She thought Johnnie belonged to her only and that I was getting in the way of that. So, we fought..."

"How did it end?" Madeleine asked equably.

"With her threatening to kill me if I didn't back off from pursuing him," the witness stated, her brow furrowed as she glared at the defendant.

"No further questions," Madeleine uttered, having set the tone intended in exhibiting the defendant's proclivity for bullying and violence.

* * *

Jessica didn't want to spend too much time with the witness, believing she had been somewhat effective in demonstrating a pattern of aggressive behavior for Stephanie. *I need to diminish its impact on the jury,* Jessica told herself, knowing that her client hated picking a fight with a high school classmate over a guy that Stephanie conceded was never really into her.

Giving the witness the benefit of a cordial look, as though they weren't on opposite sides in a court of law, Jessica said smoothly, "I understand that you and the defendant had your differences when you were in high school. Looking back on it now, would you agree that high school rivalries pretty much came with the territory, especially when it came to fighting over boys?"

"Yeah, I guess," Kimberly responded.

"Did you ever get into fights with other girls over guys?"

"Yes," she admitted.

"Would you agree that most people say things they really didn't mean in the heat of battle?" Jessica posed to her.

Kimberly waited a beat, then answered, "Probably."

"Do you think that people can change over time—especially growing up after those turbulent high school years?"

The witness glanced at the defendant. "Yes, I suppose."

Lastly, Jessica asked her poignantly, "If it was you on trial today, would you want to be judged by a mistake you made in high school?"

Madeleine objected as leading the witness. Jessica withdrew the question and indicated she had finished her cross-examination.

* * *

The prosecution's last witness was an expert in jealous rage, Doctor Roxanne Paige. African American, the thirty-seven-year-old, with a PhD in criminology, was trim with black hair in a crochet style with blonde highlights. Madeleine went through her impressive credentials, including several bestselling books on homicidal rage, before getting to her take on the destructive dynamics of intimates and rage.

"Jealousy can do things to people like you wouldn't believe," Roxanne testified. "When it comes to intimate relationships and love triangles, some individuals cannot process normally the sting of betrayal or otherwise feeling aggrieved due to infidelity or attachment. This loss of proper perspective is what can cause one to lash out irrationally." She took a breath. "Such behavior typically manifests itself in aggressive behavior, including verbal aggression, mental cruelty, tossing things around, and physical aggression—such as violence that can result in murder."

I couldn't have summarized this any better myself, Madeleine thought satisfyingly. Now she needed to relate this line of testimony to the defendant. "What is your take on the current case, Doctor?"

Roxanne glanced at the defendant and back. "Well, I have read the medical examiner's report and police report on the multiple stabbing fatal attack, and watched as the trial has unfolded," she began. "Based on this, in my expert opinion, I believe that the defendant, Ms. Dozier, simply lost it, in laypersons' terms, in going on the attack after learning that someone she trusted had betrayed her in the worst way... Only payback in the severest sense would suffice before the fury receded.

"Violence involving infidelity can be especially harsh. I've seen it in so many cases... A loss of control, pathological rage, and loathing, and a thirst for revenge... Where it concerns a man caught between two women, it is the women who more often than not bear the brunt of a violent response against one or the other. Though this is typically nonlethal violence, in the current case, the response apparently resulted in a homicide."

Madeleine asked a few more questions with solid and detailed answers, before deciding she didn't want to overwhelm the jury by going any further, potentially defeating the purpose in zeroing in on the correlation between jealousy and deadly rage in the conduct of the defendant in taking the life of Kristine McVeigh. "Thank you for your expertise, Doctor Paige," Madeleine said kindly, turning her over to the defense counsel for cross-examination.

* * *

Jessica was admittedly impressed with the witness's strong performance on the stand and convincing effort to link jealous rage and homicidal expression to the defendant. How might the jury be interpreting the expert testimony of Roxanne Paige? In her mind, the damage had been done. But Jessica refused to believe that it would make or break the case on its own merits. Particularly when considered with the other aspects of the trial, which included the inadequacies on the prosecutor's side and Jessica's own alternative perspective on the victim and others who might have it in for her.

I won't give the witness any more of a platform than necessary, Jessica thought, as she approached the box. "When you speak of homicidal rage, Doctor Paige, are the dynamics the same, more or less, whether the motivation is jealousy, revenge, or just plain old-fashioned anger?"

"Yes, the dynamics are largely the same," Roxanne concurred. "There may be subtle differences in how the rage is internalized and the impetus to let it out is manifested, but rage is still rage at the end of the day, especially where it concerns homicidal rage and the willingness to see it through till it's done..."

Jessica had hoped she might say that, giving herself more momentum in the cross. "So, if I understand you correctly, if someone other than the defendant had 'lost it,' in your words, then such person was just as capable and willing to perpetrate such a violent attack on Kristine McVeigh—whether motivated by jealous rage...or perhaps the rage that might come from losing it after being the victim of extortion or at risk for marital troubles, professional self-destruction, or public humiliation, as examples...?"

Madeleine objected, getting off her chair. "She's swimming in the wrong waters, Your Honor."

"I disagree, Counselor," Judge Kuailani-Sinclair pushed back swiftly. "When you brought in this rage expert, you opened the door to the cross-examination into the subject matter and how it might relate to types of rage other than jealous rage. The witness may answer the question—"

Roxanne nodded and responded, "Yes, that is correct, rage is certainly not limited to one kind of emotional baggage over another," she admitted. "Whoever attacked Ms. McVeigh, whatever the specific motivation, did so out of some form of rage."

Jessica was pleased with the answer, even if her opponent clearly felt otherwise. "Are people who express this type of violent rage typically suicidal as well?"

"Yes, that is often the case," the witness said, "with so many such individuals despondent enough to wish to end their own lives. But this isn't always—"

Jessica broke in, "In the defendant's case, she clearly went against the grain of this premise, calling into question the prosecution's entire narrative," she cautioned. "With the 911 call on the night in question clocked at six-nineteen and the arrival of Officer Bean at six-thirty, during that eleven-minute span the defendant would have had ample time to stab herself to death after the rampage against the victim—but she did not."

"Well, as I've said, each case of rage is different," Roxanne pointed out tonelessly.

"Is it normal, Doctor Paige, for perpetrators of violent rage to be able to simply turn it on and off, like a switch...?"

The witness lifted her chin thoughtfully. "I wouldn't say it's normal. In most cases, the rage tends to grow inside like a cancer, spreading throughout the body, and cannot be easily turned off, till such time when it can be lessened in its intensity—often through a violent outburst."

Jessica worked on this angle in making her point, "From what you're telling us, after such a brutal case of rage, as experienced by the victim in this trial, one might have expected the defendant to have exhibited at least some of this hostility when confronted by Officer Bean. Or, for that matter, Detective

Payne during his interrogation… Instead, by all accounts, Ms. Dozier did not display any aggressive tendencies along the way. Quite the contrary, she professed her innocence throughout—never giving any indication of a sense of relief that Ms. McVeigh was dead."

Before the witness could attempt to walk back her own words, Jessica skillfully put an end to the cross-examination, believing she had successfully countered the expert testimony and given the jury another reason to doubt the guilt of the defendant.

Chapter Forty-Two

When it came time to present her case, Jessica had already decided that she would rely largely on the holes she managed to poke into the prosecution's case. She believed there were more than enough reasons for the jury to seriously question whether or not they could find the defendant guilty beyond a reasonable doubt. Certainly, she was not about to play with fire by putting her client on the stand. Giving Madeleine an opportunity to go after Stephanie would be tantamount to legal jeopardy. Defendants typically made poor witnesses, even when innocent and speaking from the heart. On the other hand, Jessica saw benefit in calling some witnesses that would bolster her argument that the death of Kristine McVeigh was, more likely than not, caused by the sexual and extortionist schemes she was deeply involved in. And not the result of jealous rage, as contended by the prosecution.

Hugh Holliman was Jessica's first witness. Admittedly, she felt slightly uncomfortable having to question him as an ex-lover. But given the high stakes and his knowledge of and involvement in The Sexy Coeds Club, she really had no choice than to call him to testify.

After establishing he was married, a father, and had an occupation as a financial advisor, Jessica asked evenly, "Was art history professor Sean Quail a client of yours?"

Hugh appeared nervous as he answered, "Yes."

"Are you aware that Mr. Quail took his own life last year?"

"Yes," he said tersely.

"Do you have any information on that?" she asked mindfully.

Hugh tugged on his skinny tie uneasily. "Sean was a sex addict, spending thousands of dollars to satisfy his urges...he began having sex with one of his students. Turned out, she was part of a college sex ring that referred to themselves as The Sexy Coeds Club...Sean told me that the club had recorded him having sex with the coed and threatened to show it to his wife, the director of his department, and put it on social media if he didn't pay them to keep silent..." Hugh sighed. "Sean had clearly gotten in over his head. He couldn't handle it and killed himself."

Jessica hated for him to have to go through that, but it needed to be said. "Did Professor Quail give you the name of this coed he was having sex with and being blackmailed by?"

"He said her name was Kris." Hugh met Jessica's eyes. "I came to learn later that this Kris was Kristine McVeigh, the student who had been murdered...supposedly by the defendant."

Madeleine objected to the characterization of supposedly, while Jessica countered that the defendant had not yet been convicted of any crime and was, therefore, presumed innocent at this point. The judge agreed.

Jessica stayed on this theme with the witness. "Do you have any reason to believe Ms. McVeigh could have been killed by someone other than the defendant?"

Hugh shifted his body uncomfortably. "From what I understand, this club was specifically targeting married men...pushing them too far was a recipe for doing whatever someone might have thought was necessary to stop the blackmail and its implications—including murder."

Before another objection came, Jessica quickly moved on to another tender subject for her ex-lover. "Another member of The Sexy Coeds Club, Brittany Delray, was also murdered late last year, under suspicious circumstances—" she pointed out. "Are you familiar with Ms. Delray...?"

Hugh paused, glaring at Jessica, as though she had crossed the line with the question. In fact, he knew perfectly well that she had to broach the subject as part of her strategy on behalf of her client. Finally, he muttered, "Yeah, I was acquainted with Ms. Delray."

Jessica met his gaze head-on. "Can you tell us how?"

He swallowed thickly. "We met at a bar. I didn't know at the time that she was in college."

"Then what?" Jessica pressed.

"She came on to me and we ended up in her hotel room." Hugh ran a hand across his mouth. "After we finished things, I left, with her still alive... I found out the next day that she had been murdered...and that she had videotaped our sexual relations... I fully cooperated with the police and was cleared of the murder."

In spite of her disappointment in him, Jessica was happy that the police were quick to take him off the suspect list for the crime. "Do you believe it was Ms. Delray's intention to extort money from you?"

Hugh pursed his lips. "Yeah, I think that was the plan." His jaw clenched. "Just for the record, even if Brittany had still been alive, I would never have succumbed to blackmail... Nor would I have tried to kill her." His chin dropped. "That doesn't mean some other man, under the same pressure, might not have resorted to murdering Ms. Delray, if they thought there was no other way out, putting her in the same unenviable position as the other members of The Sexy Coeds Club, Kris or Kristine McVeigh and Danielle Osmond, who were victims of foul play."

Having gotten what she needed from him, perhaps more, Jessica spared Hugh from more painful testimony and exclaimed, "No further questions."

* * *

Jessica next called Cecelia Temple to the stand. Like Hugh, she was nervous, but willing to do her part to expose The Sexy Coeds Club's dirty secrets, which may have played a role in several murders, including the killing of Kristine McVeigh.

After talking a bit about her educational status as a student at Wryer College, Jessica got right to the point. "I understand that you were once a member of The Sexy Coeds Club. Is that correct?"

"Yes," Cecelia uttered with a sigh.

"Tell us about the club."

She paused, ill at ease. "Well, it was originated by Kristine McVeigh as a way for a few attractive and sexy coeds to take advantage of our looks and sexuality to go after married professors to have sex and make money from it."

"As prostitutes...?" Jessica asked, mainly for effect.

"No," she insisted. "We weren't sex workers. Not really... We were businesswomen."

"What type of business?"

Cecelia smoothed an eyebrow. "We recorded the sex acts with the professors and used it to blackmail them."

"For money," Jessica pressed.

"Yes."

"And if they didn't pay up?"

"We threatened to ruin their lives by revealing just what they were up to with college girls," Cecelia confessed, "including telling their wives and putting the sex recording on social media sites..." She put her face in her hands. "I know it was wrong and regret it now...especially after what happened to Kristine, Brittany, and Danielle."

Jessica gave her a moment to gather her composure, before saying keenly, "Let's talk about what happened to these coeds...all three were homicide victims."

"Yes," she acknowledged, "and I'm sick about it. They were my friends."

"At the moment, the authorities seem to believe their deaths may have been isolated incidences." Jessica paused. "I have strong reservations about that."

"Me too." Cecelia squared her shoulders.

"Did any of the professors you slept with ever threaten you with bodily harm?"

Her lower lip shook. "Yeah, we were threatened by some of the men, once they knew we wanted more than just to go to bed with them," she admitted. "At first, we thought they were just blowing hot air, hoping to get us to back down. But then, when the deaths kept piling up, I could see that someone was deadly serious about putting The Sexy Coeds Club out of business for good...starting with Kris—"

After an objection by Madeleine was overruled by the judge—perhaps, if for no other reason, to allow the jury to consider a plausible alternative to the one presented by the prosecution—Jessica asked the witness point blank, "Do you believe that the defendant killed her roommate and your friend and former club member?"

Cecelia gazed at Stephanie contemplatively and responded in a steady voice, "No, I do not!"

"And why is that, given that she's the one on trial for the murder?"

"Because she and Kris were cool, no matter what they are saying. Even if they had their differences, some more serious than others, what college roomies didn't? Yes, Kris fooled around with Brody—everyone knew about it—but that was just who she was, playing the field, for the hell of it. She loved sex. If she wasn't having paid sex, she gave it up for free. But Steph retaliating by stabbing her to death? No way. What would that accomplish, other than sending her to prison. Believe me, Brody isn't all that special." Cecelia looked directly at Jessica. "I'm convinced that the defendant—Stephanie—did not murder Kristine, no matter the evidence that seems to indicate that. Evidence can be faked. Especially when every former member of the now defunct Sexy Coeds Club has a big X on her back and it's obvious that someone wants us all dead—"

The same powerful words were echoed by other ex-club members, Aimee Atkinson, Georgina Perez, and Lacee Sheridan, who testified in succession about their own experiences, shaking down married professors, and the sense of vulnerability in believing they were now under attack for their ill-advised activities. Jessica allowed this to sink in with the jury, as she herself weighed how this might impact the verdict, before calling her final witness, English professor, Conrad Ramsay.

"Are you familiar with The Sexy Coeds Club?" Jessica got right to the point.

"Yes," he answered tersely.

"How?"

Ramsay scratched the hair on his chin. "I was approached by two of my female students, who, let's say, introduced me to the club..."

"When you say 'introduced', you mean invited you to have sex with them?" Jessica asked straightforwardly.

"Yes."

"What were the names of these students?" She peered at him. "And remember, Professor, you are under oath—"

"Kristine McVeigh and Brittany Delray..." Ramsay lowered his eyes. "Believe me when I tell you, and this court, I'm deeply ashamed of what I did and have no excuses. Other than the fact that my wife, Marilyn, was dying of cancer and the coeds caught me in a moment of weakness..."

Jessica felt for him in that moment. Yet, she still believed it crossed the line to become sexually involved with students, even if your wife was in desperate straits and perhaps unavailable to him that way. Infidelity was still infidelity, which she knew all too well, being the other woman once upon a time regrettably. "Was there an attempt to extort money from you?" she asked him firmly.

"Yeah, they came after me," he admitted.

"And did you pay?"

"No. I couldn't even if I wanted to. I was up to my eyeballs in debt from the portion of my wife's medical expenses not covered by insurance." Ramsay pulled on his nose. "I told them as much and was prepared to have this go public... But they withdrew the demand that I hand over twenty-five thousand dollars and that was it. I sure as hell didn't make the mistake of getting involved with any of those vultures again—"

Good for you—and them, Jessica thought. She looked him in the eye. "Did you have anything to do with the murders of three of those vultures, as you put it?"

"No, I didn't," he insisted. "I may have done something stupid by having sex with them, but I'm not a killer."

"What about some of the other married professors who may have cheated on their wives with The Sexy Coeds Club?"

"What about them...?"

Jessica responded flatly, "Did you hear anything about any who may have

216

been blackmailed and wanted payback—in the form of murdering one or all the members of the club?"

Ramsay stiffened. "This wasn't the type of thing anyone who was involved with those coeds would want to brag about," he said, "much less, talk about retaliation." He squirmed. "But once the girls started dying, there was some chatter through the grapevine that someone among us had it out for them, for obvious reasons—"

"Did any names pop up among the professors who seemed particularly interested in the coeds' deaths—?" Jessica asked pointedly.

Ramsay gave it little time before answering waveringly, "No, none. Sorry—" He gazed at the defense table. "The defendant, Stephanie, was one of my students. I can't speak for whether or not she really did what they say she did to Kris, but I can tell you that there was night and day difference between the two of them. Whereas, Stephanie was serious about her education, Kristine could care less. She was in it to please her father and find ways to destroy other people's lives... After what she and the other club members did to me, I think there's a good chance that another guy who felt himself backed into a corner took it upon himself to go after Kris and the others, with the attitude that it was either him or them..."

Jessica felt that was a strong way to end this witness's testimony and keep the notion that a killer, other than the defendant, was at large and going after the sexy coed extortionists. "No further questions," she told the judge.

Closing arguments were set to begin on Monday.

IV

The Verdict

Chapter Forty-Three

J essica sat in a booth across from Connie at Café Laney's, strategizing for her closing arguments. This was the culmination of a trial for which Jessica honestly could not say which way it would go. Her instincts told her that she had created more than enough reasonable doubt to get an acquittal. But the solid evidence the prosecution presented made her nervous that the jury would find it too much to simply ignore, even in the face of the victim's leadership role in a college coed extortion scheme and other questionable behavior that could have made her the first—or even second—target of a killer, if one assumed that there was more to Nicole Kingsley's fatal drug overdose than met the eye.

"You've got this," Connie cut into her thoughts, while sipping a cinnamon latte. "You're a pro, Jessica, and no matter which way it goes, you'll give the jury something to seriously think about in a case that leaves a lot to be desired with the prosecution's attempt to sell them on one thing at the expense of another and beyond—which makes it even more thought provoking..."

Jessica smiled softly over her mint tea. "I'll just be glad when it's over, one way or the other." She lifted her cup. "Of course, I'd like nothing better than to walk out of that courtroom with my client a free woman. Especially since it's been clear to me practically from the start, that she did not stab to death her roommate, in spite of the tensions and betrayal between them." Jessica sighed. "But trying to read the minds of a jury is like a fortune teller reading palms, you just never know what the result will be—"

"Which is why you need to chill," Connie admonished her, "and let the system do its job. As attorneys, we can only play the hand we're dealt, and hope like hell it works in our favor."

"I know," Jessica conceded, feeling her confidence start to return. "It helps to have you and Liam in my corner." Not to mention those in the community who had come to believe, like her, that Stephanie Dozier was no more guilty of stabbing Kristine McVeigh than any of them.

"I'll always be there for you, girlfriend." Connie's eyes twinkled. "Something tells me the same is true for your new squeeze too. The way he looks at you and after you—"

Jessica blushed. "Let's not get ahead of ourselves," she warned lightheartedly. "We're working together, dating, and more, but neither of us are jumping into something feet first that we may not be able to climb out of..."

"Who said anything about climbing out...?" Connie leaned forward. "Liam is not Hugh, thank goodness. You're happy in a relationship for the first time in recent memory. Don't throw it all away over past regrets. Once the trial is over, maybe you two could take a vacation. You're more than welcome to stay at my cabin near Crater Lake. I'm just saying..."

Jessica laughed. "And you say it so beautifully." She sipped more tea. Admittedly, the idea did have appeal. She sensed that Liam would go for it and it would give them a chance to see how they fared as a couple outside their comfort zones. But first things first. "Let's just see what happens when a verdict is reached," she uttered reflectively, "and everyone involved can breathe again."

"Deal," agreed Connie spiritedly, lifting her drink.

Jessica did the same, while wondering where things would go from there as to the fate of her client. And, for that matter, even the members of The Sexy Coeds Club, who themselves were at a crossroads in their lives and choices for the future.

* * *

Liam was surprised when Juan Guillermo showed up at his floating house, armed with a six pack of beer.

"Maybe it's time you traded this in for a yacht that can take you anywhere,"

Guillermo said, tossing him a bottle.

"Why would I want to do that when I've got everything I need right here?"

"Are we referring to this place?" Guillermo eyed him. "Or a hotshot lawyer, in particular?"

Liam sipped beer and thought about Jessica warmly. "How about both?"

"Fair enough." Guillermo sat down on the sofa. "I wanted to bring you up to date on the investigation into the deaths of Brittany Delray and Danielle Osmond—"

"I'm listening…" Liam remained standing, though eager to hear any positive news that Jessica could use in her client's defense.

"Well, there's sort of good news and definitely bad news…" Guillermo uttered, putting the bottle to his mouth. "First, the bad… We think the bicycle used by the unsub responsible for the coed deaths belonged to a campus bike share program—allowing students, professors, and even other staff at Wryer College to pretty much come and go as they pleased. It's made it damned near impossible to link this one bike to anyone in particular—in spite of fingerprinting, DNA, and even reviewing surveillance cameras… Bottom line is the trail has run dry as far as bringing in a suspect—"

"You think we're looking at a student as the perp?" Liam looked at him inquiringly.

"Possible," he theorized. "Maybe a disgruntled boyfriend of one of the coeds decided to take out his frustrations on all of them." He paused. "But it's just as likely, if not more so, that if this is in retaliation of some sort, a professor or someone else involved with the group could be the culprit."

Liam considered this and then asked keenly, "So, what's the sort of good news…?"

Guillermo sat back. "Through the ATF's ballistic comparison system and the department's own firearms examiner, we were able to match the bullets and casings used in the Delray homicide with those collected at another local crime scene. Better yet, last week a fisherman scooped a Sig Sauer 1911 .22 caliber pistol out of the river. Ballistics linked the firearm to both those crimes and traced it to the gun owner, a man named Victor Alonzo. He's a bartender at the Shakes Tavern on Mallory Road. He claimed the gun was stolen and didn't realize it till recently when he reported it as such. Personally, I have my doubts, but he's been largely uncooperative with the police. I figured he might sing a different tune with you."

"Worth a shot," Liam agreed, "figuratively speaking."

"My thoughts exactly. What do you have to lose?" Guillermo finished off the beer and stood up. "Let me know if you get anything useful out of Alonzo…"

"Will do." Liam took another sip of the beer. "Another one of these has your name on it the next time you drop by."

Guillermo grinned. "I'm counting on it."

Liam saw him out and wasted little time before texting Jessica to meet him at the Shakes Tavern for a little chat with Victor Alonzo.

Chapter Forty-Four

"Y ou think this Victor Alonzo can really tell us anything useful?" Jessica questioned, sitting behind the wheel of her car.

Liam had waited in the parking lot of the Shakes Tavern for her arrival, before sliding into the passenger seat, where he brought her up to date on his conversation with Detective Guillermo. This included the cooling off on the search for the bicycle used by a killer and ended with the discovery of a supposedly stolen Sig Sauer 1911 that was linked to the shooting death of Brittany Delray. "We won't know till we talk to him," Liam answered cryptically, knowing he owed her more. "In my experience, people will often bottle up when speaking to the police, for fear that whatever they say will somehow ricochet back on them adversely. Sticking with the weapon being stolen theme can usually avoid that. My guess is there's another explanation for how his weapon ended up in the hands of a killer, short of him being the culprit—"

"Well, let's go inside and see what he has to say..." Jessica sounded hopeful this time.

Liam nodded, while tempering his own expectations, in spite of what he told her. But at this point, any leads were worth pursuing in trying to crack the case that had an innocent woman on trial, in essence, for her life.

They left the car and went inside the tavern. There was not much going on at this time of day, but a few drinkers were present nonetheless. Liam spotted a tall, fortysomething Hispanic male behind the bar, wearing a gray pocket T-shirt and faded jeans. His brownish blonde hair was in a rope ponytail. They approached, and Liam asked, "Are you Victor Alonzo?"

He narrowed brown eyes. "Who's asking?"

This was where it got tricky for Liam. He didn't want them to be viewed as a threat to the man as authority figures. But they couldn't afford to walk away empty-handed either, if he was the right person. "Liam Reed," he told him, "private investigator. This is my associate..." Liam added, sticking to a need-to-know basis in keeping Jessica's name out of it for now. "We're looking into the death of a college student named Brittany Delray."

"Yeah, so what's that got to do with me?" The bartender peered at them suspiciously and, whether intentional or not, verified that he was, in fact, Victor Alonzo.

"We were told that the stolen gun used in the crime was registered to you," Jessica spoke up.

"I had nothing to do with that," he said defensively. "The gun was reported stolen."

Liam leaned forward. "I get that this is your official story and you're sticking to it, but as we believe there may be a serial killer on the loose that used your gun to take at least one life, we could really use your help in trying to get a lead on the perpetrator. If not for us, do it for Brittany Delray's family..." Liam hoped this angle might somehow jar his memory.

Alonzo pondered the notion for a long moment, and then said opportunistically, "Just how much is this information worth to you—?"

Liam had anticipated this possibility. Though he didn't make a habit of paying for information, in this instance, he would make an exception if it led to something worthwhile. He took out his wallet and removed two hundred-dollar bills, sliding them onto the counter. "That's all I have," he lied with a straight face. When Alonzo eagerly reached for the money, Liam slapped a hand on it. "Not so fast, pal. What can you tell us...?"

The bartender pursed his lips. "Okay. I do know something, but don't expect me to ever repeat this to the cops..."

"No one's asking you to," Jessica said tartly. "We're listening—"

Alonzo pinched his long nose. "A while back, this good-looking lady came in here and, well, we ended up back at my place, in bed..." He slanted his face thoughtfully. "While engaged in pillow talk, she asked about a firearm...

Said something about needing to protect her daughter—" He leaned against the counter. "I handed her a loaded Sig Sauer 1911 I wasn't using any longer. Didn't think anything of it, till the cops came around and said it was involved in a homicide... So there you have it—" He reached for the money once more.

Intrigued by the story and the unexpected twist that a female had, in fact, been given the firearm and used it to kill Delray, Liam again blocked his hand. "Do you happen to have the name of this lady?"

"Just Brenda," he answered curtly.

"Can you describe her?" Jessica asked, a catch to her voice.

Alonzo fidgeted. "Yeah, about forty, tall and slender, just like I like them, with short brunette hair, cut straight... Her eyes were a blue and gray combo." He wrinkled his nose. "Now do I get the money, or what—?"

Liam exchanged glances with Jessica as the description registered for them at once. *Sounds a hell of a lot like Brenda Kingsley,* he told himself, the Wryer College librarian and, more importantly, the mother of OD victim Nicole Kingsley. He removed his hand and allowed Alonzo to scoop up the bills like a vulture zeroing in on the decaying remains of a dead animal.

As he tried to come to grips with this possibility, Liam watched as Jessica took out her cell phone and texted someone. She assured Alonzo it wasn't the police and whispered to Liam that she was texting Cecelia Temple to see if she might have a photograph of Nicole's mother. Within moments, Cecelia responded with a picture of Nicole with Brenda Kingsley.

Jessica showed it to Alonzo and asked, "Is this the Brenda you gave the gun to?"

He studied it for only a moment, before replying, "Yeah, that's her—"

"Thanks for your help," Liam told him plainly.

"Where can I find Brenda?" he asked hotly, as if privy to something they were not.

"If she's the person we fear she may be, you're better off not knowing, trust me," Liam cautioned him. On the other hand, he was sure the authorities would be very interested in this new development.

Just as they were about to leave, Alonzo stopped them when he said ominously, "I almost hate to say this... Though I willingly parted with the

Sig Sauer 1911, while I was sleep, the bitch helped herself to another one of my handguns, a SAR Compact 9-millimeter pistol, along with the ammo for it—" He frowned. "Haven't reported it," he admitted. "Just thought you might want to know. She may have dumped the Sig Sauer in the river, but she's still packing heat..."

That was just what Liam was afraid of as he and Jessica assessed the threat suddenly posed by Brenda Kingsley, who may have been gunning for survivors of The Sexy Coeds Club, whatever her as yet unknown motivation was. Assuming the police couldn't get to her first.

Outside, Jessica furrowed her brow as she said musingly, "During the trial, a retired dentist testified that she had seen a woman pacing about at the apartment complex around the time the 911 call came in. Though she believed it was Stephanie that she saw, what if it was actually Brenda at the apartment just before or after she murdered Kristine?"

"It would certainly fit," Liam entertained the thought. "Particularly when pieced together with the other killings of The Sexy Coeds Club members—"

"I was thinking the same thing," Jessica confessed.

"Now we just need to find Kingsley and get some answers," he uttered, feeling the sooner the better, all things considered. He walked Jessica to her car, where she headed off to see her client.

In his own car, Liam phoned Guillermo with the news linking the gun that killed Brittany Delray to Brenda Kingsley, with the college librarian a possible serial killer. At first, the detective was skeptical on the serial murderer angle. "Why would Kingsley target these girls?" he questioned.

"I'm guessing it has something to do with her daughter, Nicole," Liam responded. "Maybe her fatal drug overdose and blaming The Sexy Coeds Club for it—" At least that was as good a preliminary explanation to him as any. "Kristine McVeigh was the initial leader of the club. As a result, that put an X on her back for someone to go after."

"Even if that were true, how does any of this help Stephanie Dozier?" Guillermo asked bluntly. "As of now, she's still on trial for the murder of McVeigh—with no indication Kingsley or anyone else was directly or otherwise involved in the homicide..."

"I get that," Liam conceded sourly, knowing time was still running out to prove the innocence of Jessica's client, in spite of the latest revelations. "And that's why Kingsley needs to be brought in for questioning...to see just how far and wide her actions have been—" Even so, he wasn't ruling out that any of the men the coed club extorted money from were still capable of exacting vengeance through the eliminations, one by one. Beginning with the stabbing death of Kristine McVeigh.

Based on what he had given Guillermo, particularly in relation to the killing of Brittany Delray and likely, Danielle Osmond, at the very least, Liam was told that a BOLO was issued for the serial murder suspect, Brenda Kingsley.

Chapter Forty-Five

Jessica tried to wrap her mind around the concept that Brenda Kingsley, the mother of Nicole Kingsley, may have been behind the murder of Kristine McVeigh and other former members of The Sexy Coeds Club. But why? What reason would the librarian have for targeting her late daughter's friends? It was something Jessica intended to ask Stephanie as she waited for her client to enter the room, with Stephanie's own fate still hanging in the balance. But they suddenly had a new reason to have hope for a desirable outcome.

When Stephanie walked in, Jessica could see that she was wary of the impromptu meeting. "What's wrong?" she asked nervously.

"Actually, there's been a positive development," Jessica told her, and waited for Stephanie to take a seat.

"Really?" Her voice was suddenly full of anticipation that someway, somehow, she could come out of this without being unjustly convicted of a violent crime.

Jessica sat up straight. "Did you know Nicole Kingsley?"

Stephanie hesitated in hearing the name. "I only knew her as a friend of Kristine's," she answered. "We didn't hang out together, or anything."

"Do you know what happened to her?"

Stephanie nodded somberly. "She died of a drug overdose. Everyone on campus was talking about it." She paused. "Why are you asking about her?"

"I'm getting to that," Jessica said evenly. "Before her death, Nicole was a member of The Sexy Coeds Club, according to other members."

"I'm not surprised." Stephanie frowned. "Seems like I was the only person

230

in Nicole's inner circle that wasn't invited to the party."

"Believe me, that's a good thing," Jessica said, assuming she believed otherwise. "Extorting money from sex-crazed married men is not a smart move. Especially at the risk of one or more of them retaliating." On that note, she couldn't help but wonder if anyone the club was blackmailing might still be involved in one or more of the coed murders.

"Yeah, I suppose you're right," Stephanie allowed. "It definitely wasn't my thing."

"I'm sure Kristine picked up on that in deciding to bypass you for her sex club..." Jessica paused musingly. "Getting back to Nicole... Did you ever meet her mother, Brenda?"

"No, not that I can recall." Stephanie made a face. "Why would I have?"

Jessica pulled up the photograph on her cell phone of the woman and her daughter, showing it to Stephanie. "Here she is with Nicole. Do you recognize her?"

Stephanie blinked. "Yeah, I think she works in the school library."

"Bingo!" Jessica voiced animatedly. "Her full name is Brenda Kingsley."

"Why do you care about her?" Stephanie asked curiously.

"She may be at the center of everything you're going through," Jessica pointed out.

Stephanie shook her head. "I don't understand."

"I have reason to believe Brenda is the person who shot to death Brittany Delray..." Jessica let that sink in, before adding, "That same person is linked to the death of Danielle Osmond." Jessica eyed Stephanie. "I think she may have also been the one to kill Kristine and left you to take the wrap for it..."

Stephanie stared at the notion. "Why would Ms. Kingsley do any of that?"

"I honestly don't know," confessed Jessica. "I think it has something to do with her daughter's OD death. She may be blaming it on The Sexy Coeds Club members."

"But I'm not a member of the club," she pointed out.

"Maybe she didn't know that." Jessica considered this. "Or maybe she did know and deliberately set you up to throw the police off her trail."

"Wow." Stephanie's eyes popped wide. "This just keeps getting weirder and weirder."

"Tell me about it." Jessica leaned forward contemplatively. "How often did you engage with Brenda Kingsley at the library?"

"Not much. I just asked her where to find books every now and then."

"Did she ever seek you out?"

"Not that I can recall..." Stephanie touched the table. "Once maybe... She asked me about bicycles...if I could recommend one. Said she was thinking about trading in her car to get more exercise."

"Did you?" Jessica gazed at her thoughtfully. "Recommend a type of bicycle?"

"Yeah, I think so," Stephanie mused. "I just told her the first thing that came to mind. Most everyone I know pretty much rides the same bike."

"Like the ones used in the campus bicycle share program?"

"Yeah." Stephanie narrowed her eyes. "What does that have to do with anything?"

"Maybe nothing," Jessica said, an edge to her voice. "Or maybe everything... Do you remember when you last spoke to Brenda?"

"It was the same day that Kristine was killed..." Stephanie sucked in a deep breath. "I was at the library to bring a book back and just said hello."

"Could she have been within ear range when you were on your cell phone?" Jessica asked, in recalling Brody's testimony under cross-examination.

Stephanie pondered this. "I called Brody to tell him I was on my way to his apartment," she uttered. "Ms. Kingsley, who was putting books on a shelf, might have heard me." Stephanie fluttered her lashes. "What does any of this mean?"

"It means she could have used this information to track your movements," Jessica surmised. "If so, Brenda would have known Kristine would be alone, and was able to put the wheels in motion to murder her and set you up to take the fall."

"Wow." Stephanie's voice shook. "That's insane."

"Or quite clever—in a homicidal way," Jessica calculated.

"Are you going to be able to prove any of this before a jury can find me guilty of killing Kristine...?"

"I don't know," Jessica had to be honest with her client. "The retired dentist that testified she thought she may have seen you lurking around the apartment building around the time of the murder, may in fact have actually spotted Brenda at the complex...the police are looking for her. When they find her, maybe she can provide the answers... Until then, I'll keep fighting for you and do whatever I can to see to it that justice is served."

"Okay," Stephanie uttered with a hopeful sigh.

Jessica offered her a tender smile, belying the fact that her own heart was beating like a drum as she awaited the apprehension of Brenda Kingsley and how that might impact the case against her client.

As Stephanie's life remained on hold, Jessica left the building and texted Liam to meet at her office to discuss the latest revelations. When she arrived there and headed inside toward the elevators, Jessica came face to face with a stern-faced Brenda Kingsley, who was armed with a handgun, pointed at her.

Chapter Forty-Six

J ust as Liam was about to make his way across the street to head to Jessica's office, he spotted her leaving the building. Only she wasn't alone. Standing behind her, but very close, was another woman he instantly recognized as Brenda Kingsley. By the way, her arm was positioned against the back of Jessica, it was obvious to him that she was directing her at gunpoint. Liam's first instinct was to reach into his shoulder holster for the Smith & Wesson M&P Shield EZ 380 Auto pistol. But, apart from not wanting to endanger Jessica any more than she already was, he didn't want to take down Kingsley. Especially if she was the key to solving the mystery of Kristine McVeigh's murder, along with that of her fellow The Sexy Coeds Club members. So, instead, Liam chose to follow the two women and wait for an opportune moment to get the jump on Brenda Kingsley. In the meantime, he took out his cell phone and called Guillermo to pass along the spotting and location of the murder suspect.

* * *

Jessica was sure she saw Liam out of the corner of her eye, as she was forced out of the building by the gun-toting Brenda Kingsley. "Where are we going?" she asked her toughly.

"Away from here," Brenda snorted. "We'll take your car."

Jessica didn't make any sudden moves as she obeyed her, moving toward the vehicle parked on the street. "You don't have to do this." She tried to reason with the librarian.

"Shut up!" Brenda snapped. "Whatever happens, you brought this upon yourself."

"I don't understand." Jessica played dumb. "What did I ever do to you, besides try to get some information on your daughter, Nicole, in the course of defending my client in a murder trial?"

Brenda sneered. "You should have left well enough alone. Instead, you had to stick your nose where it wasn't wanted—screwing up everything..." She poked her in the back with the gun. "I intend to put a stop to it."

Jessica winced from the force of the gun barrel. Again, she pretended to be none the wiser to her position when responding, "I'm not sure I understand..."

"I think you do," Brenda pushed back as they reached the car on the passenger side. "You first, I'll follow..."

Jessica complied, sliding over into the driver's seat. She put on her seat belt and prepared herself for a wild ride.

As Brenda got in, she was momentarily distracted, looking to see if anyone was onto her, before saying petulantly, "Let's go."

Jessica asked curiously, "Where to...?"

"Just start driving," she responded vaguely. "And remember, I have the gun and will use it if you try anything funny."

Jessica didn't doubt that for one minute, all things considered, as she started the car and pulled onto the street. "You mean the same way you shot and killed Brittany Delray?" she had to ask, wanting to get as much out of her as possible.

Brenda turned to her, as if surprised. "How did you know?"

"I put it together after having a chat with Victor Alonzo, who gave you the gun," Jessica said boldly. "The police linked it to the bullets and shell casings involved in Brittany's murder. I'm guessing that's why you ditched the gun, which was pulled out of the river..." She glanced at her. "And replaced it with the SAR 9-millimeter pistol you stole from him."

Brenda muttered an expletive under her breath. "That bastard should have kept his mouth shut."

"He did, as far as the police." Jessica eyed her. "So, I take it you were responsible for the death of Danielle Osmond as well?"

Brenda didn't deny it. "Of course," she hissed. "That bitch deserved it. They both did…after what they put Nicole through."

Jessica glanced at the rear-view mirror and could see that Liam was close on their tail, but with enough distance to keep Brenda from figuring it out. *Keep her talking,* Jessica told herself. "You're blaming The Sexy Coeds Club for your daughter's overdose death?"

"You figured it out—hooray for you," she said sarcastically. "If not for them recruiting Nicole for their stupid club and turning her into an addict, my daughter would be alive today. Instead, her life was taken away in the cruelest of ways, when you need a fix so badly that you can't think straight. Nicole had everything to live for—till she didn't. They needed to pay for this."

"Did that include Kristine McVeigh?" Jessica got right down to the nitty gritty. "I mean, you are the one who stabbed her to death and not my client, right?"

"Yeah, I did it," she admitted without preface. "At this point, it doesn't matter if you know the truth. It won't be of much help to you…or Stephanie Dozier."

She intends to kill me, Jessica thought, not too surprisingly. Well, if that were the case, she certainly was not going to go down without one hell of a fight. She increased the speed gradually.

"As the Queen B of the bunch, Kristine needed to take the full brunt of my anger for what she and her cohorts turned my little girl into, nothing more than a whore and drug addict," Brenda expressed, dangling the gun haphazardly.

"But why set up Stephanie to take the fall?" questioned Jessica. "Or was that not part of the plan?"

"If you must know," Brenda said, nostrils flaring, "the plan was to kill that bitch too. She had to have known what was going on and didn't lift a finger to stop it. That made her just as guilty as the others…" After a heavy sigh, she continued, "But that stupid cop had to show up in the nick of time… saving her life."

CHAPTER FORTY-SIX

Jessica cocked a brow. "You mean you were there all along?"

"Yeah, I was there," she practically boasted. "The fact that Stephanie chose to pull the knife out of that bitch was on her—not me. It worked out well enough, with her being charged with the murder. Maybe she'll still be found guilty—in spite of your best efforts to convince the jury otherwise. Including trying to make those other whores from their blackmail club appear like saints in court."

"That was never my intention," Jessica pointed out truthfully. "Whatever they did illegally, the girls will be held accountable for. I only wanted to help my client, whose only crime was choosing the wrong person to room with."

"And choosing the wrong person to represent her," Brenda spat testily.

"What do you plan to do to me?" Jessica increased the speed again, once they were on the open road.

"You need to even ask?" The librarian chortled mockingly. "You're going to have a little accident in the river—with no one to save you from drowning…"

No one but myself, Jessica thought, as she once again checked out Liam's car in the rear-view mirror. He had kept pace and was now narrowing the gap. Not confident in his heroic efforts, she pressed down on the accelerator.

Brenda noticed. "Slow down," she demanded. When Jessica refused, she pointed the gun at her face and said menacingly, "I mean it, slow down now, or I'll kill you and take my chances."

Deciding this was the right time to honor her wishes as someone not wearing a seat belt, Jessica pressed down hard on the brake pedal and swerved sharply at the same time. The car came to a sudden stop and Brenda was thrust forward, slamming her face against the dashboard. The gun went flying and, though shaken, Jessica unlocked her door and got out of the car as her dazed kidnapper tried to recover.

Liam drove up behind them, sprang out of his car, and ran up to Jessica, who was standing on wobbly legs. "Are you all right?" he asked, the strain of concern etched in his face.

"Yes," she assured him, while feeling comfort in having him near and ready to defend her from an enemy.

"Good. If anything had happened to you, I..." His voice broke.

"I know." She met his eyes emotionally. "I wasn't going to make it easy for her to finish me off."

Liam half grinned. "I think she learned that the hard way."

Jessica glanced at her car and could make out her assailant, who seemed to be stirring. "Better check on Brenda Kingsley, before she somehow manages to get away and disappear forever."

"No chance of that," he promised. "Her days of murder and madness are over."

Jessica watched as he removed his firearm from a holster and approached her vehicle, just as Brenda stumbled out. Liam made a citizen's arrest as the police arrived, handcuffed her, and took her away.

* * *

Jessica brought her client up to date on the arrest of Brenda Kingsley and the failed attempt on her own life by the vengeful-minded librarian.

"I can't believe she tried to kill you!" Stephanie's eyes widened. "Or that she planned to kill me after using the knife on Kristine."

"The entire twisted scenario does boggle the mind," Jessica admitted, still shaken at the thought that Brenda would take such drastic measures to settle the score against anyone she believed played a role in her daughter's death, or offering assistance to those she saw as responsible for Nicole's fatal overdose.

"So, what's going to happen now?" Stephanie asked anxiously. "Will she pay for what she's done?"

"Well, for starters, the police will want to interrogate her and see if Brenda will stand by her confession that it was she—and not you—who actually stabbed to death Kristine." Jessica sighed as she sat next to her client. "Then they will want to try and corroborate this with any solid evidence the police can obtain."

Stephanie's shoulders slumped. "But what if they can't find anything to support her confession? Will I end up still being convicted for what she did to Kristine?"

Jessica put a comforting arm around her shoulder. "I'm sure they will be able to build a convincing case against Brenda Kingsley," she tried to reassure her. "The woman kidnapped and planned to murder me and has been implicated in the deaths of Brittany Delray and Danielle Osmond. It stands to reason that the police and the D.A.'s office will tie this together with the death of Kristine McVeigh, in relation to Nicole Kingsley's death and The Sexy Coeds Club, as motive for murder."

At least this was what Jessica was counting on in an expedited manner, with everything coming to a head as the jury considered the case as it now stood.

Chapter Forty-Seven

M adeleine was not particularly comfortable giving her closing arguments, in spite of what she still believed was overwhelming evidence of Stephanie Dozier's guilt. But with the arrest of Brenda Kingsley and, according to Jessica Frost, an as yet unverified confession to the murder of Kristine McVeigh, along with a full-fledged police investigation into a related campus sex ring, extortion, illegal drug use, and serial murder, in Madeleine's mind all bets were suddenly off. Yet with no desire to delay the proceedings prematurely, she was obliged to press forward, with the presumption that the defendant was actually responsible for her roommate's death, unless proven otherwise.

When the judge motioned for her to proceed, Madeleine looked at her opposing counsel and the defendant, trying to read their minds as to where this might be headed, before she took measured steps toward the jury and said coolly, "Ladies and gentleman, this trial is about to reach its conclusion... I'm sure you're eager to return to your normal lives. But before you do, you have an important decision to make. You must decide whether or not on the evening of Friday, October fourteenth, of last year, the defendant, Stephanie Dozier, did in fact willfully and maliciously commit coldblooded murder in the first degree in stabbing to death the young woman with whom she shared an apartment, Kristine McVeigh.

"Now I know that the defense has argued that Ms. McVeigh's death came as the result of being part of a campus sex ring that targeted married professors and engaged in blackmail and the like, causing someone to lash out at the victim as a consequence..." Madeleine considered the most recent twists to the story weaved by Jessica. "There's even the suggestion that Ms. McVeigh may have met her demise at the hands of a crazy and vindictive mother of one of the members of this group called The Sexy Coeds Club.

"Well, folks, this trial is not about dealing with conjecture and wild theories," she maintained. "It's your job as the jury to look at the facts of the case and the hard evidence to support these facts before rendering your verdict... This violent crime comes down to one thing, jealous rage." Madeleine paused theatrically. "Ms. McVeigh is dead today because she made the mistake of having sex with the defendant's boyfriend, Brody Krane. This act of betrayal enraged the defendant to the point that she wanted her roommate dead and made that happen."

Madeleine eyed Stephanie with a mixture of determination and uncertainty, before turning back to the jury and continuing in her prosecutorial form. "The victim, Ms. McVeigh, was stabbed fourteen times with a ten-inch serrated knife, with the clear intent to do a lot of damage in the process of taking away her life. The defendant was caught by the arresting officer, holding the murder weapon while hovering over the victim triumphantly," she reminded them. "Ms. McVeigh's DNA was all over the knife, along with her fingerprints. The only other DNA on the murder weapon came from the victim, as the result of the knife entering her body repeatedly. The motive and means were there in black and white, ladies and gentlemen, to carry out this crime of passion.

"For someone other than the defendant to have perpetrated this violent act, one would have to believe that this person somehow magically appeared and then vanished like a thief in the night, without leaving a trace of evidence to this effect." Madeleine sighed dramatically. "I don't believe in magic and I don't think you do either. As such, I am sure you will come to the only decision you can when combining the evidence and common sense in finding the defendant, Stephanie Dozier, guilty beyond a reasonable doubt."

Madeleine stepped away, confident she had made her case, while nervous at the same time that another person may well have pulled a rabbit out of the hat in murdering Kristine McVeigh. Meaning, it could cause the entire scenario that pointed solidly at the defendant as a murderess to fall apart.

* * *

Investigator Payne had once thought it was an open and shut case against Stephanie Dozier in the murder of Kristine McVeigh. Now he was having some serious second thoughts in the face of new considerations to contend with. They had picked up a suspect, Brenda Kingsley, after Detective Guillermo had managed to link her to the gun used to kill Brittany Delray. And according to a statement by attorney Jessica Frost, whom Kingsley abducted at gunpoint, the mother of college student, Nicole Kingsley, who died of an OD, had confessed to murdering McVeigh as part of a revenge plot against The Sexy Coeds Club. Kingsley apparently blamed the club for turning her daughter out and into a drug addict.

Payne had yet to interview the suspect but, given the implications involving three murders of coeds he was investigating, he had gotten a judge to sign off on a warrant to search the home of Brenda Kingsley for any evidence that might support her being a single or serial killer. Though Kingsley purportedly lived alone, Payne and the rest of the team were taking no chances as they descended upon the ranch-style home on Clarkson Lane. Armed with a Glock 26 pistol, he knocked hard on the door and yelled, "Police! We have a search warrant. Open up."

With no response, he repeated this, and again there was no answer. There were no sounds to indicate someone was inside. Still, it was possible, so they prepared themselves for a confrontation before Payne gave the order to use a battering ram to force open the door. Storming inside, they spread across the acacia hardwood flooring of the single-story house, quickly determining that there was no threat to contend with.

Putting on nitrile gloves, Payne searched for possible evidence in the tidy residence with contemporary furnishings and flowering house plants. When he entered a room where the door had been closed, he was surprised to see what amounted to a shrine, with articles about Nicole Kingsley, her life, and her death; along with numerous photographs and candles. Payne lifted a framed photo, gazing at the good-looking coed, tall and slender, with blue eyes and a long reddish-blonde mullet hairstyle. He gazed at another picture of her as a high school cheerleader. Other photographs of her were at various ages, some including her mother, Brenda Kingsley. It was more than enough to convince him that the woman was unnaturally obsessed with her daughter. That type of obsession, in his experience, made the person capable of anything. Did that include serial murder and other violent criminal behavior?

"That's some serious fixation," Detective Imogen Loughlin caught his attention.

"Tell me about it." Payne turned away from the disturbing site and faced the petite junior detective with cropped sandy-colored hair and hazel eyes.

"There's something else you need to see..." she spoke ambiguously.

Following her to a door off the kitchen that led to the garage, Payne immediately laid eyes on a black bicycle with red drop handlebars.

"Are you thinking what I'm thinking?" Imogen challenged him.

"Very much so," he responded musingly, as Payne saw what could be the bike used by the person responsible for the deaths of Brittany Delray and Danielle Osmond.

Chapter Forty-Eight

"Your closing arguments, Counselor…" Judge Kuailani-Sinclair eyed Jessica as it was time for her to rebut what Madeleine said to the jury as her parting shot in trying to convict Stephanie.

Even with the opposing counsel's persuasive arguments, Jessica sensed that Madeleine's heart wasn't in it like before, now that there was credible evidence that someone other than the defendant might have murdered Kristine McVeigh. But like the prosecutor, Jessica had to go through the motions in presenting her summation. She understood that, in spite of the fact that Brenda Kingsley had brazenly admitted to stabbing to death Kristine, and the murder of her two friends, Brittany Delray and Danielle Osmond, all part of The Sexy Coeds Club, in a convoluted vendetta to avenge her daughter's death, this was not necessarily enough in and of itself to get the charge against Stephanie dropped. Jessica could only pray that, with Brenda now in custody after kidnapping her with the full intent to kill her, the police found the corroborating evidence that would implicate the unstable and dangerous woman in Kristine McVeigh's murder and allow justice to prevail. *Until then, it's business as usual*, Jessica told herself as she made her way toward the jurors, hoping to convince them to take her side on the merits of the too hard to ignore holes she presented in the prosecution's case.

"Ladies and gentlemen," Jessica began, maintaining a level, respectful tone of voice, "we're all here for one reason and one reason only. That is to see to it that justice is properly served. Not denied. And certainly not misjudged. The prosecution's case has been largely based on the premise that the defendant, Stephanie Dozier, in a jealous fury, stormed from her boyfriend's apartment—in a time frame that defies the laws of nature—arrived at her own apartment, where she grabbed a knife from the kitchen and went straight to the bedroom of her roommate, Kristine McVeigh, and proceeded to stab Ms. McVeigh to death where she lay sleeping. Then, against all logic, the defendant supposedly remained there, knife in hand, waiting for the police to arrive—as if she had built-in radar to that effect—just so she could be arrested and mess up the rest of her life." Jessica made a sarcastic face. "Does any of this really seem logical to you? It doesn't to me. People don't just commit such heinous acts and say frivolously, So, here I am—you caught me. Do with me what you will.

"Let's talk about the jealousy angle that is supposed to be the centerpiece of this murder," Jessica said calculatingly. "Or, more specifically, a love triangle, which is what we're talking about. Well, folks, I can tell you from firsthand experience, it happens. Some men turn out to be assholes, okay? Some women too. Even high school girls and boys experience this with crushes and rivalries, as has been alluded to during this trial. It's part of life and love that many of us have to deal with. But that doesn't mean we use this as a justification to take the life of another out of spite, misguided feelings, or just plain old indignation. None of these were the case in this instance," she insisted. "I submit to you that the only thing Stephanie Dozier is guilty of is naivety and trying to help her best friend. The defendant was twenty-one at the time, an age when most of us dream of reaching for the stars, but not being faced with seeing someone close to us suffering greatly. She didn't take the time to think about DNA, fingerprints, being caught red-handed, so to speak, with a weapon of murder in hand innocently and hardly with malicious intent. She made an honest mistake for all the right reasons and shouldn't have to pay for it for the rest of her life—beyond the heavy toll it's already taken on her these past months."

Jessica gazed at Stephanie in earnest, knowing that the very cop that was responsible for her current predicament had also, in an ironic twist, inadvertently saved her life, as Brenda Kingsley had fully intended to snuff it out like a candle. Thank goodness, her diabolical plans had fallen flat. Eyeing the jury again, Jessica continued her final remarks. "So, if the defendant did not kill Ms. McVeigh, as the prosecution would have you believe, then who did, given everything that's been laid out to you during this trial? Well, as the defense attorney, I have laid out a credible case for McVeigh's murder being associated with her leadership role in a college sex ring, where a group of so-called sexy coeds were seducing married professors and blackmailing them for money to keep it quiet... It made sense that one of these men would retaliate against such a threat to their marriage and reputation."

Jessica took a moment to gather her thoughts as to just how far she should go from this point on. *I don't want to get too ahead of myself before the police can announce their own conclusions in the investigation,* she told herself, *possibly hurting my client's chances for an acquittal in the process.* Yet, it was imperative that she lay enough cards on the table to give the jury the necessary and relevant information to work with before they began deliberations. Assuming it got that far. "My views, in this regard, as to the killing of Kristine McVeigh have shifted... You will soon learn that another person not only had a strong motive for committing the murder, but the means to carry it out. I, myself, was quite recently abducted at gunpoint by a woman whose daughter was a former member of The Sexy Coeds Club and died from a drug overdose. The mother had a serious beef with the club and Ms. McVeigh, in particular—holding them accountable for her daughter's death. She intended to make the coeds pay, one by one, beginning with Kristine McVeigh...then with two other members of the club, who were murdered in the past few months... I barely escaped the vengeful woman's wrath alive. The same is true for the defendant, whom my abductor told me she had planned to do away with—in some mistaken belief that she was part of The Sexy Coeds Club—after finishing off Ms. McVeigh in the knife attack. Had Officer Bean not arrived at precisely the right time, none of us would be here today with the defendant on trial after being falsely accused of murder."

Jessica took in a deep breath and then finished evenly with, "I understand that your job as jurors is to weigh the evidence and testimony against the defendant and not another person who is not on trial today...but given the very real likelihood that such a person will have her own day in court in the future, it is incumbent upon you to consider this during your deliberations. Unless you're able to say in good conscience that the defendant, Ms. Dozier, is guilty beyond a reasonable doubt, then you have no choice but to find her not guilty. Thank you for your service and I trust you will make the right decision."

Jessica walked away feeling good about putting her best feet forward in presenting her case and laying the groundwork for an appeal, in the unlikely but still possible event that her client would be found guilty, all things considered. Especially given the arrest of Brenda Kingsley and imminent charges to follow—not the least of which was kidnapping and attempted murder. But her own ordeal notwithstanding, it was Brenda's role in the death of Kristine McVeigh that left Jessica most on edge with the seconds ticking like a time bomb as her client's fate hung in the balance.

* * *

"Any news from the police...?" Jessica asked Liam anxiously, as they sat in the waiting room while the jury began its deliberations.

"Only that Detective Payne is currently interrogating Brenda Kingsley," he told her, having been on and off his phone to his contact in the department, Detective Guillermo. Seeing the uncertainty in Jessica's eyes, Liam added reassuringly, "Hey, they got their suspect and, from what I hear, she's talking... They also confiscated a bicycle from her garage that the authorities believe was used by the person who gunned down Brittany Delray and pushed Danielle Osmond in front of a moving car. The wheels are turning, no pun intended," he said confidently.

"Maybe they could turn just a bit faster," Jessica muttered wryly, wringing her hands. "My client should not have to sweat it out any more than necessary while a jury holds her fate in its collective hands."

"I couldn't agree with you more." Liam took her trembling hand. He admired how committed she was in defending her clients to the point of making it personal. Though he tried to maintain a healthy distance between him and his own clients, Liam felt that if he ever needed a lawyer, he would definitely want to have Jessica in his corner. For now, he happily settled for just having her in his life and giving him reason to believe she felt the same about him and was ready to tackle the future together. This sense of longing and gratefulness was especially true with her close brush with death. If Kingsley had her way, Jessica would have been submerged, along with her car, in the Creighton River. And his journey with the beautiful attorney would have been over before it had been given the proper time to blossom. "Whatever happens, Stephanie is the better for it with you representing her interests," he stressed. "Let the system of checks and balances work and good things will happen."

Jessica smiled at him tellingly. "You're right and I will..." Now she took his hand. "Good things are already happening."

Liam grinned. "There you go," he jumped on the moment. "Justice will prevail, even if it can sometimes be justice delayed." As he sat on that thought, Liam was admittedly just as eager to receive information on the status of the police investigation into Brenda Kingsley as a possible serial killer and, with near certainty, the person responsible for the death of Kristine McVeigh; before the jury came back in.

Chapter Forty-Nine

P ayne sat across the table from the suspect in the interrogation room. He had let her sit alone for a little while, as he conferred with his colleagues on the other side of the one-way mirror. There was good reason to believe that Brenda Kingsley was a bona fide serial killer, with at least two murders that could be linked to her, as well as kidnapping and attempted murder. But it was a third possible murder that was particularly significant to him, given the trial underway and, he understood, the jury already in deliberations. Had the forty-three-year-old suspect actually been the killer of Kristine McVeigh, as alleged in the full statement given by Jessica Frost, who was representing Stephanie Dozier, the one on trial for the murder? Or would Kingsley deny this when given the opportunity to come clean officially?

May as well get to it, Payne told himself, realizing time was of the essence. The suspect had already been read her rights, including having an attorney present, but refused representation. *A good sign*, the investigator thought. "Do you mind if I record this?" he asked routinely.

She shrugged. "Whatever you need to do."

He took that as a yes, turning on the recorder. "State your name, please?"

"Brenda Kingsley," she muttered.

"Do you understand why you're here?" he asked in a polite tone, as though speaking to a child.

She grimaced. "Of course. I'm here because that bitch attorney pulled a fast one on me before I could do what I intended to with her."

"Which was?" Payne peered at the suspect.

"What do you think?" she hissed, wincing from the bruise on her forehead she'd received after hitting her head on the dashboard of the defense lawyer's vehicle. "Kill her by forcing her to drive her car into the river, where I would get out safely and she wouldn't—"

He glanced at the mirror and back, while musing about Jessica's smart maneuver with her vehicle that probably saved her life. "Why did you try to kill Ms. Frost?"

Brenda, who was handcuffed, glowered scornfully. "She got in my way."

"How so?"

"By aligning herself with those bitches from The Sexy Coeds Club. She offered them advice and protection. I couldn't let her get away with that."

But she did get away—at least from you, he thought. "Let's talk a little about The Sexy Coeds Club..." Payne glanced at some notes before him. "I understand that your daughter, Nicole, was once a member. Is that right?"

"Yes, she belonged to the club of whores, drug abusers, and extortionists," Brenda growled like an animal. "I tried my best to get Nicole out of it, but she was hooked on the sex, drugs, and money. Eventually, it killed her."

Payne didn't doubt that, knowing the coed had OD'd last year. But the suspect had given him some context, from her point of view. "So, you wanted to avenge her death by going after other members of the group?"

"Yeah, that's right," she admitted. "They had it coming—all of them."

He leaned forward. "We used a search warrant to find a bicycle in your garage. Surveillance video picked up a bike matching this description ridden by someone who shot to death Brittany Delray. We were able to recover the murder weapon and link it to the three bullets fired into the victim at point blank range. Were you the bicyclist and shooter?"

"Yeah, it was me." Brenda curled her lip bitingly. "I followed her from the hotel where she had sex with another sleazebag that the whore intended to blackmail to keep his secret from the wife."

Payne took that as a confession to murder. "The bicycle also matched the description of one involved in the death of Danielle Osmond, who was pushed into oncoming traffic, resulting in a fatality." He met her cold eyes. "Was that you, too?"

Brenda nodded, as if nothing more than a walk in the park, instead of murder. "Yeah, I killed her...or made sure someone else did. Just like the others, the bitch thought she could just continue to play with other people's lives, without paying the price. Doesn't work that way. Not for her any longer."

Chalk up another homicide case solved, for all intents and purposes, Payne told himself gladly. Those were the easy ones, relatively speaking. Now came the one that wasn't so cut and dried in his mind. "Let's talk about Kristine McVeigh."

Brenda sighed. "What do you want to know, other than she's the biggest bitch of them all as the first leader of their sordid and greedy group..."

Payne couldn't argue with the suspect that the coeds got way over their heads in their sex-based illegal actions—and some paid the ultimate price. But in McVeigh's case, who was the culprit in her death, Stephanie Dozier, charged with the crime? Or the woman before him? "You know that McVeigh's roommate, Stephanie Dozier, is on trial right now for her murder..."

"Yeah... It worked out that way..." Brenda said, a catch to her voice. "It wasn't part of the plan."

Payne narrowed his eyes musingly. "Did you kill Ms. McVeigh?"

Brenda pursed her lips. "Yeah, I admit it. I took her life and would do so again, if given the chance. That bitch brought my beautiful Nicole into their stupid sex club, introduced her to fentanyl, watched as she got hooked, and then basically dropped her like a hot potato when Nicole needed her and the other girls the most."

Payne looked at the mirror, imagining the eyes rolling with shock over the suspect's statement and coldhearted manner. His instincts, combined with the other murders, had him believing that she stabbed to death Kristine McVeigh. But there was still the little matter of Stephanie Dozier and the evidence that pointed toward her as the killer. He gazed sharply at the suspect. "How did you kill McVeigh?"

"I stabbed her to death," Brenda boasted.

"With what?"

"A serrated knife I took out of a knife block in the kitchen."

Those details had become common knowledge by this stage, more or less, Payne knew. "How did you get inside the apartment?"

"Just walked right in," she admitted. "It wasn't locked. I knew that after overhearing Stephanie tell someone that over the phone when she was at the library..."

"What day was that?"

"The same day I killed that bitch—Kristine McVeigh."

Payne ran a hand across his chin. "I believe you...just need to clear up a few things." He met her gaze. "Since Stephanie Dozier was found holding the knife over the victim when a police officer arrived, can you explain how you killed McVeigh and escaped detection?"

"It's not that complicated, really." Brenda gave a sardonic chuckle. "I walked into the bedroom with the knife while she was asleep. After I plunged the knife into her so many times, my hand hurt, I was about to yank it out, when I heard someone enter the apartment. Panicking, I hid in the closet. That's when I saw through a crack, Stephanie come into the room. I hadn't expected her back quite so soon, after hearing her on the cell phone at the library tell her boyfriend she was coming over." The suspect grinned crookedly. "Actually, I thought that worked out perfectly, as I had intended to wait for Stephanie to return so I could kill her too—" Brenda frowned. "I couldn't believe that bitch was still alive when she begged Stephanie to pull the knife out. Like a dimwit, she did. I was about to take the knife from her, when the officer entered the room... I remained quiet as a mouse while he forced her to drop the knife and arrested her. I waited till the coast was clear before making my getaway."

Payne again glanced at the one-way mirror and back at the suspect with some qualm. "You're telling me that throughout this scenario you were hidden in the closet, with no one being the wiser?"

"Yeah, it's true," she insisted. "Between the time the officer took her away and others arrived, I managed to slip out and head back through the woods, where I had my bike. I rode home and no one suspected a thing."

"There was no other DNA on the knife, aside from Stephanie Dozier's and the victim," he pointed out. "Were you wearing gloves?"

"What do you think?" Brenda rolled her eyes. "I'm not stupid. Everyone who's ever watched any of those crime shows on TV knows you wear latex gloves to keep from leaving DNA and prints at the scene of a crime... So that's what I did. Oh, and before you ask, I got rid of the gloves and the clothes I wore, burying them."

Payne cocked a brow. "I don't suppose you could tell us where you buried these items?"

"I'd be happy to," she surprised him by saying. "But I want something in return."

He wasn't interested in making a deal prematurely with a serial murderer, but asked anyway, "And what would that be?"

"I want my daughter to have a headstone for her grave." Brenda lowered her head. "After she died, I couldn't afford one. I hated that." She lifted her face. "So, do we have a deal...and in writing?"

All things considered, Payne was sure that if she could truly lead them to the damaging evidence that could only have come from Kristine McVeigh's real murderer, the department would be happy to spring for a gravestone. Especially if it meant getting an innocent woman off the hook and a guilty one behind bars, where she belonged.

"You've got yourself a deal," he told Kingsley, "provided you deliver on the goods..."

Less than an hour later, Payne phoned Madeleine Griffin and said contritely, "We've got a problem with the case against Stephanie Dozier."

Chapter Fifty

"Are you sure about this?" Madeleine asked as she paced in her office, heart skipping a beat. She had just listened to the investigator tell her over the phone that the case against Stephanie Dozier had fallen apart like a house made of sand. Though this threw her for a loop, frankly, Madeleine had mentally prepared herself for the likelihood, given what had unfolded of late. Still, she needed to hear more.

"Yeah, I'm afraid so," Payne told her in a straight tone of voice. "Turns out, Stephanie Dozier is innocent after all in the death of Kristine McVeigh."

"Go on," Madeleine pressed, the wheels already spinning in her head as to what this meant in moving forward.

"We've filed charges against Brenda Kingsley," the detective informed her, "for not only the murder of McVeigh—but also for the murders of Brittany Delray and Danielle Osmond, as well as the kidnapping and attempted murder of Jessica Frost."

"Let's just stick with McVeigh's death for the moment," Madeleine stated anxiously, though sorry to hear about Jessica's frightening ordeal. "Talk to me."

"All right. Kingsley confessed to stabbing to death McVeigh," he pointed out. "She led us to where she buried the bloody clothing and the gloves she wore when carrying out the murder. Her and McVeigh's DNA were present on both." Payne sighed. "Kingsley hid in the closet after killing McVeigh and backed Dozier's story about pulling the knife out of the victim at her own request, just before Officer Bean arrived on the scene and made the arrest."

Madeleine blinked, a slice of skepticism remaining. "Could Kingsley and

Dozier have been in on it together?"

"No, Kingsley orchestrated and carried out the entire murder on her own," Payne insisted without hesitation. "It was part of a convoluted vendetta against the females involved in The Sexy Coeds Club. Kingsley blamed them for the overdose death of her daughter, Nicole, who was a member of the club, and for turning her into a sex worker, in effect. As the ringleader and the one who brought Nicole into the group and introduced her to drugs, McVeigh was targeted first by Kingsley, and bore the brunt of her rage… She confessed to planning to murder Dozier too, for rooming with McVeigh, whether a member of the club or not." Payne made a grunting sound. "Bottom line is we no longer have a case against Stephanie Dozier, so you need to end this trial before the jury reaches a verdict, and we can all get on with our lives. Especially, the defendant."

Madeleine heard him loud and clear. Having no grounds for arguing further, she called Jessica and requested that they meet in the judge's chambers pronto, while knowing that this changed everything, for better or worse.

* * *

"Madeleine has asked to meet with me in Judge Kuailani-Sinclair's chambers," Jessica informed Liam.

"That can only mean one thing," he told her confidently. "The charge against your client is being dropped."

This had, more or less, been confirmed by Detective Guillermo, Jessica knew. He had kept Liam in the loop as Detective Payne grilled the suspect and got the full confession he sought and the hard evidence to back it up. They had no choice but to do the right thing, even at this late stage in the legal proceedings. But she wasn't about to put the cart ahead of the horse. Not until this near miscarriage of justice was over for Stephanie and her family.

"I should go," Jessica said thoughtfully.

"Yeah." Liam gave her a supportive grin and then a kiss, as though to seal the deal. "Good luck."

"Thanks." She nodded appreciatively, touching her mouth where his lips had been. The tingling sensations were something she was getting used to and liked very much. Just as she liked him and what he was doing to her. Jessica knew she was doing just as much to Liam and it showed. Once they were past her current case, maybe they could work on that some more.

Ten minutes later, Jessica sat tensely beside Madeleine in the judge's chambers, as Judge Kuailani-Sinclair said with an edge to her tone, "This had better be good."

Madeleine swallowed thickly and said, "There's been a development." She laid out everything in a clear and concise way that left no doubt as to who the guilty party was in the death of Kristine McVeigh. And, more importantly, who was not.

The judge arched a thin brow. "Unbelievable," she uttered.

"Believe it," the prosecutor maintained respectfully. "We put the wrong person on trial, for what were all the right reasons at the time..."

Judge Kuailani-Sinclair gazed interestedly at Jessica. "And what do you have to say about this, Counselor?"

Instead of laying out a detailed diatribe of she told them so, Jessica responded evenly, "I have always maintained that my client was innocent in the death of her roommate. I'm delighted that the prosecution and police are now on board and have acted swiftly to prevent any further damage to the life of Stephanie Dozier."

"Well put, Ms. Frost," the judge said. "I agree that the important thing at this point is to do what is right." She took a breath. "Let's get this over with."

* * *

The jury was called back into court, before reaching a verdict, as Jessica whispered to her client, "You're about to get your freedom back and I couldn't be happier for you."

Stephanie forced a smile and said tentatively, "I'll believe it when I see it."

"You will," Jessica promised as the judge got everyone's attention.

"Ladies and gentlemen of the jury," Judge Kuailani-Sinclair said, "thank you for your service and considering the case as presented to you. Unfortunately, that case has proven to be highly misleading... New developments have emerged that have turned upside down everything we thought we knew..." She gazed at the defendant and asked, "Please stand, Ms. Dozier."

Stephanie rose to her feet, along with Jessica, and held the attorney's hand. "It's come to the attention of this court that another person has been charged with the murder of Kristine McVeigh," the judge continued. "It is believed that she acted alone and this belief is supported by the strong evidence pointing toward her guilt as the sole perpetrator in the young woman's death."

Judge Kuailani-Sinclair sighed. "There's not much I can say to justify the ordeal you've been put through," the judge spoke in earnest, "other than that I am very sorry. The justice system failed you and your family. Perhaps by reversing this injustice before it was too late and giving you your life back, it can in small measure make up for what was taken from you. The case is hereby dismissed. You are free to go, Ms. Dozier. I wish you well."

"Thank you, Your Honor," Stephanie voiced, as she broke into tears and hugged her lawyer. "And thank you for believing in me when no one else did."

"It's my job to do so," Jessica said modestly, her own eyes watery as she hugged her back, feeling both vindicated in the faith she had in her client and the justice system's remarkable ability to correct its own shortcomings. She wondered if Judge McVeigh and his wife felt the same as they headed out of the courtroom, seemingly defeated in their inability to control their daughter and the poor choices she made that ultimately proved too difficult to pull away from before tragedy struck.

As Stephanie raced to hug her parents, Madeleine came over to Jessica and said apologetically, "What can I say? We screwed up...big time."

"Yes, you did," Jessica told her flatly. She allowed that to sit for a moment, before letting her opponent down gently. "That said, you were only doing your job, Madeleine. Don't beat yourself up about it. The important thing is that my client was not convicted and sent to prison for something she didn't do. Everything else is part of the process we all go through in making sure mistakes such as this can be corrected in time, sparing the innocent from further suffering."

"I suppose." Madeleine nodded. "I'll try to do better the next time."

Jessica took that as a warning shot for future battles to come. "See you in court!"

As the prosecutor left, Liam came up to Jessica with a broad grin on his face. "Looks like justice has prevailed!"

"It has." She smiled back. "Thanks for all your help with this case. Couldn't have done it without you," Jessica surprised herself by saying. She was normally independent minded in her desire to go it alone. But he had made her have second thoughts about that. And she relished this feeling.

"Happy to do my small part in helping you to get your client off the chopping block," he said smoothly.

"We'll have to team up again sometime," she teased him.

"I'm game, whenever you need me or my services."

Jessica took that for what it was worth, which was plenty in her book. "That's good enough for me."

"What do you say we get out of here and celebrate this victory?" Liam looked at her ardently.

"Good idea," she agreed. "But first, there's a little more unfinished business to attend to—"

In front of the courthouse, Jessica stood alongside Stephanie and her parents to give a brief statement to the media and public, believing it was necessary to close out this case, arguably the most challenging of her career, thus far. "I would just like to say that my client has been through a painful experience that neither she nor I would wish on any innocent person thrust into a nightmare not of their own making. But, as a fighter, Ms. Dozier never gave up on the truth coming out and exonerating her. Neither did I. Now that she has been given her freedom, my client needs time to readjust to society, resume her college education, and properly grieve for the loss of her roommate and best friend, Kristine McVeigh. As such, I ask that you respect her privacy. Thank you."

Without taking any questions, Jessica ushered Stephanie away, knowing they both needed time to unwind and look ahead for whatever may come their way.

Epilogue

Two months later, Jessica stood in her new office at the Creighton Hills law firm of Nelson, Martinez, Frost, and Associates. The floor to ceiling window wall offered an amazing view of the river and sunny skies. After giving it much thought, she had decided to take her friend, Connie, up on her offer to join her practice as a partner. Though going it alone had brought her much satisfaction, Jessica found she was ready to share in the defense of clients and pursuit of justice, no matter how arduous the process might be. It was something she needed and it had worked out very well for her and the firm. Right away, she had been swamped with new and diverse cases that tested her skills and, at times, patience. She wouldn't have had it any other way.

Jessica sat down in her ergonomic desk chair and again gazed out the window thoughtfully. Her former client, Stephanie Dozier, was now back in school full-time, having put the ordeal of going on trial for the murder of her roommate, Kristine McVeigh, behind her. Jessica had heard that Stephanie was back together with her boyfriend, Brody Krane, with both apparently willing to let bygones be bygones. The former members of The Sexy Coeds Club faced disciplinary measures from Wryer College, including suspension; as well as extortion charges at the state level. In need of a good lawyer, Jessica had volunteered her services and secured a plea deal that kept them out of jail, with a fine, restitution, and doing community service, while helping the school devise policies to deter future such campus-related activities.

As for Brenda Kingsley, the confessed killer of Kristine McVeigh, she pled guilty to the crime, along with the murders of Brittany Delray and Danielle Osmond; as well as the abduction and attempted murder of Jessica, and received a life sentence for her crimes. Jessica was grateful for her own second chance at life, wishing the same could be said for the others targeted by Brenda as a vengeful mother gone berserk.

"Hey, there," Connie said, breaking Jessica's train of thought.

"Hey." She smiled at her friend standing in the doorway.

"A few of us are going out for drinks to celebrate the latest big win for the firm. Are you up for it?"

Though tempted and loving the camaraderie, Jessica had something better in mind. "Rain check?"

"You've got it," Connie said.

"Actually, I need a favor…" Jessica sat up. "Do you think I could borrow your cabin for the weekend? I could use a little break—"

"Of course." Connie flashed her teeth perceptively. "Is a certain hunk accompanying you…?"

"I'll have to ask him," she answered slyly. "With those PIs, you never know what their work schedule is like these days."

Connie laughed. "Something tells me he'll find a way to fit it into his schedule."

Jessica giggled. "We'll see…" *Now I wonder where I might be able to find Liam,* she asked herself playfully.

* * *

"Buy you a drink?" Jessica asked the good-looking man sitting at the bar in Dusty's all by his lonesome.

"Sure, why not?" Liam offered her a charming grin.

"What are you having?"

"I usually prefer scotch on the rocks, but I'm open to suggestions."

"Your preference works for me," she teased him and ordered two of his preferred drink, with one for herself.

"I'm guessing you don't come in here often?" he said coolly.

"Not too often. But this seemed as good a time as any—"

Liam smiled crookedly. "Is that right?"

Jessica smiled back flirtatiously. "Yeah, I think so."

After the drinks arrived, he tasted his scotch and asked curiously, "So, is there something on your mind...?"

"As a matter of fact, there is..." Jessica tasted her own drink, before getting down to business, of sorts. "I was wondering if I could entice you into spending the weekend with me at Connie's cabin near Crater Lake? I could use a break..."

Liam pretended to think about it. "Uh... Okay, you talked me into it."

She laughed. "Wasn't exactly that hard to do."

He chuckled. "What can I say, I'm a sucker for a gorgeous lady with a legal mind and a sparkling personality."

Jessica blushed. "If you keep that up, I just may have to keep you all for myself."

"Hey, I'm yours for the taking." His gaze locked on her sinfully. "What do you say we get out of here...?"

"I was thinking the same thing," she admitted, feeling turned on by his mere and near presence.

"Your place or mine?" he asked, sipping his drink.

Jessica grinned coquettishly at him. "Yours, of course. That floating house is for some reason beckoning me... I'll follow you—"

He stood. "Hmm... Why does this seem like déjà vu?"

She sipped the scotch. "Looks like someone's about to get lucky—again..."

Liam smiled as they locked eyes. "Some things in life are worth repeating themselves," he spoke affectionately.

"I couldn't agree more," Jessica told him warmly, taking his proffered hand as she rose and they headed out.

A Note from the Author

Good day,

As a longtime literary criminologist and crime novelist, I am thrilled to be able to bring you my latest novel, *Exposed Evidence: A Jessica Frost Legal Thriller.* It has enough twists and turns and surprises along the way to keep you riveted from beginning to end. I also invite you to check out some of my previous legal thrillers, that are equally gripping in their stories.

Best,

R. Barri Flowers

Acknowledgements

I would like to thank Shawn Reilly Simmons, Verena Rose, and Harriette Sackler, the Dames of Detection, at Level Best Books and Lee and Denene Lofland of their imprint New Arc Books, for taking me on with *Exposed Evidence*, in adding this thriller to a long career in legal and crime fiction for readers to discover.

Printed in the USA
CPSIA information can be obtained
at www.ICGtesting.com
LVHW092257300924
792598LV00032B/150

9 781685 120603